The
Black Cloister

The
Black Cloister

A Novel

MELANIE DOBSON

Kregel
Publications

The Black Cloister: A Novel

© 2008 by Melanie Dobson

Published by Kregel Publications, a division of Kregel, Inc., P.O. Box 2607, Grand Rapids, MI 49501.

The persons and events portrayed in this work are the creations of the author, and any resemblance to persons living or dead is purely coincidental.

Scripture quotations are from the King James Version, or from the *Holy Bible, New International Version*®. Copyright © 1973, 1978, 1984 by International Bible Society. Used by permission of Zondervan. All rights reserved.

Library of Congress Cataloging-in-Publication Data
Dobson, Melanie B.
The black cloister : a novel / by Melanie Dobson.
    p.   cm.
1. Women college students—Fiction. 2. Americans—Germany—Fiction. 3. Family secrets—Fiction. 4. Cults—Fiction. 5. Mothers and daughters—Fiction. 6. Sisters—Fiction. I. Title.
PS3604.O25B57   2008   813'.6—dc22   2008006534

ISBN 978-0-8254-2443-4

Printed in the United States of America

08 09 10 11 12 / 5 4 3 2 1

To Windy—
for your kindness, friendship,
honesty, and relentless quest for truth

Acknowledgments

DELVING INTO THE mind of a cult leader and the actions of an abusive cult is an emotionally and spiritually exhausting endeavor. I'm grateful to the many people who prayed me through the darkness of this story and back into the light.

To the editorial and marketing staff at Kregel Publications—Dennis Hillman, Steve Barclift, Amy Stephansen, Leslie Paladino, Janyre Tromp, Wendy Yoder, Miranda Gardner, and Dawn Anderson. Thank you for not only believing in this novel, but also for your encouragement and support through the entire process. It's an honor to work with you.

To an amazing group of readers and editors. Thank you Christina Nunn, Vennessa Ng, Kelli Standish, Windy, Laura Walter, Dave Lindstedt, and Brian for sharing your stories and insight.

To those who cheered me on as I raced toward deadline. Thank you to my parents, Jim and Lyn Beroth and Dobby and Carolyn Dobson, and to Wendy Lawton, Tosha Williams, Nancy Jo Jenkins, Melanie Wells, Heather Cotton, Teri Stone, and Lynda Shields for your kind words and inspiration.

To my patient daughters, Karly and Kiki. Here's to celebrating the end of this book with hugs and kisses and a special ice cream date.

To my husband and best friend, Jon. Not only do you encourage my dreams, but your Saturdays spent in the trenches enables me to pursue them. I love you!

And to my Lord, Jesus Christ, who died to give me freedom and eternal life. Darkness flees in the warmth of his light.

Set me as a seal upon thine heart,
as a seal upon thine arm: for love is strong as death;
jealousy is cruel as the grave: the coals thereof are
coals of fire, which hath a most vehement flame.

SONG OF SOLOMON 8:6

Prologue

NOVEMBER 15, 1991

THE WOMAN EDGED along the dark hallway, testing each floorboard with her bare toe until she reached the nursery. She stopped and placed her ear against the peeling door. The only sound she heard was the wind rattling against the windows of the old house.

Turning the knob, she hesitated in the shadows to see whether Phoebe or one of the children had heard. No one moved.

Last week, she had stolen up to the third floor during dinner, but Phoebe had caught her hovering over her baby's crib, mesmerized by the green flecks in her little girl's eyes. She had endured the punishment like a true follower, until Solomon banned her from seeing her children for a month. Phoebe was in charge of the kids, and if she needed any help, she would ask.

And every one that hath forsaken houses, or brethren, or sisters, or father, or mother, or wife, or children, or lands, for my name's sake, shall receive an hundredfold, and shall inherit everlasting life.

She'd become too selfish, loving her girls more than she loved God, and Sol knew it. He had purchased a train ticket for her—one-way, to Berlin, so he could direct her daughters' spiritual growth without interference. She would leave in the morning.

She wanted to feel God's presence, to obey his will, but every time Sol left her room, she felt empty instead. She'd failed God. And she'd failed her family.

Her fingers brushed over the seal that marked her arm. They could beat her to death if they wanted; she was ready to die. But she couldn't leave her children alone. Not with him.

Moonlight swept across the room, and she glanced over the line of twenty small beds crowded into the icy room. The older children slept on mattresses along the floor, and the younger ones were secured in the cribs by the drafty dormer windows.

Johanna slept in the third bed along the wall.

She tiptoed across the wood, knelt beside her daughter, and threaded her fingers through her hair until Johanna stirred in her sleep and opened her eyes. "Mommy?"

She leaned down and lifted her little girl. "I've got you, sweetheart." Johanna wrapped her arms around her neck and nestled into her shoulder. The child's long legs dangled down to her knees. When had her baby grown into a girl?

A cloud darkened the room, and she waited until the cloud passed. Then she whispered into Johanna's ear. "Where is she?"

Johanna lifted one of her arms and pointed to the first crib along the window.

"I'm going to pick her up," she said quietly, "and then we're going to run."

Johanna squeezed her neck, her gentle voice trembling. "Don't drop me."

She kissed her daughter's cheek. "I won't let you go."

She took a careful step toward the window and then a second one. Wind blasted through a crack in the glass, and Johanna shivered in her arms.

Another soft step.

The crib was only a few feet away now. She moved Johanna to her left hip so she could snag her baby with her right arm.

One of the boys cried out in the darkness behind her. She took a step back and saw Michael's curly blond hair thrashing on the pillow. She placed her hand on his head until he stopped shaking. She wished she could rescue all the children, take them someplace where they would be safe and warm.

Maybe she could come back later and steal all the little ones away, but tonight she needed to focus on saving her girls.

Another step forward. Johanna's hair was soft on her cheek, hands wrapped around her neck.

God had entrusted her with these children. No matter what Sol or anyone else said, she had to get them away from here.

The floorboard groaned under her weight, and her shoulders shook as she leapt back and waited in the silence. And the darkness.

There were three more steps between her and her baby. She would pick her up and run toward the forest. Once they made it to the trees, Sol would never catch them.

As she stepped forward again, Michael bolted up. She bent down to comfort the boy, but it was too late. He shrieked as if he'd seen a ghost.

A flash of light blinded her for an instant, but it wouldn't stop her. She lunged toward the crib.

Phoebe slapped her hand away from her daughter. "What are you doing?"

A few other children cried out, but not her daughter. She could see her sleeping between the wooden slats, her black hair tangled around her forehead.

Phoebe held out her arms. "Give Johanna to me."

Her heart pounded as fear snaked through her skin. She would not leave her daughters with Sol.

Phoebe shone the light in her eyes. "I'll call him if you don't hand her over right now."

Adrenaline shot through her body, and she lurched forward. Phoebe couldn't stop her. She would grab her baby and run.

Phoebe stretched her arms across the crib and screamed. "Sol!"

She pushed forward, but Phoebe blocked the crib and yelled again for Sol.

She squinted through her tears to see her baby one last time. God help her. If Sol caught her, she'd never see either of her girls again.

She turned and ran—out the door, down the hall. Sol called out to

THE BLACK CLOISTER

her, but she didn't stop. She stumbled down the winding steps and into the kitchen.

The cold tile jolted her bare feet, but she didn't break stride as she raced toward the back door. Freedom.

The door smacked the wall behind her as Sol threw it open. He pointed his cane at her. "Where are you going?"

Johanna trembled in her arms as she turned and locked his gaze. His velvet robe hung crooked over his shoulders, and his long, graying hair made him look several decades older than forty-five.

"I'm leaving," she said.

"You're not leaving." He took a small step as he steadied his words. "You belong here with your family."

She pressed her palms into Johanna's back as she moved toward the door. "She is my family."

"You're too young to raise her." His cracked lips eased into a smile, his outstretched arms welcoming her back into the fold. "There's so much you need to learn."

Johanna's tears soaked through her mother's clothes and puddled on her shoulder.

"They need someone strong to care for them." His voice dropped to an eerie calm. "Someone to show them the way."

She froze, her legs anchored to the tile. He knew her obsession to be a good mother, her insecurity that her children wouldn't grow up with faith. He knew her too well.

"You can leave if you want, but don't force Johanna into the world." His bad leg faltered, and he grasped the kitchen counter to steady himself. "She will be safe with us."

She shivered. Sol would teach her daughter about sacrifice and sin and purity—and most of all, how to love as Christ loved the church.

His gaze moved from her to Johanna, and he devoured her with his stare. "I'll take care of her until you return."

With her daughter clutched in her arms, she threw open the door and raced down the steps. She didn't care what he did to her, but she would never let him have her girls.

12

The frosty grass stung her toes as she raced toward the forest. Wind pierced her skin.

"Damnation!" Sol shouted from the open door. "Is that what you want?"

Light flooded the yard, and she wheeled around for one last glance at the man who had embodied God's love for her. His cane batted the sky as he blasted her with a vulgar round of words.

She switched Johanna to her right hip and ducked into the shelter of brush and leaves.

"God will kill you!"

She could hear the rush of the river, the seduction in the wind.

She'd take Johanna to a safe place. Then she'd come back to rescue her baby before Sol hurt her too. She'd care for her family. Far, far away from here.

Sol's curse carried in the wind. "And he'll kill the girl!"

Chapter 1

Seconds after Elise Friedman stepped onto the concrete platform, the doors slammed behind her and the train raced toward a dark tunnel. Wind flooded the underground station, and she shivered as she moved away from the tracks.

Her dad had told her about the bone-chilling air that settled on Berlin in the fall, but she'd forgotten his warning until she stepped outside the hotel this morning and was blasted by the brisk wind rushing through the German capital.

The platform vibrated as another train rushed into the station, and Elise pushed through a mob of tourists, toward the light that carved a channel through the passage.

When she'd called her dad from the airport last night, she'd answered his latest inquisition about her travel plans. Of course, the only reason she was here was because *he* wouldn't answer any of *her* questions.

He wouldn't answer questions, but he had no problem dumping advice on her. He warned her against all the evils of a big city. Traffic. Crowds. Dark streets. Men. Not any specific man—he thought they were all bad. She assured him that she'd be too busy studying to get into trouble. Of course, he thought she'd come to Germany in search of information for her honor's thesis, but today's research was personal.

The tunnel swerved right, and she followed the dim passageway. She'd read about this station in her guidebook. After the Berlin Wall went up in 1961, the U-bahn had continued to speed by this platform on its course between western stations, but it never stopped. For twenty-five years, armed guards had ensured that no one got off the train—and no one got on.

She jogged up the concrete stairs and emerged onto the busy Unter den Linden. Colorful tourist shops and cafés had replaced the browns and grays of the former East Berlin, and lime trees lined the grassy strip in the middle of the road with cars, buses, and bikes speeding down both sides.

At the end of the street, the quadriga atop the Brandenburg Gate blazed gold in the sunshine, the majestic horses claiming victory over the city below. Elise stared up at the gilded gate as she waited with the crowd of tourists at a crosswalk. Her tourist book had devoted two entire pages to the gate. A symbol of Nazi power in the 1940s, it later became a symbol of freedom.

Some Germans had joined the Socialist Unity Party without a fight after World War II. Those who balked were forced to toe the party line. But a divided family cannot stand, and in 1989 thousands of East Germans gathered on this street, at this gate, to demand that the government tear down the border that had severed their city and country from the free world.

When the wall finally came down, East Berliners raced to the other side of the gate and discovered that the western side had left them behind. Though some East Germans thrived in the new world, others wanted to return to the safe arms of Communism.

She was shocked when she read how many Germans wanted to revitalize Communism, swapping their freedom for the security of the East German days. She didn't get it. There was nothing more important to her than freedom. If she'd been born behind the Iron Curtain, she would have escaped or died trying.

The bright green Ampelmann, one of the few symbols left over from East Germany, flashed on the crosswalk signal. Elise crossed the street and kept walking with the crowd until she saw the sign for the Hotel Adlon at the base of the Brandenburg Gate.

The entrance was guarded by two bellmen with shiny gold buttons on their uniforms and caps. This place was an obvious fit for an ambassador, but not for a country girl trying to glean information about the past.

The clock over the bus stop beside her read ten minutes past noon. Through the hotel's window, she could see the in-house restaurant. Addison Wade was probably sitting in there, drinking a wine spritzer and rechecking her diamond-studded watch.

If only she had gotten up when her alarm rang this morning instead of succumbing to jet lag. She'd wanted to be early to this meeting. Confident. Prepared.

The wind blasted down the street, and she batted the wisps of dark hair out of her eyes. When she brushed her fingers over her wrinkled white blouse, she saw a faded patch of sepia that had smeared across the buttons and stained the left side.

She groaned. A half hour earlier she had grabbed a cup of coffee and a muffin from the hotel lobby before she dashed toward the train station. Now she was wearing her breakfast.

She wouldn't care if she were meeting with one of her professors today, or another student, but lunch with the U.S. ambassador was a different story. How could the ambassador take her seriously when she looked as if she'd been splattered with mud?

She'd gone for a classic look—a simple white blouse and black skirt—and ended up with a scary resemblance to one of the pigs that her dad kept on the farm. Whenever she tried to dress up, something always happened to bump her back to the status of a country girl. Not that she minded, not usually. She loved her family's farm and the country air and all the cats that she'd rescued over the years and brought home. On days like this, though, she wished she could manage to stay stain free for just an hour.

With both arms crossed over her ribs, she marched toward the hotel and tried not to think about her blouse. If she didn't hurry, Mrs. Wade would call for her car, and Elise would lose the chance to ask about her mother.

She rushed up the trail of red carpet and in through the hotel's glass doors before the bellmen could stop her. The lobby was painted a stark white with wrought iron balconies overlooking the tile floor. The smell of cigar smoke clung to the chairs that were grouped in twos and threes, each one upholstered with the red or yellow shade of autumn leaves.

In the middle of the room, water cascaded from the tusks of four elephants into a marble fountain. A lone woman sat by the fountain, her chestnut hair pulled back in a twist. She dangled an ebony-colored sandal off her toes as she skimmed a newspaper.

Elise rushed toward her. "Ambassador Wade?"

The woman stood up and reached out her hand. "Please call me Addison."

"I'm Elise Friedman. Catrina's daughter." She grasped the ambassador's hand, her nerves rattled. "I'm so sorry I'm . . ."

Addison glanced down at the stain on her blouse and tried to repress her smile. "You look just like your mother."

She pointed at her blouse. "Minus the coffee?"

"I thought I'd missed out on a new trend."

Elise grinned. Maybe Mrs. Wade wasn't wound as tight as she'd imagined.

The ambassador folded her newspaper. "Your e-mail surprised me."

"I'd like to ask you a few questions about my mother."

"I don't know how much I can help you." Her gaze shifted between Elise and the newspaper. "I didn't know her very well."

Elise pinched the zipper on her backpack and pulled it open. She was tired of people stumbling around the truth. Tired of the lies.

She rifled through the top of her pack until she found the picture that had sat on her parents' dresser for years. Her parents' wedding day.

With a quick glance down, she handed the photo to the ambassador. Her mother's dark hair was swept over the shoulders of her red and white sundress. Sand covered her toes, and she waved a straw hat toward the camera with a rare smile. Her arm wrapped around the shoulders of another woman, Addison Wade.

Addison's voice cracked as she took the faded picture. "Where—did you get this?"

"I want to know what happened to her."

Addison motioned her toward the restaurant at the side of the lobby, the picture clutched in her hand. "Surely Steve already told you the story."

"He told me *a* story." She stopped walking and faced the ambassador. "But I want to know the truth."

Chapter 2

ADDISON DIDN'T WANT to look at the picture, nor did she want to plod down memory lane with Catrina's daughter. She was weeks away from going back to the States for her next confirmation—this time as ambassador to the United Nations. She'd spent most of her life preparing for just such a position.

When her assistant had shown her Elise's e-mail, her first reaction was to ignore the request for lunch. She'd put a lock on her past fifteen years ago when she'd run for office in Virginia's General Assembly, and no one had ever asked questions about the year she'd spent abroad.

Now Elise was asking questions, and if Addison ignored her, the girl might ask questions in the wrong place. Like Heidelberg. She had to convince Elise that the past wasn't worth excavating. If the girl dug too deep, Addison could say good-bye to her nomination and her career.

She shoved the picture back toward Elise as they stepped into the restaurant. Tall ferns framed beveled glass windows, set off against burnt orange walls. Brown wicker chairs surrounded ten covered tables, each cushioned seat hosting a celebrity or dignitary or executive.

The girl tucked the picture into her backpack. "Tell me about their wedding."

Addison followed the maître d' toward a table by the window and sat down. "Didn't Steve tell you?"

"He doesn't like to talk about her."

So Addison told her about the ceremony. It was on the Virginia Beach pier, and she, Richard, and Elise had been there to watch Catrina and Steve exchange vows. Elise was six years old at the time and wore a red- and white-swirled sundress to match her mother's. She mimicked Catrina's every move, including nudging her aside to give Steve a kiss on the cheek when the pastor told him it was time to kiss the bride.

Elise smiled as she reached for the flute of bubbly water on the table, and Addison studied the grown-up version of the girl she had played with so long ago. Her straight hair was windblown, and her slender nose was sculpted from the same mold as Catrina's.

The thing that struck her most, though, was not Elise's resemblance to her mother. It was her green eyes, tinted with yellow. The eyes of Bethesda, Elise's grandmother.

She pinched the crystal stem of the water glass. As much as she had loved Catrina, she despised Bethesda.

A waiter stepped beside her, and she ordered for both of them. If anything could help her redirect Elise, it would be the duck salad.

"How did you find me?" Addison asked when the waiter turned toward the kitchen.

"I used to stare at that picture when I was a kid." Elise smoothed her napkin over her lap. "I always wondered who you were, but no one would tell me."

Addison took a sip of water, but her mouth still felt dry. At least Steve and Catrina had honored their end of the deal.

"Then I saw a clip in the newspaper about your nomination," Elise continued. "With a picture."

Addison smoothed her fingers across the white tablecloth.

It had been almost three decades since she'd run away. She had almost stopped worrying about them finding her. But if Elise had connected the dots . . .

The water sloshed against the sides of her glass as she set it back on the table. "I hope you didn't come all this way to talk to me."

Elise shook her head. "I'm going to Wittenberg to research my honor's thesis."

"About Martin Luther?" she asked. She'd rather talk about almost anything than Catrina.

Elise swept a strand of hair back over her ear. "About Katharina von Bora."

"You must be majoring in history."

"Women's history." Elise paused. "I want to teach women how to succeed in spite of their circumstances."

Addison could discuss this topic for an hour. "You're going to teach them how to overcome oppression?"

"Oppression or anything else that keeps a woman from doing what God wants her to do."

Addison smiled. If Catrina were still alive, she'd be proud of her daughter. She seemed to have the strength and drive that Catrina had always desired.

Elise leaned forward. "Could you tell me what my mother was like?"

Addison closed her eyes for an instant and saw the nine-year-old girl with a bruise on her cheek. Catrina had been shattered. Lonely. Scared. But she couldn't tell that to her daughter.

"Caring." She took a long sip of water. "And kind."

"Did you know my birth father?"

She crossed her legs. This conversation was for Steve, not her. "Surely Catrina told you about him."

"She said I was born in Heidelberg. Her boyfriend was an air force pilot."

"There you go . . ."

"The only air force base in Heidelberg was British." Elise tapped the table. "According to my mother, this guy was from Montana."

Addison took a deep breath. If neither Steve nor Catrina had told Elise the truth, she wasn't going to be the one to expound. "Heidelberg has a huge army garrison. Hundreds of pilots from the States go through there."

"And I want to know which one was my father."

Addison squelched a sigh. "You should talk to Steve about this."

"He won't talk about it."

"Elise—"

"So I'll have to find out what I can on my own."

Her shoulders locked. "You're going to Heidelberg?"

"This afternoon," she said. "To get my birth certificate."

Addison didn't even look at the waiter when he grazed her shoulder with the duck salad. If Elise went to Heidelberg, she might find the house. And if she found the house . . .

Following that trail could destroy them both.

She cleared her throat. "You've done your homework."

"I've had to. No one will tell me what I want to know."

Addison looked down at her salad, crisp slices of duck and toasted pecans on a bed of dark greens, but she didn't take a bite. "I'm sure Steve has told you plenty."

"He told me that my mother died of a stroke."

"We were all very sad . . ."

Elise shoved her salad to the side of the table and set a photocopy of Catrina's obituary on the table in front of them. "But he's lying."

"Your father wouldn't lie."

"He also said my mother was twenty-two when they got married."

Addison didn't say anything.

"According to this, she was only twenty when she died. That means she got pregnant when she was like eleven or twelve and married my dad when she was seventeen."

Addison arched her back. "Eighteen."

"Is Catrina really my mother?"

"Of course . . ."

"Then what was her maiden name?"

"I can't tell you that."

Elise leaned forward. "That's all I want to know."

Addison shoved her fork through her salad. "Sometimes it's better not to dig around in the past."

Elise groaned and collapsed back in her seat. "Now you sound like my dad."

Addison couldn't control her racing heart, but she could steady her breathing. One of the reasons the president had nominated her to represent the United States at the UN was because of her tough negotiating skills. She enjoyed haggling about trade agreements and security and preserving the environment.

However, when it came to her personal life, she rarely negotiated. Those close to her usually did what she asked, and if they didn't, it was easier to cut the tie than bother about the back-and-forth. She had enough red tape to untangle in her professional life; she didn't need it outside the office as well.

Her cell phone rang, and she dove into her purse like it held a lifeline. She glanced at the ID and saw it was Jack, her assistant. Unless she needed an excuse to leave, she ignored his calls during a meeting.

She mouthed an apology to Elise and lowered her voice to talk on the phone. "What's up?"

"You asked me to remind you about your meeting with the director of the Florian Schmidt Center this afternoon," Jack said.

"Hold on," she said as she sprang from her seat. She glanced at Elise as she grabbed her briefcase. "I'm sorry. It's an emergency."

Elise pulled her fingers through her hair. "Of course."

"I wish I could help you, but I'm not the one you need to talk to."

"Then who?" Elise asked as the ambassador rushed from the room, but she didn't turn around to answer.

"You've got a half hour," Jack said as Addison pushed open the hotel's front door.

The new embassy was right around the corner, but she flagged down a cab instead of walking back to her office.

"Reschedule the meeting for tomorrow," she told Jack. She pressed the mute button to give the driver her home address.

Jack paused. "Is everything okay?"

"I need you to check a timetable for me." The cabbie swerved around a bicyclist and turned right toward Charlottenburg.

"No problem."

"When does the next train leave Hauptbahnhof for Heidelberg?"

She heard him clicking on his keyboard. "One left twelve minutes ago, and there's one at 4:05 this afternoon."

She rubbed her finger over the plate of her watch. The train would leave in three hours.

They didn't have much time.

Chapter 3

BALSAMIC VINAIGRETTE dripped off Elise's fork and onto her skirt, pooling on her leg before seeping through the fabric. She groaned as she reached for her napkin and dipped it into the bubbly water. Forget Etiquette 101. She didn't need an oil stain to accent the coffee on her blouse. It was the only skirt she'd brought to Germany, and it had to do double duty—for her meetings with the ambassador in Berlin and the professor in Wittenberg.

She redipped her napkin and tried to attack the coffee stain as well, but she only succeeded in expanding it. She'd have to find a way to do laundry before she went to Wittenberg.

As she carefully scooped up another bite, she wondered why she had even bothered to dress up. Addison Wade hadn't cared about her attire or her questions. All Elise wanted to know was the basics about her past, yet her dad and his family, and now the ambassador, kept tap-dancing around the truth.

She had tried to talk to her dad one last time before she left for Germany, but he was even more evasive than Addison. Instead of answering her questions, he chipped every one of them out-of-bounds and redirected the conversation toward safe topics like school, church, and the six cats that paraded like royalty around their farm.

She'd mastered the science of researching other people's history, so she decided to stop pestering him and apply a little fact-finding to her personal history. No matter what he was trying to hide, she'd unearth the answers by herself.

She downed two more bites of salad without splattering herself and then set her fork on the plate and waved at the waiter. The man smiled at her bumbling attempt to ask for the bill in German before he explained to her in English that the ambassador had an account.

At least Addison had bought her lunch.

She strung her backpack over her shoulder and left the hotel.

Back on the street, Elise followed the steady current of tourists flowing toward the Brandenburg Gate. The crowd bottlenecked at the plaza in front of the gate and then slowly moved through the giant arch. She had plenty of time to retrieve her suitcase from the hotel and get to the train station—enough time, at least, to play tourist while she was in the heart of Berlin.

With a quick glance at her guidebook, she turned left on the sidewalk at Ebertstrasse and followed the thick line of trees in Tiergarten until she reached the city block that was Germany's memorial to the Jews killed in the Holocaust.

She squinted over the chunky gray plaza and wondered whether a couple thousand pieces of granite was really an appropriate tribute to the victims. She stepped toward the square and began moving across the pavement.

The slabs were low, the path wide. Most of the granite was as short as her ankles though some pieces climbed as high as her knees. At least a hundred other tourists shuffled across the memorial, and she scooted easily around the slabs as she worked her way toward the middle.

To her left was Tiergarten, and to her right were tall city buildings and condos. She caught her wind-whipped hair with one hand and held it out of her face as the blocks around her grew taller.

From the description in her guidebook, she'd expected a grand display of regret and remorse, but this was just a sea of rectangle blocks that looked like they'd tumbled down from the sky and fallen haphazardly across the square. Hardly a fitting tribute to the six million who had died.

Her pace quickened as she continued toward the center. She would walk to the other side and then cross the street and head north to visit the Reichstag before she left Berlin.

She glanced at the trees to one side again and realized that she was walking down into the memorial instead of staying level. Her path became steeper as the granite rose even higher, and the pathway became so narrow that it felt as if the blocks were now towering above her.

With her next step forward, both of her shoulders touched cold stone. The granite walls blocked both sunshine and wind. Even though she knew there must be other people nearby, she didn't hear anyone.

For ten minutes, she pushed through the maze, trying to decide which path would take her back to freedom. The designer had made his point. She was ready now to look down on the city from the glass dome in the Reichstag instead of being trapped underground.

A guy with a backpack and a ponytail came around the corner, and she jumped, her dad's many warnings reverberating in her head.

"Scary, isn't it?" he asked.

She mumbled a yes as she swallowed hard to stifle a cough. It smelled as if he hadn't showered in a week.

He stepped toward her. "It's like they didn't know what was happening until it was too late."

She turned to the right, away from the backpacker, and chose a new path through the granite maze.

The pathway began to widen as she climbed back into fresh air, and the slabs around her shrank in size until they were knee-high again. The breeze massaged her face, and she reveled in the sunshine.

It was never too late to find a way out.

She pushed the hair out of her eyes, and when she looked down again, she saw a tiny mound of white huddled by one of the slabs, its fur mangled and worn. She knelt down and held out her hand, but the kitten cowered, dragging one of his legs behind him. His blue eyes pleaded with her not to hurt him.

She rubbed his head. "What's your name?"

The kitten slowly lifted his head and then raised his tiny paw up and wrapped it around her finger.

Elise smiled as she stroked his fur. "It looks like you need a friend."

She glanced at her watch—about ninety minutes to get her suitcase and make the train. She probably should find the nearest U-bahn station and get back to her hotel, but she couldn't leave the kitten alone. If she didn't find shelter for him, he'd get trampled.

With a gentle swoop, she picked him up and cradled him as she rushed along the wide path and across the street. All she needed was to find one compassionate person who loved cats as much as she did.

She buzzed around some office buildings and turned onto an alley behind them. Painted doors lined both sides of the narrow street, and she jogged up the stairs and banged on the first door.

The woman who answered had a weathered face with dark age spots dotting her cheeks. Her body was tightly wrapped in a burgundy robe. "*Ja?*"

"*Sprechen Sie English?*"

The woman shook her head in annoyance and started to close the door.

"Wait." Elise struggled to remember the German words she'd spent the past three years trying to learn. She held out the kitten. "*Hilfe.*"

The woman slammed the door in her face.

She scratched the kitten's ears as she hustled back down the stairs. She wouldn't let the unkindness of one woman deter her. She'd find a place for the kitten, and then catch the train. Surely someone on this street liked cats.

"Don't worry," she mumbled as she moved down the street. "We'll find someone to take care of you."

She knocked on four more doors, but no one answered.

She petted the kitten again. If she didn't find someone to care for him in Berlin, he'd be taking a trip to Heidelberg this afternoon.

The next door along the alley was painted black, and she skipped over it and opted for the one doused in a midnight blue. Ascending the stairs, she tried to spot life inside the lace-covered windows, but nothing moved.

She rang the bell and waited. Someone peeked at her through the curtains, and then the door clicked before it opened. The woman who answered wasn't much older than she was, but she looked tired, deep lines circling her eyes and lips. Her blonde hair hung in rings around her neck, and she wore a black choker and a silky emerald dress.

The woman didn't seem self-conscious about her dress or even aware that Elise was standing on her stoop. Her eyes were focused on the kitten, and the hard lines on her face softened into a smile when the kitten batted her silk sleeve with his paw.

She'd found the right door.

The woman reached out to pet the kitten. "Isn't he sweet?"

Elise sighed with relief, grateful that the woman spoke English. "I found him by the hotel. His back leg is broken."

"Are you from Berlin?" the woman asked.

"The U.S."

The woman leaned over and plucked the cat out of her arms. Then she shooed Elise back out the door.

"You need to leave," she whispered.

"But the kitten . . ."

The cat nuzzled into the woman's shoulder. "I'll take care of him."

"But, I . . ."

The woman glanced behind her and then looked back at Elise. Her voice was urgent. "Please go."

The woman closed the door, and Elise turned around. Was it normal to slam the door in Berlin or did they just do that to Americans? She supposed it didn't really matter. At least the kitten would be safe.

She brushed the cat hair off her hands and pulled the map out of her pocket to find out where she was—a block south of Unter den Linden. If she hurried, she would still be able to catch the train.

Chapter 4

THE EXPRESS TRAIN PULLED out of Hauptbahnhof at 4:06 PM and trekked toward the west side of Berlin. Pink light reflected off the city's glass towers and settled on the battered shells below, brick buildings scarred with graffiti murals and battle wounds.

Carson propped his backpack over his shoulder and wandered down the train's aisle. The crowded car was buzzing with Italian, German, and French. Every once in a while, he would hear someone speak in English, and he'd stop and look for the pretty American girl. But the people talking were mostly Brits, and not one was a young woman with dark hair and green eyes.

The conductor stopped him, asked for his ticket, and reminded him that his seat was four cars back. Carson responded with a nod and thanked him in English so the man would think he was a tourist and not bother telling him to turn around.

He continued his trek through the line of first- and second-class cars, but he didn't see Elise Friedman anywhere.

When he reached the last car, he set down his backpack. It wasn't that heavy, but he'd been lugging it around for the past hour as he'd waited on the platform and then boarded the train during the final call.

He stretched his neck and picked up his bag before wandering back down the aisle and through the crowded dining car.

At a table by the window, he saw a woman sitting by herself. Early twenties. Dark hair tied up in a fancy knot. She was eating soup and crackers and watching the sun fade over the city.

He stowed his bag at the side of the dining car, and from the side pocket he slipped out a book. Then he sat down at a table across the narrow aisle from the girl and ordered bratwurst and potatoes for dinner.

When the food arrived, he set down his book and turned toward the woman. "Do you speak English?"

She glanced over, and when she saw him, she smiled. "Maybe."

He resisted the urge to roll his eyes and reached out his hand to shake hers instead. "My name's Carson."

She looked down at his hand, but she didn't take her fingers off her spoon. "You can call me Amy."

"Okay, Amy." He drummed his fingers on the table. Even if it was annoying, his job would be easier if she kept flirting with him. "Where are you from?"

"Los Angeles."

He studied her eyes—more blue than green—and wondered whether she was lying about her hometown as well as her name. "Are you on vacation?"

She smoothed her hand over a loose tendril. "It's a business trip."

"What do you do?"

She studied him for a moment and turned the question back on him. "What do *you* do?"

He took a bite of the brat and chewed it slowly. "I'm a translator." It might take the entire five-hour ride to get this girl to admit she was Elise.

"For tourists?"

"Mostly for businesses and universities."

"Impressive."

He shrugged. It was a good job when he was translating a meeting or business negotiations or even a lecture, but sometimes the university socked him with mounds of research papers to translate. After a week or two of sifting through complicated paperwork, he was ready to look for another job. Some days, he wished he could bail on his job and come up with a new shtick, like guiding tours around one of Berlin's famous destinations. He could make enough in tips to fund his travels.

He grinned as he looked down at his plate, imagining the conversation where he would tell his mom that he was ditching his dual degrees in German and business administration to become a tour guide. After all, when he wasn't working, he was out conquering the Alps across Austria, Switzerland, and Bavaria. Maybe he could look for a new gig near the mountains.

"What's so funny?" the girl asked.

"Just thinking of a way to freak out my mom."

She glanced back down at her soup, clearly not impressed by his thoughts. But then again, she didn't know his mom.

"So you're working in Heidelberg?" he said, trying to get the conversation back on track. If he wasn't careful, he would freak her out as well, and then he'd have to resort to stalking her through town.

"You could say that."

"Do you need a translator?" he volunteered.

She laughed. "You're bold, aren't you?"

"I thought you might want some company."

She propped up her chin on her fingers. "Maybe I do."

Carson cut off another piece of sausage and ate it. He'd been warned that Elise might be hard to befriend, but this girl wasn't putting up much of a fight. Maybe her name really was Amy.

He motioned to the server, and the man brought him his bill.

"Carson?" the girl asked as he dug ten euros out of his wallet and handed it to the waiter.

He turned toward her. "Yep."

"My name's really Kate, from Seattle."

He stood up and grabbed his backpack. At least he didn't have to follow this woman around Heidelberg. "It's nice to meet you, Kate."

"Do you have plans for breakfast tomorrow?"

"Yep," he said as he walked toward the door.

He would be waiting at the registrar's office before it opened, and if Elise didn't show up, he would scour Heidelberg until he found her.

Chapter 5

CHURCH BELLS ECHOED through the valley as Elise looked down at the river that separated Heidelberg's Old Town from the new. The river's lazy current loped under the arches of the medieval bridge and threaded toward the golden hills outside town.

On the other side of the river, terra cotta roofs stepped up the hill until they plateaued at a sandstone castle that reminded her of a sleepy sentry who'd nodded off after battle and never woke up.

She hopped up on a brick wall and dangled her feet.

She had missed her train yesterday by three minutes, but another one had left for Heidelberg last night and she had slept the entire trip. The train had reached Heidelberg before the sun came up, and she'd slept another hour in the hotel room before venturing out.

As she looked down at the medieval town, she could hardly believe she was here. Her mother had roamed these streets as a child. She'd probably played in the parks, dipped her feet in the river, savored chocolate pastries at the local bakery.

Was her family still living in the town? If not, where had they gone?

Somewhere in the midst of the winding streets, Catrina had met a phantom man from Montana who'd faded away like the ringing bells. Someone around Heidelberg had to have known her mother. Maybe someone had even celebrated the day Elise was born.

Even if her dad and Addison Wade tried to hide the information about her past, she would find out. Someone other than the two of them had to remember and she would start getting answers today. Her original birth certificate would have her mother's maiden name on it . . . and maybe even the name of her birth father.

The registrar's office opened in fifteen minutes, and this time she wouldn't be late.

She clutched her hands together and watched a ship cruising down the channel and under the bridge.

What she didn't understand was why she had to come to Heidelberg to track down her family. Surely her mother would have guessed that someday her daughter would wonder about her birth family and where she'd been born.

It was only last month that she'd learned there was much more to her mother's story. Her dad had decided to throw her a birthday party even though birthdays had been avoided in their house for years, especially hers. The last time they'd celebrated was on her seventh birthday. Her mother had made a Strawberry Shortcake cake and decorated the house with hot pink balloons. Then her dad had opened the back door and in bounded her favorite birthday gift of all time, the kitten she'd named Penguin. It was the happiest day of her life.

Her next birthday was the worst day of her life, and her dad never threw her another party until—surprise—he decided to celebrate her twenty-first birthday in style. A barn dance. Barbecue. And a bona fide hayride around their horse farm.

Behind the house, he'd built a raging bonfire, and Elise had crouched down on a damp log between her college roommate and her cousin Kristen to roast marshmallows.

Kristen's younger sister, Stacy, was on a rock behind them, and she'd brought a guy—Jeff something—from Hampton. In true Stacy form, she was keeping him entertained with the tabloid heads from their family's archive of secrets. Their grandmother's affair. A cousin's surprise pregnancy. Their uncle's abrupt move to Portland.

Then Stacy had taken a quick breath and turned her sights on Elise.

"Her mother died on her eighth birthday," she whispered.

Elise stuck a marshmallow on her carved stick and shoved it into the hot coals circling the campfire. The terror of that day clenched her chest, and she took a deep breath to squelch it.

Kristen nudged her. "So you're headed to Germany."

Elise tried to drown out the emerging image of her mother. "In two weeks."

"What happened?" Jeff asked behind them.

Kristen raised her voice to drown out the conversation. "Are you going to Berlin?"

"And Wittenberg."

Stacy cleared her throat. "They said it was a brain aneurysm, but . . ."

Kristen whipped her head around. "Could you please talk about something else?"

Stacy and Jeff both jumped.

"It's okay," Elise told Kristen as she swung her leg over the log to face the couple. In the firelight, she could see a wave of red welling up Jeff's neck. "It was actually a stroke, but if you have any other questions I'd be glad to answer them."

The guy shook his head.

She leaned closer to him. "For example, you could ask why I didn't call for help right away."

He scooted back. "No, that's okay."

"Or you might be wondering how someone so young could die so fast."

"I—I wasn't," he stuttered.

"Do you want me to tell you exactly what I saw in the room?"

Jeff jumped to his feet. "I'm going home."

He backed away from the fire and when he turned toward the car, Elise called after him. "But I'd hate for you to miss all the gory details."

Stacy glared at her as she stood up. "Thanks a lot."

"If you're going to gossip about my family, you should get the facts straight."

Stacy slipped a denim jacket over her arms. "My mom said she died of an aneurysm."

"It was a stroke."

Stacy's blonde hair flung forward as she leaned into Elise's face. "Are you sure?"

"Shut up, Stacy!" Kristen snapped.

Stacy shrugged her shoulders as she followed Jeff to the car.

Elise turned toward her cousin. "Do you know something?"

"Elise . . ."

"Because if you do, you had better tell me."

"There are just differences of opinion as to what caused your mom's death."

"How could there be differing opinions? A stroke is a stroke."

"Right."

Kristen pointed toward the fire, and Elise's fingers trembled as she pulled her stick out of the coals, the marshmallow blazing like a torch. What was her cousin implying?

She blew out the flame and stared at the blackened sugar. "They would have examined her after she died."

Kristen stared at the fire. "Have you seen her death certificate?"

Of course she hadn't seen the death certificate. She'd never even thought to ask. Her dad had told her it was a stroke. Nobody's fault.

But she grew up knowing it was her fault.

Kristen hugged her. "You okay?"

"Fabulous." She stood up from the fire, the images of her mother trapped in her mind. No matter how hard she tried to erase the scene, it had been seared into her brain.

She'd spent the past thirteen years trying to purge it, but the pictures flashed back with sound and color. The sirens blaring outside the window. The paramedic who knocked over her mother's prized lamp as he tried to revive her. And the stretcher that they rushed into the room while Elise slumped helplessly in the corner.

A few other college friends waved to her from the hay-filled wagon as she crossed the dark yard toward her dad. He flipped another round of hot dogs on the grill, gave her a hug, and then pointed to the parking lot as Jeff backed up his Jeep.

"Did you say good-bye to Stacy?"

"Sort of." She paused. "Hey, I have a question for you."

"Shoot."

She leaned against a patio chair. "Do you have a copy of Mom's death certificate?"

He looked at her like she'd pulled a gun and demanded the keys to his F-250.

"Why do you need that?"

"I just realized I've never seen it before."

He plucked a hot dog off the grill and onto a plate. "I'll look for it later."

She nodded before she turned back to the fire.

As far as she knew, he had never looked.

The mailman had delivered a copy of the death certificate the day before she left for Germany. Cause of death: *suicide*.

Her dad hadn't just embellished the story. He'd flat-out lied.

You'd think if her family was going to lie about the death, they could at least coordinate their stories. A stroke? An aneurysm? Maybe a blow to the head? It must have been hard to keep the lies straight.

The question was—which of her aunts and uncles and cousins knew about the suicide? Had they convened a family meeting to agree on a cover story? And were they ever going to tell her what happened, or were they going to let their lies evolve into fact?

The church bells rang out again in the valley, and Elise threw her backpack over her shoulder and waited with a dozen other people in front of the registrar's office. When someone propped the door open, she marched into the lobby, wrote her name on the waiting list, and asked the woman at the front desk for an application to get her birth certificate. The woman didn't look up as she handed over a piece of paper.

Elise stepped to the right and into a brightly lit lobby with brick walls and five long tables. She collapsed into a chair at the table closest to the door and stared down at the lines on the application.

She answered the easy questions first.

Name? Elise Layne Friedman.

Adresse? Chesapeake, VA, USA.

Then she pulled out her German-English dictionary to begin the slow process of translation.

"Do you need some help?"

She looked up to see a college-age guy standing across the table from her. He flipped back messy bangs that hung like caramel-colored fringe above his eyes and slipped into a seat.

She shook her head.

When she opened her dictionary, he leaned closer. *"Verstehen Sie Deutsch?"*

She flashed him a quick, polite smile, and then focused on the application. *"Ein bisschen."*

"So would you rather talk in English or German?"

"Right now, all I want to do is fill out this application."

"No problem." He leaned back in his chair. "And congratulations."

She glanced over at him. "For what?"

He pointed at the application in front of her. "Your marriage."

"Marriage?"

Now he was the one who looked surprised. "You're applying for a marriage license."

She groaned. "I'm trying to get a birth certificate."

He whipped the paper out of her hand and returned it to the desk. Minutes later, he walked back with a new application, and this time he sat down beside her.

"Put your name and address at the top," he instructed and pointed to the next line. "Date and place of birth. Your parents' names."

She pulled the application closer to her. "Thank you."

"No problem." He started scribbling on a sheet of paper he'd set on the table in front of him. "Just let me know if you need anything else."

Someone called her name and she picked up her paper and backpack to follow the woman to the other side of the lobby. The woman pointed her inside a small office, and Elise slipped into the cramped room, which smelled of cigarettes and butterscotch. The woman sat down at the desk across from her, and Elise slid her the application.

The woman took one look at all the white space and pushed back the paper.

"I need the surname of your mother," she said in perfect English.

"I don't know it."

"Then I need the name of your father, please."

Elise ground the heels of her boots into the tile floor. "I only have my birth date."

The woman motioned to a man waiting outside the door, and he stepped into the room. "Without a name, it is impossible to find your record."

"Could you just look up the date?" Elise persisted. Even if she was one of ten or twelve babies born that day, she could at least narrow down her search.

The man set an application on the desk, but Elise didn't move. The woman took the paperwork and began typing on her keyboard. "Did you visit the army base?" she asked Elise.

"I called them."

"The consulate in Frankfurt?"

"They told me to come here."

The woman stopped typing for an instant. "I am sorry, but we need more information."

Elise stuffed her hands into her jacket pockets as she slogged back through the lobby. The army hospital needed a name too—a name her dad probably knew but refused to provide.

After he'd adopted her, the state had issued a new birth certificate, and she was officially the child of Steven and Catrina Friedman. Born September 28, 1987. Heidelberg, Germany.

But where in Heidelberg? And to whom?

Chapter 6

A FIRE ROARED IN THE corner of the stone room, and Solomon Lucien stoked the logs with an iron poker. The blaze should have smothered the chill in the air, but the room still felt like an icebox. The damp air soaked through the velvet on his robe and settled on his skin.

Autumn wind rushed through the corridors of the old abbey and enveloped the members of his family. Cold was good for their souls. It made them more aware of their sacrifice, their devotion to the call.

With the darkness of winter approaching, he had to stamp out any thoughts of desertion that seemed to culminate with the shorter days and gray skies. He knew what his children were thinking; he knew them better than they knew themselves, and he'd learned to recognize the signs—the hope that flickered in their eyes, the curiosity about the world, the requests to visit town. Only those who hated to leave the home were sent into town to solicit donations.

The hinges on his door squeaked as it opened, and Jozef Ogitzak walked inside. The man placed a small box on Sol's desk and then sat in a chair.

Sol eyed the box, and then used the poker to balance himself as he walked back toward the desk. "I called for you two days ago."

Jozef nodded at the box. "I got what you wanted."

"I need new girls in Berlin."

Jozef drummed his fingers on his chunky legs. "It's not like I can advertise for them."

He slid into the leather chair behind the desk. "You know exactly where to look."

"Right here." Jozef placed both of his swollen hands on the mahogany desk. "If you want more workers in Berlin, send the rest of your women with me."

Sol carefully moved the box to the side of his desk and reached for the onyx paperweight. His fingers rubbed over the stone.

Five million people lived in and around Berlin, and that didn't include all the tourists who weren't as particular as the locals. Traveling to Berlin had its perks, and he used to be one of the top suppliers. But many of the girls he'd sent as missionaries had grown old and tired, hardly the allure needed to attract new clientele.

Their revenues were lower than ever right now, weeks before the slow, winter season. Most tourists stayed clear of Berlin after the Christmas markets disappeared, and the men who visited the Christmas markets usually brought their wives or girlfriends.

He made the decision last week to have Jozef recruit women from the streets of Berlin. Unlike the pimps in Mitte, they took care of the women in their house and gave them decent food, new clothes, and a place to sleep in return for their hard work. He needed them to support the family like King Solomon had needed the heathen slaves to build his temple.

Someone tapped the door knocker, and he motioned for Jozef to open the door. Sara lowered her head as she walked inside, and in her hands, she balanced a sterling silver platter with fried eggs, toast, and two mugs of hot tea. She was a pretty girl, but the vibrancy in her green eyes had dulled years ago.

Sara didn't look at him as she set lunch on the desk, but she shivered when he touched her arm. He'd chosen her from the entire flock to be his.

As she waited, he sipped the tea and set the mug on the desk. Seconds ticked by before he responded. "It's barely warm, Sara."

Her shoulders slumped forward. "I'm sorry, King Sol."

"It's your job, Sara, you must take it seriously."

"Yes, sir. I thought—"

He clasped her elbow. *"Whether therefore ye eat, or drink, or whatsoever ye do, do all to the glory of God."*

She reached down and picked up the mugs. "I'll make it again."

Sol turned and watched Jozef's eyes follow her out the door. He would never let Jozef touch Sara.

"Why isn't she in Berlin?" Jozef asked.

"I need her here."

"She should be in the city."

Sol shook his head. He'd never let Sara go any further than town to solicit food, and even that was rare. "Sara is special."

"I can see that."

Sol fingered the sheath that hung from his belt. Paul would have axed Jozef out of the ministry years ago, but Sol needed him. For now.

In the earlier days, Sol had run the most lucrative home in Europe. His tithe back to headquarters in Amsterdam had swelled Paul's pockets for years and provided the resources to evangelize the world—until Paul reassigned him to Frankfurt.

Several different elders had run the Berlin mission until the group moved their operations to South Africa, and Sol had had to recruit someone to help him run both homes. Jozef might be from Poland, but he knew Berlin, knew the girls, and he knew the politicians who liked their palms greased.

Lately, though, Jozef had failed to meet his monthly quota. And he'd certainly failed at recruiting new women. When his young lieutenant, Michael, was ready, Sol would throw Jozef back to the dogs in Mokotów and let Michael take over.

A mouse raced by the corner of the room, and Sol stood up and grabbed the poker. He slammed the poker on the stone floor, but the mouse got away.

"I could put an end to your mouse problem," Jozef said.

Sol rubbed his hand over the wound on the front of his leg. "I don't allow guns in this house."

Jozef eyed the sheath on his waist. "I know, you prefer more primitive weapons."

He wondered what the blade would feel like against Jozef's neck.

"Let me take Sara to Berlin for the winter," the man insisted. "Just until we can find someone new."

"When she is older."

"Isn't she seventeen?"

Sol stepped toward the fire. "Barely."

"Two of my girls are younger than her."

Sol moved over to the fire and ground the tip of the poker into the burning wood. "She stays here."

"You push me into a corner, my friend."

"Do your job, Jozef, and let me do mine." He stirred the blaze, and flames sparked when he shoved a log.

Sara knocked on the door and returned with two mugs. With her head bowed, she handed them to the men and backed toward the door.

"Wait," Sol said, and he saw the familiar flicker of fear in her eyes. "I need you to go to town this afternoon."

She cringed. "Yes, sir."

"And this time I need you to bring back some food."

She nodded, but he would make sure Phoebe enforced his words. Most of the family hadn't eaten in two days, and if they got too hungry, they might stop listening to him and let their stomachs dictate their actions.

He set down his mug of tea to let it cool, but Jozef chugged his in spite of the heat. Then he held out his mug. "Don't you have anything stronger?"

"*Be not drunk with wine,*" Sol quoted.

"Black coffee." Jozef wiped his mouth with his sleeve. "I was up all night."

Sol glared at the man across from him. He despised weakness, and in spite of his bravado, Jozef was a coward. Almost a decade ago, Jozef had bolted with a cocaine shipment that was supposed to have been delivered to the Polish mafia. The money had lasted for a couple years, but he was still a hunted man.

Sol rolled the metal poker in his palms. Jozef would have to learn how to control his tongue. He may not be a member of the flock, but he would show respect for God's authority. It would only take a few calls to get rid of the man and send Michael to Berlin.

Sara would stay here with him.

Chapter 7

ELISE PACED UP AND down the walkway that overlooked the river and village. On the plane ride to Berlin, she had been confident that Addison would supply her mother's maiden name, and she would then use the information to get her birth certificate in Heidelberg. It would be easy—or at least easier—to track down her family with that information in hand.

Now she'd slammed into a barrier, and she had nothing. No names or addresses or even a glimpse into her past.

She rubbed her temples. Library research was so methodical. Orderly. But walking through Heidelberg in search of her mother was like sweeping her fingers along a beach in hopes of snagging a pearl.

Maybe one of the local teachers had had her mother in class. Surely one of them would remember the pregnant, dark-haired girl who rarely smiled.

"It's called the Neckar."

Elise recognized the voice of the college kid from the registrar's office, but she didn't move.

He kept talking. "The river will take you through the Neckar Valley and the Odenwald Forest."

"Fascinating," she mumbled.

"I guess you aren't here to learn about the landscape . . . or get married."

Just what she needed—an English-speaking guy who thought he was funny.

"Would you like to get some lunch?" he asked.

She folded her arms over her chest. "I wouldn't be good company."

"An American woman who was born in Germany, but doesn't know German." He grinned. "I'm intrigued."

"I know German," she insisted. "Some German."

"Glad to hear it," he said. "Then I won't have to worry about you."

"I don't recall asking you to worry about me."

"My name's Carson Talles." He stuck out his hand, and she shook it. "I'm from Norfolk."

She didn't mention that she was from Virginia too. "Are you here for school?"

"I'm backpacking my way across Europe."

She recrossed her arms. At least he didn't smell like the backpacker at the memorial. "Do all backpackers stop off at the registrar's office?"

"Probably not." He shrugged. "I had a question about my visa."

She hesitated. The backpacker in Berlin had given her the creeps, but this guy didn't seem weird. Of course, according to her dad, most predators were later described as "nice guys." He had warned her about all the dangerous men in Europe, but he hadn't said anything about American boys. Even though this guy was in his twenties, he was all boy.

"I'm Elise."

He put his arms into his fleece jacket and pulled it on. "So you're looking for your birth certificate?"

"I'm going to get lunch." She stepped away from him and nodded toward a row of shops at the end of the street. It was none of his business why she was here.

"What do you think about fish?"

She hesitated. "Are they still swimming?"

"Fried beyond recognition."

Her stomach rumbled. She supposed it wouldn't hurt to have lunch with him. He pointed left, and she followed him down a lane ribbed with wrought iron fences and hurricane lanterns. The street was rutted with broken bricks, and hardy violet and pink geraniums splashed color on the stucco houses that were crossed with timbers.

At the corner of the street, they passed a teenage girl who was leaning up against an iron railing, her long legs patched with fishnet. Her eyes were lined with black to match the stringy black hair piled on top of her head, and her shoulders drooped forward as she drummed her ruby red heel on a step.

Elise stopped, a chill stinging her spine as she watched a man in an expensive business suit approach the girl. He whispered in her ear, and she looped her black-painted nails around his elbow and led him toward the door.

Carson turned and looked at her. "What's wrong?"

She pointed up to the door as it closed behind the girl and her client. "Ahh . . . culture shock."

She faced him, her shock turning to anger. "It's got nothing to do with culture."

"Nobody's making her sell her body."

She snorted. "No woman would *choose* to do that."

"Prostitution is legal in Germany."

It felt like he'd punched her in the gut. "It's not—"

"The law is supposed to stop pimps from forcing women to work as prostitutes."

She shook her head as she backed away from the woman's door. "God bless Germany."

"I'm not saying it's right." Carson directed her through another courtyard. "It's just different here."

Instead of standing on street corners and waiting for men, these women could walk away and find real jobs where they didn't have to sell their bodies or live trapped inside a brothel. There were plenty of opportunities available for a woman who was willing to work.

Carson pointed up at a tin sign that dangled above a dark wooden door in front of them. She couldn't read the name of the restaurant, but she could smell the cigarette smoke even before he opened the door. Covering her mouth, she coughed as she followed him inside.

Carson motioned toward a booth, and she slid across from him on the hard bench. "I don't suppose they have a nonsmoking section?"

"You'll get used to it."

She opened the menu and blinked rapidly as she tried to read it. She might be able to cope with the smoke, but she'd never get used to it—just like she'd never get used to the idea of legalized prostitution. Just because the government condoned it didn't make it right.

Carson reached over and swiped her menu from her hands. "You don't need that."

Seconds later, the server appeared at their table. "Two fish and chips?"

Carson nodded and ordered a local brew.

"Just water for me." Elise coughed again and fanned her face to clear the air. "A lot of water."

Carson leaned back against the booth. "So you're in Heidelberg to get your birth certificate?"

She cringed. "I'm on a research trip for school."

"I thought those study tours were just an excuse to play."

She shrugged. "Not if you like to study."

"And the birth certificate?"

"That part's personal."

"I'd be glad to help you."

"No, thanks." The server set down a glass of water in front of her. She guzzled it and handed it back. "Do you always backpack by yourself?"

He grinned. "I meet all sorts of interesting people along the way."

The waiter served up two plates with an aluminum foil bundle wrapped in twine. She unwrapped the twine around her fish, and the salty steam gushed out over her face and hands. "What high school did you go to?"

"Norfolk Collegiate."

"Pricey."

"It was decent . . . for a school." He peeled back the foil on his fish. "Have you been to Norfolk?"

She reached for the vinegar bottle and sprinkled it over her meal. "I grew up in Chesapeake."

"We're practically neighbors."

She tasted the vinegar soaked meat. "Not bad."

He pulled his hand to his heart like she'd insulted him. "You're kidding, right?"

"Okay, it's pretty good."

"Let's hope the cook doesn't speak English."

She bit into a wedge of potato and thought about the woman who'd handed her the application for the marriage license. "I thought everyone around here spoke a little English."

"Most of the students."

"And the shop owners," she added.

He stopped eating. "Who told you that?"

"I just figured . . ."

"You're not in the States anymore." He reached for another piece of fish. "People here aren't required to know your language."

It hadn't occurred to her that she'd have trouble talking to people in Heidelberg. "What about the teachers?"

"Most of the younger ones would know English."

"I need to speak to the teachers who were here twenty years ago."

He wiped his hands on a napkin. "Do you want me to help translate for you?"

She eyed the stranger across the table. She didn't want someone tagging along, yet she might need help with the language, especially if anyone recognized the picture of her mother. If he had time, maybe he could come along with her for a couple of hours—just until she got the information she needed.

She bit into a soggy french fry and swallowed. If he was going to help her, she had to be honest with him. "I'm adopted," she explained. "And I want to find out about my birth parents."

"Fair enough." He crumpled his greasy tin foil into a ball. "The birth certificate would have been a good place to start."

She took her last bite of fish. "Don't you have someplace you need to be?"

"I leave for Switzerland on Sunday."

"We may not find anything."

He shrugged. "Most of the fun is in the hunt."

She crunched her fingers. She wasn't doing this for fun.

Chapter 8

SARA'S STOMACH RUMBLED as she smelled the warm scent of yeast drifting out the open door of Café Sperl. She inhaled, pretending the aroma could fill the emptiness in her belly. She could almost taste the buttery flakes of a croissant on her tongue.

It was an hour before dinner, yet there was nothing to eat at home. Food had been scarce over the past month, most of it reserved for Sol and his guests. When she pleased him, he would give her part of his steak or bratwurst, but now, even when she tried to please him, there was no meat left.

She wasn't picky today. Any kind of food would satisfy the gnawing in her gut and stop the pain.

The owner of the café had a daughter, and when her father wasn't there, the woman would slip her a roll over the counter. When her father was working the counter, he wouldn't even give her a crust of leftover bread.

Her stomach groaned again as she peered at the lemon pastries, chocolate éclairs, raisin marzipan, and iced cookies in the glass case.

Something moved inside the window, and Sara looked up from the case and into the face of the owner. He was staring right at her, his right arm batting the air like he was swatting a swarm of flies. Sol said the man used to donate food to their family years ago, but he'd never given a crumb to Sara. And she'd asked him over and over again because Sol insisted that she try.

There was no reason to wait near the café. Even if the owner's daughter were there, she wouldn't be doling out food with her father nearby.

Sara turned and moved toward the meat shop two doors down, her feet dragging under her torn cotton dress. Though he didn't know English, the butcher sometimes gave her a dry sausage or a slab of pork.

She didn't have the strength to visit all the shops today. When she went for a day or two without food, her energy faded away. Sol said that God would fill her with power during these times of fasting, yet she could barely get out of bed.

Surely God knew how much she wanted to serve him. Every night she lay in bed and pleaded with him to forgive her for her many sins. Her doubts. Her disobedience. Even when all she wanted to do was serve him, she failed.

Her mission today was simple. All she had to do was ask for food from some of the local merchants, enough to feed her and the others who lived in the house. It was an easy task, but she had never been good at begging.

When she eased open the door to the meat shop, the butcher was standing behind the counter, a cleaver hoisted above his head. His white hat hung crooked over his gray hair as he thrust the steel blade into a large roast. The smell of spicy meat filled the air, and she felt faint for a moment. She couldn't remember the last time she'd had a sausage.

She greeted him in German, and he nodded his head. He rarely spoke to her, and his eyes always looked tired and sad. If only she could speak better German, she would tell him that Jesus could wash his sadness away.

"Haben Sie vielleicht bitte etwas Essen für meine Familie?" She used one of the few phrases she had learned from Sol. *Do you please have some food for my family?*

Her stomach growled again, and she was embarrassed that he heard. He didn't say anything, but he slowly nodded his head as he reached into the glass case and pulled out a roll of salami.

"Für dich," he said as he put the meat into a bag and handed it to her. Her fingers shook as she took the meat from him. She was so hungry.

She lowered her eyes as she quoted a verse from Matthew to him.

"Who then is a faithful and wise servant . . . to give them meat in due season?"

He stared at her in frustration, like he did every time she blessed him with a Scripture. And she understood his frustration. She'd been raised in Germany, yet she knew only a few basic words and phrases in German. Everyone in her family spoke English. She didn't need to speak German until Sol sent her to town, and he believed that the locals would be more sympathetic—and generous—if she didn't know the language. So whenever she came into town, she stumbled through the same spiel, asking again and again for food for her family.

She'd asked Sol once how she was supposed to tell people about God if she didn't know German, but he said she needed to let the missionaries in Berlin do the witnessing—where most people spoke English anyway. God was using the other women in the family to spread God's love, but he wasn't using her. With her whole heart she wanted to please God . . . and Sol.

I am crucified with Christ: nevertheless I live; yet not I, but Christ liveth in me: and the life which I now live in the flesh I live by the faith of the Son of God, who loved me, and gave himself for me.

Like Christ, Sol had given himself for her. He'd loved her, and she had to give back to him and to God.

Her stomach rumbled again, and she tried to ignore the paper bag in her hand as she strolled toward the river. She hadn't eaten a full meal in weeks.

During the fall and winter, they usually had enough income coming in from Berlin to feed the entire family, but not this month. Even the squash and pumpkins and greens from their fall garden were gone.

Sol had been sending someone into Grimma and Leipzig and Dresden almost every day for the past week to ask for food and money, but the banks of generosity were almost bankrupt. He usually demanded that they solicit food in teams of two or three, but he was making an exception to that rule lately because they needed more food. Before she'd left the house today, Sol had prayed in desperation that God would provide for his chosen people.

For we walk by faith, not by sight.

The enemy was punishing them for their devotion, and she wouldn't let him win. She may hate begging for donations, but God asked so little of her. He just wanted her to love him and his people. All she had to do was squelch her pride. Overcome her weakness. She had so far to go before she could please God. Some days it seemed like it was impossible to win his favor.

Every time she sought the light, it disappeared.

Michael was hunting food on the east side of town. She had taken the west side so she could watch the river. It was a respite for her, the current reminding her that the persecution in this world would only make her stronger. If she proved her love in this life, God would welcome her home for eternity.

A group of teenage girls in pressed navy and white uniforms sat in front of a café, sipping drinks and squawking like chickens.

Sara leaned against the wall and tried to beat back feelings of jealousy as she watched them. What must it be like to be so carefree—drinking coffee and eating chocolate biscotti with a couple of friends? These were worldly girls. They didn't know God. Yet they seemed to have the happiness that she craved—maybe she'd be happy too if she were allowed to eat chocolate.

One of the girls elbowed her friend, and suddenly the entire table was looking at her. Laughing. She looked behind her to see what was so funny, but she was alone on the sidewalk, entertainment for a horde of schoolgirls. Not that she could blame them—she was a spectacle in her ratty brown dress and tangled hair.

Yea, and all that will live godly in Christ Jesus shall suffer persecution.

Jesus didn't promise warmth or security. He promised hardship and persecution. She could live her life dedicated to Christ, or live her life in selfishness, like the world.

She blinked back tears as she turned and ran down the sidewalk. Jesus may have drawn crowds, but she didn't want an audience. She wanted a friend.

She wasn't like those worldly girls. She had been called out from the world. Chosen by God to live in righteousness with the true believers.

Blessed is the nation whose God is the LORD; and the people whom he hath chosen for his own inheritance.

God had marked her from the beginning, selecting her to be his bride. She shivered as she crossed the cobblestone street. No matter how hard it was to serve him, she was devoted.

And he that doubteth is damned . . . for whatsoever is not of faith is sin.

She'd memorized hundreds of verses, quoting them as she cooked and served and combated the demons that stole her sleep. The verses kept her mind pure when the doubts plagued her; the words held her faith intact and kept her plodding down the narrow road to heaven.

She crushed the quiet seeds of disbelief before they became rooted in her soul. There was no room for questions. No time to lose faith. The risk was too great. If she lost her faith, she'd lose her soul.

And if thine eye offend thee, pluck it out: it is better for thee to enter into the kingdom of God with one eye, than having two eyes to be cast into hell fire.

She shivered. God help her—she was terrified of spending eternity in hell. The fire. The darkness. Damnation.

She dug her rough fingernails into the skin under her loose sleeves, punishing herself for her thoughts. She'd cut out both eyes if she had to in order to purge herself of her offense.

For, behold, the LORD cometh out of his place to punish the inhabitants of the earth for their iniquity.

The Mulde River bubbled up around the pilings after the night's hard rain. A man cruised by on a fishing boat, and a swan circled under the bridge. On the other side of the water, the red roofs of the churches and houses bled into the trees.

Some days, she dreamed about throwing herself into the river and letting the water envelop her in its current until it reached the waterfall downstream. Then it would plunge her over the edge, and she would fall into a world free of hunger and pain.

A string of clouds blew in across the river and blocked out the sun. The fall might free her from her earthly pain, but the depths of hell would be even more painful than life on this earth.

If there was a hell . . .

She dug her nails deeper into her skin, battling for control. She could feel the warmth of the blood on her fingertips.

So then because thou art lukewarm, and neither cold nor hot, I will spue thee out of my mouth.

Tears pooled in her eyes.

"Don't leave me," she pleaded quietly. She could bear the pain if it would make her closer to him.

The breeze stirred the aroma of the salami from her bag, and her stomach raged with desire.

One bite was all she needed. The meat would calm her anxiety. Clear the doubts in her mind. Stop her shakes.

She gripped the bag to her side, pleading with God for strength. It was food for the whole family, not just for her. She would chop it into a soup or slice it for sandwiches, alongside whatever food Michael had gathered.

Stepping toward the river, she untied her shoes and eased her bare feet into the muddy banks. The cold mud sucked on her toes like it was savoring the taste, but the chill didn't bother her. Nor did the dirt. She lifted her skirt and trudged toward the water. The current was strong today. Decisive.

She stuck her toe in the water, icing her skin. If she relinquished control, maybe it would carry her away to a safe place of warmth and security.

Her stomach roared again. Even louder. Her hunger was making her lose focus.

For many are called, but few are chosen.

God had placed her in Sol's family, and she would never run away. She was called. Chosen. One of the few who were privileged to marry not only a messenger of God, but a king.

Her belly ached. She had to get away from the river before she lost her throne in the next kingdom.

Muddy water splashed the hem of her dress when she swiveled toward the street. She quickly laced her shoes and rushed back toward town, turning onto Langestrasse to avoid the crowd of girls by the café. Perhaps she could find some more food before Michael finished his rounds.

With the bag of salami still clutched between her fingertips, she visited four more shops, but she left each without adding to her rations.

And whosoever shall not receive you, nor hear you, when ye depart thence, shake off the dust under your feet for a testimony against them.

She wiped her feet on a small patch of fading grass and continued toward the center of town. She wouldn't take the rejection personally. Jesus wasn't popular either, but he was strong. Once, he went forty days without food even though the Devil tempted him . . . just like he was tempting her now.

And just like Jesus, she wouldn't give in to the temptation. She would be strong.

On her right was a pizza shop. The pungent scents of oregano and cheese and tomato sauce were heavy in the cool air. She slipped into the narrow alley beside the shop and ducked behind a metal staircase. She couldn't think about the repercussions. Food was what she needed right now. A few bites and she would be fine.

With a loud rip, she opened the bag and bit the end off the salami roll. Chewing wasn't necessary. She just swallowed and inhaled another bite. And another.

She barely tasted the meat, but she couldn't stop herself from eating it. It was what she needed to feel better. To stop the pain.

She devoured the entire roll and collapsed back against the staircase, her stomach finally full. Then she hiccupped and rubbed her greasy hands onto her skirt. What would Sol do if he smelled the meat on her? He would know she had been weak, and he would send Phoebe to remind her that Satan was winning the battle for her soul.

She rubbed her hands over her arms. Maybe Sol wouldn't notice the smell over the stench of mud and sweat.

The church bells rang out. It was four o'clock. Time to go home.

She clutched her skirt and ran toward the town center. She could see Michael standing beside the beat-up tan Volvo that they used to haul donations back to the house. His long blond hair was pulled back in a rubber band; his dusty boots crossed at the ankle. Sol had molded him into a strong lieutenant over the years, but she still caught glimpses of the scared, abandoned boy in his gaze—the one whose father had left him with their family when he was two and never returned.

When they were both kids, they would sneak down under the convent together and revel in the quiet. They'd both been lonely, and they'd both been terrified about the future.

But they'd grown up quickly, and when they did, they discovered the realities of being chosen. Sol selected her to be one of his wives and designated Michael as his lieutenant. She'd watched her best friend turn into a stern soldier as his influence grew in the house. Neither of them asked questions, unlike some of the other kids in the family—they'd both done what God required.

He glanced at her empty hands. "Where's your food?"

She dug her fingernails into her palms. God forgive her lie. "No one would donate today."

"Did you even ask?"

She cringed. What had happened to the kindness that had once pervaded his heart? "I'm sorry, Michael."

She glanced into the back seat and saw three bags filled with food.

Michael reached for the door handle. "He'll be angry."

"I know," she muttered as she climbed into the car.

Michael opened the driver's door and slid into the seat, but he wouldn't meet her eye. "I'll tell him you got one of these bags."

Sol wouldn't believe him. The last three times he had sent her into town, she'd come back without food, yet he kept sending her.

"Tell him the truth," she insisted. If he didn't, Michael would be punished for her sin.

"He won't let you eat tonight."

She held her breath to stifle her hiccup. "I'm not hungry."

Chapter 9

RAIN POUNDED THE FRONT window of the coffee shop as Elise stirred her latte with a spoon. The drops glided down the glass beside her, weaving an erratic pattern in their race to the ground.

She and Carson had spent the afternoon tromping down the hallways in Heidelberg's schools and quizzing the teachers. Elise would show the picture, and if the teacher didn't understand English, Carson would ask in German if they knew her mother. Carson was right—most of the teachers didn't know enough English to answer her question, but they usually chatted with Carson for ten or fifteen minutes.

At first she had gotten excited that he was talking so long, but each time they left a classroom, he would relay their conversation and inevitably they had spent their time talking about German history or football or great places to climb near town. After four hours of searching, no one had recognized Catrina.

Carson had volunteered to hit the row of stores in Old Town with her tomorrow, and she had taken him up on the offer.

A group of students passed the coffee shop, their faces hidden behind umbrellas and brown bottles of beer. She closed her eyes for a moment and quietly asked God for guidance. She was floundering right now. Scattered. The plan she had arrived with had crumbled, and she was left with nothing but her determination.

If any of you lack wisdom, let him ask of God, that giveth to all men liberally, and upbraideth not; and it shall be given him. But let him ask in faith, nothing wavering. For he that wavereth is like a wave of the sea driven with the wind and tossed. For let not that man think that he shall receive any thing of the Lord. A double minded man is unstable in all his ways.

It was one of the many Bible verses her mother had taught her; verses that came back to her when she needed them most.

Carson sat down across from her, a mug of black coffee in one hand and a bagel in the other. "So, are you ready to come clean with me yet?"

She sighed. "I already told you why I'm here."

"Why don't you just call your mom and ask her for her maiden name?"

She swirled her drink in the mug. "I can't."

He stared at her face, waiting for an answer.

"She died a few years ago . . . from a stroke."

His mouth dropped. "I'm sorry."

She shrugged off his sympathy. "A lot of people die from strokes."

He reached for her hand, and she pulled it away. "We'll find someone else who can help you."

"Right . . ."

She took another sip of her latte. This week was not about reveling in the past, but discovering the truth so she could move beyond the past. The memories would only serve as a guide.

Carson leaned toward her. "Do you have any other relatives?"

"My dad adopted me when I was six, and along with him came scads of family members; but whatever they know about my mother's past, they're not talking."

"Does he know you're trying to find out what happened?"

She bristled. "No."

"That doesn't sound fair."

"It's the right thing to do." She glanced up at a clock. Four o'clock in Germany. Ten in Virginia. She was supposed to have called her dad before nine.

She guzzled the last of her drink and pulled a khaki-colored parka out of her pack. At least her dad had prepared her for the dreary weather. "I need to find a phone."

"There's a booth over on Hauptstrasse. A block or so away."

She tugged the hood of her parka over her head. "I'll see you tomorrow."

He shot her a look like she'd lost her mind. "I'm coming with you."

"Your hostel is the other way."

"Let's see . . ." He ticked off his fingers. "Darkness. Rain. An American girl who doesn't know the language . . ."

"I know enough."

He zipped up his Gore-Tex jacket. "I won't be able to sleep tonight unless I make sure you get back to your hotel."

She strapped her backpack over her shoulder. Heidelberg was hardly riddled with crime, but even if it was, she knew how to take care of herself. "I know my way."

He flashed her a puppy dog grin. "Yeah, but it would make me feel a whole lot better."

She wasn't giving in. She had gotten all the way to Heidelberg without Carson's help; she didn't need an escort now. Besides, she didn't want some guy she'd just met walking her back to her hotel.

"Thanks for your help," she said as she opened the door.

"I'm not letting you go alone."

She stepped out into the downpour and clutched her pack to her side. "*Gute nacht.*"

She couldn't understand exactly what he muttered in return, but he didn't return the good night.

"I'll meet you at nine," he shouted into the storm. "By the town hall."

Rain drizzled down the sides of the plastic hood and soaked her face as she plodded toward Hauptstrasse. Black clouds masked the fading rays of daylight.

The phone booth stood at the corner of an empty courtyard. Apparently, whoever built it decided they didn't need even a sliver of a roof, like it never rained in Germany. She and the phone would have to weather the storm together.

It would be much easier if she had her cell phone, but when she'd taken it into a phone shop yesterday to buy an international chip, the man had informed her that even if he sold her a chip, she wouldn't be able to use a locked phone in Germany. So instead of a chip, he had sold her a phone card, and she had called home last night from a phone booth in Berlin. Her dad wasn't happy about the situation, but she had promised him that she would check in every night by nine.

Now she was an hour and a half late.

She searched her pockets and found the phone card in the back of her jeans. She had at least eight minutes left to chat—a good excuse to say good-bye before he asked too many questions. It wasn't the time to try to explain that she was a five-hour train ride from Berlin.

She brushed the water off the plastic and held it up toward the dull glow of a streetlamp as she punched in the code.

Her dad answered. "I was worried about you."

She shivered under her parka. "You're always worried about me, Dad."

"Where are you?"

She brushed water off her forehead. "At a freezing cold phone booth."

"It was sunny here today. Seventy-five."

The water clung to her eyelashes. "How's my crew?"

"Missing you," he said. "Rags refused to eat this afternoon."

She stopped smiling. "Please don't tell me that Devin fed him the dry food!"

When he hesitated, she knew her half-brother hadn't listened to her precise instructions. The minute she got home, she'd fire her dad and her brother, even if he was only seven.

"That stuff makes him sick."

"I'm sure it was a mistake."

She shook the water off her icy hands and buried them back under her parka. Even though she wrote down what each cat could and couldn't eat, Devin was too young to get it straight.

"I specifically told him that Rags gets the prescription food and the supplement instead of milk."

"Are you sure you don't want to come home early?"

"Nice try, Dad. Did you tell Devin to feed Rags the wrong food?"

"I would have if I had thought of it." He paused. "I miss you even more than the cats do."

Even when he hounded her with opinions and advice, she missed him too. He was her cheerleader. Her strong arm when she needed help. It would be easy to give up the search and rush back to the safety of home, but if she didn't pursue her story now, she'd probably never do it.

"Only eight more days." Rain dripped down the collar of her parka, and she rubbed her neck. "Can you please make sure Rags gets the right food tonight?"

"I'm trying to teach Devin more responsibility."

"And I'm trying to keep my cats alive," she huffed.

"I'll make sure Devin feeds him the right stuff."

She shifted her shoulders. "Thank you."

"How's Berlin?"

"As rainy as you said it would be."

"And your German?"

She grimaced. "*Nicht sehr gut.*"

"You'll get used to it by the time you go to Wittenberg."

She wiped off the phone with her hand before she spoke again. "Dad . . . do you know if Mom was ever in Berlin?"

Seconds passed before he responded. "Not that I know of."

"I was just thinking that while I was here I could go visit some of the places where she went or see some of her old friends or her favorite parks or even her family."

He stopped her. "Your mother hated big cities."

She glanced across the desolate plaza in front of her. "What if I went to Heidelberg?"

He didn't hesitate this time. "Stay away from there, Elise."

She braced at his tone. He was four thousand miles away, but she knew his mouth was locked in a frown and he was grinding the heels of his cowboy boots into the floor.

"I know you can't possibly understand," he continued, "but it's not safe."

She switched the phone to her right ear. "Why won't you tell me what happened to her?"

His voice softened. "She didn't want you to know, honey."

"I can handle it, Dad."

He sighed. "It's not a matter of handling it."

The phone beeped to signal the end of her time. He quickly said that he loved her, but the connection ended before she could tell him she loved him too.

She hung up the phone and wandered down the dark street toward the muted light of a cast-iron lamp. Her jeans were drenched up to her knees, and her arms shivered under her sweater.

She'd been angry when he had lied to her and yet she was now doing the same thing to him. If she were honest with him, though, he'd be irate. And she had no idea why.

When her mother died, she had left Elise alone with a man whom she'd known for only a couple of years. Fortunately, she'd chosen the man well.

As much as Elise wanted to find out what happened to her mother, she'd never risk hurting the man who'd loved her like a daughter for the past fifteen years. Her birth father may have been a hotshot pilot from Montana, but he could never replace her dad.

She tugged her hood over her eyes and trudged through the downpour, toward the hotel and a hot cup of tea and a dry bed. The rain pelted her bare face, stinging her skin.

After four blocks of fighting the wind, she ducked under an awning and clutched her side as she gulped in the wet air. The fatigue from lingering jet lag fogged her mind. If she pushed herself the three more blocks to the hotel, she'd probably end up in a gutter.

She would have to wait until the wind died down.

She glanced up the street and saw a few lights, but no pedestrians. She was alone in the darkness. In Heidelberg.

She leaned her back against the brick wall, and the cold seeped through the parka and into her skin as the wind shot missiles of rain into her shelter.

She wished she were back at home in the warmth of the farmhouse, tucked into her cozy bed with the corner fireplace blazing and all six of her cats snuggling under the covers.

She'd only been away for three days, but it wasn't a problem of time. It was a problem of location. She'd never been this far from home.

She could hear her dad's words, telling her to be careful and to stay near crowds if she had to be out at night. She hated deceiving him, but she couldn't tell him where she was.

Prom night, her junior year, she had gone on her first real date with a guy named Trevor Vaughn. Her dad had informed Trevor that when the clock struck midnight, she was to be home and in her own bed. She and Trevor had danced under the Arabian Night stars in the school gym, and they'd lost track of time. When she asked Trevor to check his watch, he said it was 1:30.

Her dad was already out looking for her when she called his cell, and he was livid. Even though it was the middle of the night, he had lectured her for an hour and then he'd grounded her. It didn't matter that she'd never missed a curfew before, or that a couple hours later, he went to the ER because of chest pains, and the doctor performed an emergency angioplasty to open a blocked artery.

She'd overshot curfew. A mistake. But breaking curfew wasn't the core issue. It was like he was terrified that if he didn't keep a tight grasp on her life, she would slip away like her mother.

The next time Trevor had called, she had turned down the date, and when she had gone off to college, she didn't have time to date. She ran for student government her freshman year and got voted in as vice president. When she realized all the red tape she would have to blaze through in that position, she'd nixed the political track and picked up women's history instead. If she was going to convince women to overcome their circumstances, she decided that education was the key. She'd learn from the past and then teach a new generation the success stories alongside the failures.

The rain poured harder, swirling down the street like river rapids. Trash wrapped around her ankles, and she clutched her fingers in her pockets to try to keep them warm as she waited for the wind to subside.

Her teeth chattered as she looked up at the black sky. She was stuck in a storm, alone in a strange country, with only twenty soaked euros in her pocket. Her teeth chattered. If she didn't get out of this storm, she would be sick for the rest of her trip.

Maybe she shouldn't have ditched Carson back at the restaurant. He could have talked his way into someone's warm, dry home.

The gray rain blurred her view of most of the buildings across the street, but in the darkened window directly across from her, she could make out piles of apples and bananas. Next to the grocery was a chapel.

A light flickered behind the stained glass window of the church, and she took a small step toward it. And another one.

When she reached the curb, she didn't turn back. She waded through the water and stomped up the stairs to the front of the church building. She twisted the doorknob and pushed the door open.

A light glowed at the front of the small sanctuary, illuminating a wooden crucifix. A carving of Jesus hung on the cross, his eyes frozen on the ceiling as he silently pleaded with God to take away the pain.

As she stared at his face, something twisted in her gut. It didn't matter how drenched she was. Or how cold. Or sick. Christ had suffered so much more. Yet even in the suffering, Christ was a refuge from the cold and the darkness and the evil in the world.

Water pooled on the marble floor under her feet as she stepped forward. Rain hammered the stained glass windows on both sides of her, but she felt safe for the moment. Slowly, she moved down the aisle toward the light, the warmth soothing her skin.

She hung her soaked parka on a hook and sat down on the front pew. The faint scent of lavender lingered in the air. On her left was a small choir loft and a pulpit that glistened in the light. She turned her head and glanced up at the dark balcony behind her. Organ pipes crept up the wall like stalagmites from a cave floor.

She dropped her bag onto a pew and wished she could wrap herself in the aura of peace that settled over the church.

She was still alone in the dark, but she wasn't frightened. God was here. She could almost taste his sweet spirit on her tongue, feel his comfort in the spray of flowers beside the altar, the worn hymnbooks, the candelabra. No matter how miserable or alone she felt, maybe she could find peace here.

Above the pulpit was a wooden canopy engraved with a golden cross. She stood up and took a step toward the lectern, staring at the gold.

It was uncanny. Almost as if she'd seen that canopy before.

She blinked as the memory blurred.

Maybe she had seen pictures of something similar in one of her research books. After four years of study, she felt as if she'd read every book written on European history.

The rain pounded against the windows, but she barely heard it. The warmth of the room settled around her like a blanket as she stared at a familiar painting of Daniel facing the lions.

In her psych class, she'd studied the intricacy of the human psyche. A child breathes in her surroundings, soaking in her tiny environment with wonder. As an adult, memories of her childhood are triggered by the simplest things. Strips of wallpaper. A whiff of peppermint. Shutters flapping in the wind. Or a picture hanging on a wall.

She sat down again and closed her eyes.

She hadn't seen these pictures in a history book. She had been in this church before . . .

Chapter 10

THE LOCK ON THE door clicked shut. Sara stripped off her wet clothes and collapsed on the cot in the corner. Even though she had told Michael not to lie for her, she still thought he would let her take credit for some of his food. He used to do things like that for her when they were younger, and she had loved him for it.

When they were kids, he'd hold her after she'd been punished, and after he had been disciplined, she would tiptoe downstairs to find ice for his wounds. Once, when he was ten, Phoebe had beaten him because he said he was the one who had sneaked outside during the night. Sara had gone out to the courtyard to dance, and he knew it, but he endured the punishment for her.

She had given her heart to Michael that night, silently devoting herself to help him whenever she could. She never forgot her promise.

She knew she belonged to Sol, yet she wanted to tell Michael that no matter what happened, she still cared for him.

Phoebe had lit a candle stub and left it on the dresser, but the wick was almost gone. In minutes, it would burn out and darkness would envelop her, punishing her for her sin.

Next time she went to town, she wouldn't bother asking for food. She would visit the grocery store and steal some canned goods from the shelf.

Ye shall not steal.

Sol would never have to know that she stole it. She would say that after all these years of saying no, the store owner finally decided to donate some food to their family.

Neither lie one to another.

Phoebe had set a Bible and a glass of water beside the candle, but Sara didn't open the book. Instead, she stared up at the ceiling, watching the light flicker on the stone. Maybe she should have jumped in the river when she'd had the chance and let it carry her away from here.

Once she was locked in this room, escape wasn't an option. Phoebe or Sol or Michael or one of the other men in the group would catch her. Phoebe would whip her for trying to desert the group and lock her back in the cell.

If Phoebe found out she had eaten the salami, her back and legs would burn for weeks.

She rubbed her hand over her belly. In spite of the punishment, she was still glad she'd eaten the meat. She'd endured solitary confinement for weeks in the past; she could easily survive a couple more days now with a full stomach.

A cramp rippled through her abdomen, and she clenched her stomach until it disappeared. The last time she hurt this bad, she had lost a baby.

She closed her eyes and took a deep breath as she listened to the rain patter the sliver of a window near the ceiling. She didn't want to think about the possibility that she might be pregnant. All she wanted to do was pretend she was sitting with the group of girls on the plaza, sipping hot chocolate and eating biscotti. She wouldn't have to say anything. She just wanted to be a part of their laughter. And fun.

They were probably allowed to dance and play music and sing something other than the choruses that the family chanted before meals.

Sara sat up and brushed her feet against the tile.

At one time she had felt hope. Happiness. When she was a child. During the summer days, she used to escape to the courtyard by herself and dance to the music that played in her head. The trees were her orchestra. The birds her audience.

And most days, Sol would invite her into his office and share his dessert to remind her of the sweetness of God's love for her. Then he would tell her about how God had chosen her to be his bride.

The music started fading around her tenth birthday. Sol invited her into his office after lunch, and she remembered wondering if he would have any chocolate for her.

He did—a slice of mousse torte to celebrate her birthday. And then he announced that it was time for her to fully experience God's love. Phoebe had dressed her in white, and the other members of the family had gathered for the ceremony.

She shivered, remembering the excitement she'd felt as a child. And pride, awestruck that Sol had picked her to be his wife. She was special—to him and to God.

But after the ceremony, his kindness had disappeared. He had hurt her, but he told her that her pain was nothing compared to the suffering that Christ experienced on the cross. She was nothing, but she could give her body back as an offering to God.

Even though she wanted to serve God and his messengers, she'd cried for days when Phoebe forced her to visit Sol.

The chocolate vanished along with the music. And she stopped dancing.

Naomi and the other girls she had played with as children were now working in Berlin. Luke had been sent to a home in Italy, and Joshua had died two years ago. Sol told the family that Joshua had killed himself, but she never believed his story. Joshua had loved one of the other girls that Sol had chosen, and he'd paid with his life.

After Joshua died, Michael stopped talking to Sara. And he started to despise her. At one time he may have wanted her, but not anymore.

Something brushed her toe, and she pulled her knees up to her chest as tears began to fill her dry eyes. Last year, she had rescued two cats and nursed them back to health. Within weeks, the scurry of mice running through their rooms had vanished. But when spring came, Sol whisked her cats away to town, because he said that she loved them more than she loved him. After he took them, the mice returned.

Every time she went into town, she looked for the cats, hoping to find them under someone's stoop or scavenging for food in an alley. She had never found them, and eventually she slammed shut the small part of her heart that she'd opened just for them.

Sol had been right. She couldn't help loving her cats. They'd asked so little of her, snuggling with her in the darkness when she didn't think she could make it through another day.

She almost hadn't made it after they were gone, but she'd clung to her faith. God had ordained Sol as a messenger, and Sol knew when she was putting something before him and before God. The cats had taken what he thought was his place in her heart, and he wouldn't allow it. No person or animal should take the place of her husband. Not a cat, and especially not someone like Michael.

The wick on the candle burned out, and the darkness folded over her like a cold blanket.

Maybe Michael would get her out in the morning.

Chapter 11

A CRACK OF THUNDER jolted Elise, and she clapped her hands over her ears. In the moonlight, she could see other children around her. They were all in their beds along the wall. Asleep.

The thunder roared again, and she pulled the thin blanket up to her chin. How could the others sleep through this noise?

The door at the side of the room opened, and she watched as a gray cloud drifted past her and stopped over the crib by the window. The cloud hovered over the crib, and Elise watched in horror as it turned black and rained shards of glass.

Then she heard a scream. There was a baby inside the crib, and she was crying out for help. Elise leapt from her bed and ran toward the crib.

The baby's fingers pressed through the slats of her bed, trying to get away, but she couldn't get out. Elise scaled the bed in seconds, ignoring the cuts on her own skin. She would rescue the baby. Get her away from the storm.

A woman shoved her away from the crib. Elise beat the woman's arms with her fists. If they didn't help the baby, the glass would shred her skin.

The woman ignored her as she screamed.

Someone needed to save the baby.

Elise woke with a start, sweat pouring down her cheeks. She wiped her face with her wet sleeve and breathed deeply, reminding herself that it was only a dream. Even so, she could still see the baby reaching out her arms, crying for help.

She shook her head. She was at the church. In Heidelberg.

There was no baby.

Her back and neck ached, but the room was quiet. Light poured through the stained glass, streaming rivers of purple and yellow along the waxed floor.

She sneezed twice as she tried to sit up, her skin still felt damp from the storm. She needed a long, hot shower and a cup of coffee. Her fingers massaged the knot in her shoulder and then she stretched her arms and toes. Shivering, she crunched her arms to her chest.

If there were a virus within a mile of this church, she'd catch it. She was like a magnet during the cold and flu season, attracting germs wherever she went. It didn't help that she'd spent the night on a pew. In wet clothes.

She sneezed again and glanced at her watch. Carson was supposed to meet her at the Marktplatz in an hour.

A side door opened, and she turned to see a minister walking toward her. The hem of his black robe brushed the floor, and his thin hair was combed to the side. She couldn't see his eyes, but his glasses reflected in the morning light.

"*Bitte* . . ." He froze when she smiled at him. "Rahab?"

Her voice cracked. "Who is Rahab?"

The minister stepped away from her, his eyes focused on the face of Christ. His lips moved in a rapid motion but no words came out. His gaze dropped from the crucifix to the light underneath as he seemed to contemplate his next words. "Rahab was a brave woman who loved God."

Elise balled up her hands in the arms of her sweater as she tried to remember the story of Rahab in the Old Testament. "Wasn't she a prostitute?"

"Some scholars say she was a harlot, but others believe she was an innkeeper." He straightened a candle on the silver stand. "It doesn't really matter, does it? God blessed her because she risked her life to protect the people he loved."

Elise's fingers trembled under her sweater. "But you knew someone else named Rahab."

"A long time ago."

"My name is Elise Friedman." She hesitated. "Some people say I look like my mother."

The haze lifted from his gray eyes like he was coming out of a trance. He edged back and sat on the wooden pew. "Where is your mother?"

"She died thirteen years ago." It hurt to say the word. "Suicide."

The minister's shoulders collapsed back like someone had punched him. "God forgive them."

Elise's mind raced through all the questions she'd like to ask him. Most of all she wanted to know whom God should forgive.

She leaned toward him. "Could you please tell me how you knew her?"

"She visited here a long time ago."

She pointed up at the relief of Daniel. "I remember being here . . . but I don't remember why."

"Do you have other family?"

"My dad adopted me when I was six."

"And does he love you?"

"Very much."

"Go home, Elise." He reached out to her shoulder, his eyes steeped in sadness. "There is nothing here worth remembering."

"I want to know what happened to my mother."

He stood up. "The important thing is not to know what happened, but to know that your mother risked her life to protect you."

"Protect me from what?" she persisted.

"Your mother adored you, Elise. You would honor her by remembering her love and her life."

"Could you please tell me the truth?" she begged as he stepped back toward the side door and opened it.

"You can stay here as long as you'd like."

"Did you know her last name?"

He walked through the doorway and turned around. "She didn't have a last name."

Then he shut the door behind him.

Elise scooted along the pew, grabbed the doorknob, and tugged, but the minister had locked it.

She beat on the wooden door and yelled. "Who should God forgive?"

Chapter 12

TEN SECONDS WAS ALL it took for Elise to strip off her damp clothes and climb into the shower. She turned the dial toward hot and closed her eyes as the water warmed her skin and relaxed her mind.

Rahab. The name sounded familiar to her, beyond the biblical story. And the minister had seemed so certain that he knew her mother. If he was right, why had she been named after a prostitute? And how was it possible that she didn't have a last name?

The showerhead spurted her with cold water, and she hopped to the side of the shower and waited for it to turn hot again.

Even though the minister hadn't given her much information, he had confirmed that her mother had lived here, under another name. It was exactly what she had asked God for—direction and wisdom.

The shower doused her with another stream of cold, and her teeth chattered as she rinsed her hair before shutting it down. She wrapped herself in an oversized towel until she stopped shaking. Fifteen minutes later, she was dressed and dry, but her body still ached and her chest hurt when she coughed.

Today, she would roam the streets of Heidelberg, and she wouldn't sleep again until she found someone who recognized the picture of Catrina. Or Rahab.

She folded her wet parka under her arm just in case it rained again and shaded her eyes as she stepped out of the hotel and into the sunlight.

The air felt cool. Clean. Water dripped from the awnings of fruit stands and coffee shops, and with a quick hop, she skipped over a line of puddles and walked toward Marktplatz.

As she walked, she quietly prayed that Carson hadn't given up on her last night when she bolted. Even if she didn't want to admit it, she needed him, in case the one person who had known her mother years ago could only communicate in German. It was almost as if God had sent him here specifically to help her.

Her dad would have a list of reasons why she shouldn't trust him, but he was usually wrong about people. He certainly had been wrong about Trevor Vaughn.

The entire square was packed with tourists, bicyclists, and clusters of white tables topped with maroon umbrellas. A circle of giant dormer windows peered over the crowd. Meeting Carson here had seemed like a good plan; she just didn't realize that it would be so crowded.

She waited in front of the town hall for ten minutes, scanning the crowd, but he didn't show. Not that she could blame him. She wouldn't come back either if the person she had offered to help had run away.

She stepped away from the front of the hall. Even with the language barrier, she could go door-to-door on her own. It didn't matter if people continued to slam the door in her face. She would press on until she found someone else who knew Rahab.

She had just rounded the corner away from the square when someone called her name. She turned around and there was Carson, waving at her.

He jogged up beside her. "Where are you going?"

"You're late," she said before she coughed.

His easy smile turned to concern. "Did you get some sleep?"

"On a church pew."

"Elise . . ."

"I got caught in the rain."

He groaned. "I knew we should have stayed together."

"It's too late to give me a lecture."

"But not too late for an 'I told you so.'"

She sneezed. "You didn't tell me that I'd get stuck in the rain."

"If you would have stayed to listen, I'd have told you about a hundred things that could happen to you."

She dug a tissue out of her pocket. "Do you always enjoy gloating this much?"

"No." He grinned. "This time is particularly fun."

She sneezed again.

"We need to get you to the *Apotheke*."

"The what?"

He sighed and shook his head. "The pharmacy."

She followed him down a side street and into a small store lined with baskets of dyed soaps, medicine boxes, and throat lozenges.

Carson didn't hesitate at the door. He strode right to the pharmacist at the counter and fired off a rapid round of German. Elise leaned back against the wall and tried to pick through their conversation, but the only words she understood were *amerikanische* and *krank*—ill. She hoped he was also telling the pharmacist that her head was killing her.

He stepped toward her. "Are your muscles sore?"

"Every one of them."

He turned back to the woman in the white coat and translated.

The pharmacist ran her fingers across the white boxes behind her and plucked one off the shelf. She held it out to Elise, but her eyes were on Carson as she dispelled the last of her advice.

Elise paid for the medicine and followed him outside.

"Take two of those"—he pointed at the box—"every four hours."

She eyed the medicine in her hand. "How do I know this isn't arsenic?"

"Because the pharmacist doesn't recommend taking arsenic for a cold and flu."

She coughed again and opened the box.

"If you would have trusted me last night, you wouldn't be sick today."

"It wasn't just a matter of trust."

"Okay, if you hadn't been too proud to accept some help."

She wasn't proud; she was independent. Resourceful.

She peeled back the foil on the back of the medication. "Where did you learn to speak German so well?"

"Traveling around, talking to people."

She popped two pills out of the plastic packaging. "I took three years of German, and I only understood a few words of your conversation."

"You've got to immerse yourself in the language to learn it."

"That's what I've been trying to do."

He grinned. "And you almost got married."

Her chin inched up. It was time for her to take the lead again. "I'm going to do the talking today."

"No problem," he said. "I'll just be there to back you up."

When she coughed again, he pointed down at the medicine in her hand. "Are you going to take those?"

She eyed him one more time, and then dumped the pills into her mouth and swallowed.

"Now all we need is a plan." He nodded toward a row of bikes chained to a metal grate. "Should we rent bikes today?"

A cramp ripped through her leg. "I can barely walk."

"Give it a half hour—that medicine is powerful stuff."

He pointed toward a bench, and she sat down on the concrete slab. "It feels just like my bed last night."

"How exactly did you end up on a church pew?"

She glanced over at the handsome stranger who was elbowing his way into her private life. She'd never intended to make friends in Germany. She just wanted to get a few details about her past and then dive into her research.

She supposed it couldn't hurt for him to know some of her story.

She told him about the church and the light.

He interrupted her story with a groan. "You went in alone?"

"I wasn't worried."

"That's half of your problem."

She bristled. "I don't have a problem."

"What happened in the church?"

"I met the minister." The sun warmed her face as she told him about Rahab and the fragments of information she had learned.

He was silent for a moment. "Why would your mom change her name?"

"Apparently, she was trying to get away from someone who lived around here." She paused. "The minister told me there is nothing here worth remembering."

Carson hesitated. "What do you think about that?"

"He never told me why she was running."

"About leaving whatever happened to your parents in the past."

"It's not *the* past, it's *my* past. I want to know where my father went and why my mother isn't here today, showing me where I was born."

"A stroke can kill anyone, Elise. Any age."

She gulped. She couldn't tell Carson the whole truth. She'd never even told her dad that she'd researched the cause of her mother's death—acute alprazolam and alcohol poisoning.

Alprazolam, she had discovered, was a drug to treat anxiety disorders and to counteract treatments for depression. Her mother had condemned alcohol, and she'd always refused to take medication, saying God would heal her pain.

Yet somehow she had overdosed on a combination of drugs and alcohol.

How could she tell this man that her mother had killed herself? For some reason, it was a better option than raising her only child.

She stuffed the medicine box into her pocket. No one would ever understand why she needed to find out what had happened to her family.

Chapter 13

CARSON FLICKED HIS hair out of his eyes as he forced the rusty bicycle down the street. The sign on the rental shop had said the bikes were state-of-the-art, but the wheels on this piece of junk wobbled more than they spun and the handlebars were about to pop out of the socket.

He watched Elise weave around a batch of tourists, and he followed her, thankful that he wasn't having to tail Kate from the train. Elise was aggravating in her own way, but at least she was focused on the task.

They had spent their morning in the heart of Heidelberg, searching for information. Elise didn't have time to mess with being coy—or even with pleasantries. At every stop, she would pull her mom's picture out of her pocket like she was drawing a gun and force the clerk to look at it. Then he was responsible for patching up her slasher style.

She had fed her mother's picture to probably twenty locals this morning, and they all looked at her like she was loco. Yet it didn't stop her from going to the next store and the next. There were hundreds of stores in Heidelberg, but the numbers didn't seem to faze her. Most people would have given up when the registrar told her to go home.

He wasn't the one to tell her that she'd never find what she was looking for. If anyone knew how to stall, he did. And he'd already redirected the conversation twice this morning when two people told him in German that they remembered Rahab.

Elise pointed right, and parked her bike in a rack.

The situation had comedy written all over it. An American girl stumbling around Germany like she was some kind of whiz at investigation. Yet she was lousy at German and not so great with the German people either.

Unfortunately, Elise didn't think it was funny.

His bike clanked as he propped it beside hers. There was no need to lock them up. They'd have to pay a thief to take these bikes off their hands.

He unzipped his jacket. "Where do you want to start?"

"The sock store."

"Of course." He tried not to grin. "Let's go practice your German."

He held the door open as she pushed her way around him, past the overflowing bins of socks and slippers. She marched toward the woman at the counter and slapped down the worn picture. She didn't butcher her intro as badly this time, though she asked the woman if she'd eaten her mother instead of known her.

Carson didn't correct her.

The salesclerk managed a smile along with a clear, "*Nein.*"

Elise's shoulders slumped as they walked back toward the door.

"At least no one ate her," he quipped.

She stared at him like he was the crazy one and walked into the baby shop next door.

There was an elderly woman inside, hanging miniature coats along the rack. Wrinkles cascaded down her cheeks and throat, but her eyes lit up like lights on a Christmas tree when she saw them. She clapped her hands together and asked if this was their first child.

Carson laughed and then glanced at Elise, who didn't even crack a smile. He told the woman that maybe they'd be lucky enough to be expecting on their next visit.

Elise looked at the woman and then back at him. "What's she saying?"

"She asked if we were looking for a gift."

"Tell her no."

"I already did."

Elise pulled out her picture and handed it to the lady. This time she actually asked the woman if she had known her mother.

"Ja!" the woman exclaimed, and Elise jumped back.

The woman didn't pause for a breath. She spurted out a story in German about a girl who used to come to her shop many years ago and stare at the clothes. The girl never bought anything. She never had money.

"What?" Elise whispered to Carson.

He hushed her as he continued to listen to the woman.

The girl's body had swollen with child, the clerk said, but she was much too young to have a baby. The girl kept visiting until right before her baby was due. Then she never saw her again.

She'd always wondered what had happened to the girl.

Carson decided not to tell the shopkeeper that Catrina had died. She might break down crying, and Elise would demand to know why. Instead, he told her that the girl was now in the United States. He pointed at Elise and said her daughter wanted to visit her birthplace.

The woman stepped forward, kissed Elise on the cheek, and said she wished she knew where the girl had lived.

Elise reached for the woman's arm, but Carson pushed her toward the door. She stopped at the door and looked back at the woman. "I'm not ready to leave yet."

"She's about to set you up on a date with her son," he whispered.

Elise bounded down the stairs and collapsed on a bench outside. "What else did she say?"

"Nothing important."

She glared at him. "Feel free to summarize."

He brushed the leaves off the seat beside her and sat down. "Seriously, she thought you would be perfect for her son. He's forty and lives with her at home."

She ignored his taunt. "I heard her say something about a baby."

His eyebrows arched. "She said she's tired of selling clothes to other grandparents—she's ready to be a grandmother too."

Elise groaned. "You're not helping me."

"I'm trying to get you a date!"

"What did she say about the picture?"

He shrugged. "She didn't know your mom either."

Her face fell, and he felt rotten about lying to her. But no matter how disappointed she was, it was his job to protect her. Part of him wanted to hug her and the other part wanted to shake her and tell her to move on.

"She seemed so excited when she saw it."

"Your mother looked like a woman who comes into the store every few weeks. She thought something bad had happened to her."

Elise twisted the picture in her hands. "This isn't getting me anywhere."

"Maybe the minister was right."

When she looked at him, he saw a mix of determination and grief. "About what?"

"Moving on, Elise."

"I need to know what happened."

He corrected her. "You want to know."

Her eyes blazed. "Are both your parents still alive?"

"Yes."

"Any brothers and sisters?"

"Only child."

"But you have grandparents? Aunts? Cousins?"

"A few too many."

"I'm majoring in women's history, yet I don't have a clue about my own past."

She fidgeted with the zipper on her jacket.

"There's another reason, though, isn't there?" he asked quietly.

She looked up at the patchwork of autumn leaves above them. Wind chimes hung from a branch, clanging in the breeze. "I want to know why my mother killed herself."

He slumped back against the wooden slats. "Your mom committed suicide?"

"My dad told me she had a stroke."

He hesitated, skipping past all the reasons why she bugged him. If his mom took her life, he would wonder what happened too.

"I'm sorry."

She shrugged. "I've always wondered about my birth family, but I never tried to find them until I discovered that my dad was trying to hide the truth from me."

He almost wished he could tell her what the owner of the baby store had said, but that information would kick her into high gear. His job was to protect her from the truth.

She pointed toward a piano store on the other side of the street as she stood up and stepped off the curb. "Let's go."

He sighed. Maybe he should take her out to a nice dinner tonight. Try to clear her mind. Distract her from her search. He'd heard there was a posh Italian restaurant near the castle.

Elise didn't even bother to see if he was behind her when she walked through the door of the shop.

Carson hopped off the bench and followed her across the street.

White tablecloths and fine wine may work on a woman like Kate, but not on this one. Elise wouldn't stop searching until she thought she was on the right track . . . or sidetrack.

The store owner stopped tuning one of the pianos and looked at them. When Elise held out the photo, Carson saw a flicker of recognition in the man's eyes. He rushed up beside Elise to translate.

"How do you know her?" the man asked in English.

Carson tried to redirect the conversation to German, but neither Elise nor the owner paid attention.

"She was my mother."

The man studied her face. "Rahab?"

Elise glanced back at the picture and then whispered. "Yes."

"She used to come and practice on my pianos. She needed no music."

"Can you tell me about her family?" she asked.

Carson started to tell the man in German that Elise didn't really need to know, but the man continued to ignore him.

"She was always secret about her life with them."

"With whom?" Elise pleaded.

The man's voice sounded ominous. "The Chosen."

Chapter 14

THE PIANO KEYS clanged under Elise's fist, and she jumped away from the instrument as she steadied her balance and her voice. "What is the Chosen?"

The store owner shook his head as the door opened and a couple strolled inside. He mumbled something and bolted toward them, and Elise couldn't blame him. The couple might actually be in the market for a piano.

But who had *chosen* her mother? And why?

She stepped up beside the man as he played a few chords for the newcomers on the black Steinway.

"Where are the Chosen?" she asked.

He finished the song and then turned and looked at her like he was surprised she hadn't left. "They used to live in the Odenwald."

"Can anyone else tell me about them?" she persisted, but his attention was already back on the couple.

Elise stepped away from the piano and hurried out the door. Flinging her leg over the bike, she pedaled back onto the cobblestone street. Behind the row of old shops, she turned and pressed her bike up the hill leading out of town.

There were answers in the rugged forest that surrounded Heidelberg. Someone had to know where this group had lived and what exactly they were doing hidden back in the hills. And someone beside the minister had to know why her mother had been there.

Her legs burned as she churned her bike up the steep road. The wind rushed at her, ready to fight. If she lost, it would send her spiraling back into town.

She steadied the bike and pushed harder. She wasn't about to lose this fight. She was going to find out where the Chosen had lived twenty years ago, and she was going to find someone who knew their story. Someone who knew English.

"Wait up!"

She glanced behind her and saw Carson battling the wind as he tried to pedal his bike up the hill.

"I can't stop," she shouted.

"You're going to kill yourself."

His voice was quiet when he pedaled up beside her. "I'm sorry, Elise."

She shrugged off his comment, stood up on the pedals, and pressed on toward the summit. Past the last shops and houses of Heidelberg. And into the trees.

Her lungs begged for air, and she sighed with relief when her front tire met level ground.

The fierce wind calmed into a breeze, and she looked at the ruins of the Heidelberg castle as she rode through an archway and into a court of bronze statues.

"Slow down," Carson begged.

She stomped on the marble side of a murky pool and balanced her bike as she looked back at him. He wasn't going to talk her into giving up.

"I'm going to the Odenwald," she said.

"We need more information before we go into the forest."

"I've already wasted too much time in town."

He wiped his sleeve over his damp brow. "You aren't going to find anything without directions."

She stared at him. "It's not your problem, Carson."

"There are hundreds of miles of forest around here."

"Then we should split up."

He shook his head. "This time I'm not leaving you."

Since when had she become his responsibility? She was grateful for his assistance, but this was her family. Her search. She'd gotten the direction she needed, and she didn't need him telling her to go someplace else.

She sneezed as she started pedaling again.

"You're still sick," he said as he followed her.

"I'm aware of that."

"The medicine won't be able to work if you push yourself too hard."

She planted both feet on the stones, and he stopped his bike again. She had one more day left in Heidelberg, and if he was going to waste her time, he could find another tourist to "assist."

"Listen, Carson. I've really appreciated your help, but I'm going to search the forest today." She clutched her handlebars. "If you're not up for a bike ride, I completely understand."

"Point taken."

"I'm serious."

He dropped back behind her. "I'll shut up."

She didn't answer. If he wanted to tag along, that was his prerogative. She was here for answers, and she wouldn't let anyone distract her.

She pedaled past the ruins of the castle and followed a dirt trail around the back. In minutes, the trees overhead thickened and their leaves glowed in the sun.

The Odenwald.

Carson stayed a bike length behind her, and she opted to ignore him. The breeze was cool. The sky clear. No danger of rain for the afternoon. As long as the medicine kept pumping through her veins, she'd be fine.

She steered her bike around a pothole.

Her train left for Wittenberg on Sunday morning. First thing Monday, she had an appointment with Professor Sophie Reimann to interview her about Katharina von Bora and her influence on Martin Luther and the Reformation. Until then, she would trek around Heidelberg and no one, least of all Carson, would stop her.

The road curved to the right, but she turned left and then right again onto another trail. She followed the narrow track until she saw a worn farmhouse with a sagging roof and streaked clapboard. Brown grass covered the base of the walls like a tattered scarf.

She pedaled up the bumping driveway, leaned her bike against a willow tree, and marched toward the front porch. Alone. A broken screen door was propped over the grimy front window, and she squinted to see if she could detect anyone inside. When nothing moved, she knocked on the door.

As she waited, she glanced back over her shoulder and saw Carson fiddling with the branches on the willow. She was waiting for him to try to stop her or tell her the door-to-door effort was fruitless, but he didn't say a word.

Smart man.

She knocked again and heard a shuffling noise inside. An elderly woman opened the door and glared at her with eyes that were as welcoming as a bear guarding her cubs. But not all bears attacked, did they? This woman had probably lived around here her entire life. Surely she would know about the Chosen, if Elise could coax her to talk.

She wrung her hands and stared back at the woman, trying to clear her mind. She'd rehearsed her lines before she presented her mother's picture to the shop owners, but she'd been so distracted by the news about her mother, and so aggravated with Carson, that she'd forgotten to prepare for this conversation. How was she supposed to ask in German about the Chosen?

She botched her introduction, and the woman inched the door shut.

"*Bitte . . .*" Elise begged, and then asked the woman if she spoke English.

The woman glared, as if she'd been insulted. "*Nein.*"

The door was about six inches from being closed. Desperate, Elise kicked out her foot and rammed her shoe into the gap.

"I'm looking for a group called the Chosen," she said, hoping the woman had lied about her English.

The door pinched her foot as the woman unleashed a diatribe of German that she didn't need translated.

"C-h-o-s-e-n," she spelled slowly. The woman responded with another push on the door, and Elise groaned in pain.

She glanced over her shoulder and motioned for Carson to join her. He looked behind him, and with a dramatic sweep of both hands, he pointed to his chest. "Me?"

"Yes, you," she shouted. "Come here."

She looked back at the door and all that was left in the slit was the woman's wrinkled right eye.

She turned back toward Carson, and he still hadn't moved. "C'mon."

"I'm trying to stay out of your way."

"And I appreciate it, but I need you to talk to this woman."

He grinned. "But you're doing such a good job scaring her on your own."

The woman stomped on her toes, and Elise stumbled backward. The door slammed in her face, and she heard the lock click.

She limped toward the steps. "Thanks a lot!"

"I won't take credit for that." He hopped off his bike and ambled toward her. "You flopped all by yourself."

"Can you at least try?"

He stuck his hands in his pockets.

"Please!" she begged. "I'll buy you dinner."

He hesitated another moment before he scooted around her. "Deal!"

The woman didn't open the door when Carson tapped on it, so he began conversing with the wood. Then he stopped talking and shooed Elise away with his hand.

She sat down on a rock in the front yard and waited. What was she—a two-year-old?

Once she was seated, Carson started talking again. Whatever charming thing he said finally got the door reopened and the woman actually smiled at him. She began talking in a normal pitch. Like she liked the guy.

The woman pointed at her and then back at Carson. He laughed, and they chatted like old friends for ten minutes. Finally, she heard Carson thank her as he backed down the stairs.

"Do you always get what you want?" Elise asked as he walked toward her.

"People are a lot more friendly when you don't scare them."

"I'm hardly intimidating."

He laughed. "You barrel down on your victims like one of those gunslingers in a bad Western."

"I do not barrel."

"What would you call it?"

"I guess I'm bold, but I'm also friendly."

He snorted. "Right."

"Maybe I stumble a little in my approach, but it's only because I'm horrible with the language."

"No kidding."

Elise glanced at the closed door on the farmhouse and then at the windows. The old lady was probably loading her shotgun inside.

"Is it safe to get up?" she whispered.

"Very funny."

"I wouldn't want to scare her."

He kicked a rock, and it hit his bike. "I can see you're going to take my advice."

She stood up and brushed off the back of her pants. "That was actually criticism."

"Hey, I'm on your side."

She glanced back at the house and didn't see anyone move. "Does she know anything?"

"You never told me what to ask."

"Carson!"

He sighed like he couldn't believe she doubted him. "She's never heard of the Chosen."

"You guys talked for ten minutes."

"She's an avid bird-watcher."

She hopped back on her bike and pushed off. One more setback wasn't going to stop her. "Let's go to the next house."

"She's lived here for seventy years."

Elise didn't care if she'd lived here for seven hundred years. "So?"

"If the group was near here, don't you think she would know?"

"Not if she's as friendly with her neighbors as she was with me."

"Let's go get some lunch."

She hit the brakes on her bike. Even if Carson knew German, he wasn't really helping her. This was a personal journey, and she could continue without an escort or a translator.

"Why are you doing this, Carson?" she asked.

His smile looked forced. "I can't resist your charm?"

"Maybe it's time for you to go on to Switzerland."

"No problem," he said, but he didn't turn around.

"That's your cue to leave."

"So, you're saying you remember how to get back to town on your own?"

When she groaned, he pedaled his bike forward. "You're wasting daylight."

"I'm not stopping until I find someone who can give me more information—and if I need to, directions back to town."

He ducked under a tree limb. "Fine."

Fine.

They stopped at two more farmhouses with no luck. Only one person was home—a farmer who wasn't even interested in talking to Carson. Apparently, the guy had more charm with women.

After they left the last farmhouse, they rode for at least twenty minutes in the trees. No homes. No other bikes. Not even a rabbit or a deer. The peaceful wilderness soothed her thirsty heart like water on a hot day. She'd never been a city girl—her family's farm was her oasis away from her hectic college life. She'd rather be out roaming the fields and ponds around their farm than in any one of the avant-garde restaurants in Richmond's Fan District or even in one of Heidelberg's many pubs.

The path in front of her narrowed again, and a flock of birds dipped toward the west. She glanced down at her watch—they'd been gone for three hours. She'd rented a hotel room, complete with a pillow and a mattress, so she didn't have to camp out in a church or under a tree. As much as she loved the countryside, she wasn't going to spend the night stranded in the forest with Carson.

They rode toward another bend in the road, and she looked over her shoulder. "Let's head back in a couple minutes."

"My hamstrings thank you."

"And I was so worried about them."

"You need to take your medicine."

She'd almost forgotten. "Yeah . . . thanks."

As they sped around the curve, Elise gawked at the sight across an open field in front of her. It looked like an old monastery—or an abbey. The crumbling rock walls were gray with age, and patches of moss clung to its sides.

Katharina von Bora had once lived in a place like this—except Marienthron had walls to keep the influence of the world out and the nuns inside.

Chapter 15

SOL STOMPED A SPARK that flew out as he stirred the fire. He wanted Sara tonight, but he wouldn't go to her room, not until she was ready to repent. All he'd asked for was some food, an easy task. Yet she continually returned with nothing to show for her hours in town. It was almost as if she didn't even bother to ask.

He was losing her slowly, and he had to stop her before she deserted. On his watch, only two women had left for the world, and he wasn't going to lose Sara like he had lost Tirzah and Rahab.

He threw another log on the blaze.

No one missed Tirzah when she abandoned the family. She'd been disruptive, mean-spirited, an irritant to him and to all the women. After she ran, he'd sent five brothers out to search for her—not because he wanted her back, but because he wanted to demonstrate the wages of sin for the entire family. Unfortunately, they never found her.

He rubbed the scar on his leg. When he realized she wasn't coming back, he had left his arsenal of weapons in Frankfurt and moved the family to Heidelberg in case she went to the police.

But when Rahab ran away . . . he'd always thought Rahab would return to the fold. She knew too much, cared too much, to be out in the world. And Rahab had been special. She'd been Bethesda's only daughter, and he'd loved Bethesda.

Rahab wasn't his child, but before Bethesda died, he'd promised her he would care for her daughter. And he had cared for Rahab, carefully plotting God's plan for her life, spoiling her as a child. Yet after all he had done for her, she left him for the world.

He'd whisked the family away from Heidelberg after Rahab left, but he'd never given up hope that one day she would look him in the eye and recognize that he was king. Someday, she would beg forgiveness and return to her first love. When she did, he would delight in her, body and soul.

The door to his office opened, and Sol turned to see Phoebe entering quietly. She took off her gray hat and sat down in a leather chair across from his desk. She had never been as beautiful as Bethesda, but her blue eyes still held the fire and passion they'd had when she joined the Chosen.

She had been his wife and partner since Bethesda had died. He was in charge of their home, but Phoebe oversaw the details. She raised the children, maintained the kitchen, filed his paperwork, and answered the phone.

She held out the cell phone—the one means of outside communication he allowed in the house. "Jozef called."

He shut the fireplace grate as he clutched the poker in his other hand. Jozef had left a couple of hours ago, still angry that Sol wouldn't hand over Sara. "What did he want?"

"Eve committed suicide while he was here."

Sol threw the poker on the floor. They couldn't afford to lose any more girls. "He didn't have the guts to tell me himself?"

"He wanted me to tell you first."

"Go get Michael," he said, and Phoebe stood up.

If they weren't still waiting for the last package from Mokotów, Sol would fire Jozef tonight. He only needed to keep him around until he got the final shipment.

Until then, he would do everything he could to keep the remaining women working for him. He didn't even care if the women evangelized as they worked—that was Paul's and Bethesda's idea. As long as the men continued paying top dollar for their services, they could talk about the weather if they wanted, in whatever language they wanted to discuss it, but some of the Chosen Girls needed to be reminded of their purpose. If anyone could inspire them to continue spreading God's love to the men in Berlin, Michael could.

Phoebe brushed her hair back onto her hat. "You need to take Sara to Berlin."

For more than a year, she had been trying to convince him to send Sara to the house in Berlin, but he had always refused. Yet maybe a trip to the city would help Sara gain some perspective.

"Get her too," he said.

Chapter 16

ELISE FLUNG HER LEG off her bike and quietly approached the field of ruins. The entire complex looked as if it had collapsed a couple hundred years ago.

She sat down on one of the stones, and for an instant she forgot about her mother as her mind assimilated the research she'd been accumulating for months.

Katharina von Bora had been born during a time when women had no choice about their future. Katharina's mother had died when she was about five, and her father had sent her to be raised in a convent. When she was ten, she was moved to the Cistercian cloister called Marienthron.

Even as she was being raised as a nun, the urge for freedom was stirring in her soul. Eventually, she and eleven other nuns wrote to Martin Luther and asked him to help them escape the abbey's cells. And he did . . . even though helping a runaway nun was punishable by death.

Scholars had concocted multiple theories about her escape—the nuns either climbed out windows, or sneaked through a rear gate, or crept through a tunnel. How they did it wasn't as important as the fact that they actually broke out of the formidable walls without being discovered by the watchman. And then they huddled together on the bottom of a wagon, all the way to Martin Luther's Wittenberg.

Katharina actually asked Luther to be her husband, and when they married, they agreed that if both men and women were created by God, they both had value—a revolutionary concept in the sixteenth century. She became a successful gardener, landowner, spiritual advisor, and businesswoman, as well as her husband's confidante, the mother of their six kids, and the "Mother of the Reformation."

Elise stretched her back as she watched the leaves swaying over the stones. When she finished graduate school, she would be ready to teach Katharina's story to a new generation of women and inspire them to become politicians and writers and doctors and businesswomen. If Katharina could escape a prisonlike convent, there was no excuse for women today.

Carson sat down on a rock in front of her. "You like it here?"

"It's marvelous." She stared at the mounds of moss-covered rocks. "Can't you see all the nuns crammed inside these walls?"

He leaned forward. "You're being dramatic."

She squinted toward the ruins. "Forty women in white habits and veils."

"And not an available one among them."

She glared at him, and he relented. "I don't see anything."

"Martin Luther once said that 'it is very shameful that children, especially defenseless women and young girls, are pushed into the nunneries.'" She kicked a rock and watched it roll across the grass.

"I'm sure the church has changed their policy since—"

"The early 1500s. The Catholic Church was pushing the sale of indulgences for salvation and using the money to fund the renovation of St. Peter's Basilica in Rome."

Carson leaned toward her, his arms resting over his knees. "Enter Martin Luther and his message of grace."

She glanced over at him, startled that he knew that slice of information.

"Exactly," she said. "The Protestant Reformation was launched as the church tried to decide whether or not buying these indulgences would guarantee salvation."

"And this new twist on Christianity gave people the freedom to say they were Christians without ever serving God."

She turned to face him. "People can serve God around the clock, but they'll never earn their way into heaven."

He picked up a twig and threw it over the wall. "Didn't Paul say that grace without works is dead?"

"Actually that was James." Both fists flew to her hips. "And it was Jesus who said he preferred mercy over sacrifice."

"That's because Jesus was calling sinners to himself, rather than people who thought they were already good enough."

She shook her head. "God is more interested in our heart than our sacrifices."

"Yet Jesus asked his followers to give up everything to follow him."

Her gaze wandered back over the remnants of the abbey. "We surrender our hearts and our lives to a God who loves us, not to church leaders who claim that they speak for God."

"Unless that leader has a humble heart and is calling us to be accountable."

"But we are ultimately responsible to live our lives for God," she insisted. "We can't rely on other people for our salvation, nor can we pay for it."

He threw another stick. "Though we are responsible to God for how we live our lives."

"That's what I just said."

He lifted his hand in a mock toast, and she smiled at him. At least the guy knew how to debate.

Someone shouted behind them, and she jumped. She turned to look over the wall, but didn't see anyone. Then she heard another shout. And laughter.

A fleet of bikes raced over the hilltop, preteen girls waving their arms at each other instead of focusing their eyes on the road. They reminded her of a gaggle of geese—flapping theirs wings and honking their horns.

The leader of the pack was a girl with a blonde ponytail and freckles dotting her cheeks and nose. She held her shoulders high like she was prepared to skip her teen years and move right into her seat at the Bundestag.

The girl stopped her bike at the foot of the old abbey, and the other five bikes braked behind her. She propped herself up on a rock and looked over the wall at them.

"*Alles gut?*" the girl asked.

"Yes." Elise didn't even bother trying to answer in German. "We're just looking for something."

The girl eyed Carson warily before she turned back to Elise. "You are American?"

"Yes."

The other girls hopped off their bikes and flocked to the edge of the wall to see the phenomena of Americans lounging in their back yard.

"My name is Lena." The girl scooted over the rocks and walked toward her. "Do you need some help?"

"I'm looking for someone—" Elise paused. "Actually, a group of people who used to live in this area . . . they were called the Chosen."

Lena glanced back at her swarm of friends and then leaned toward Elise. "The religious sect?"

"A sect?"

"Yes—*die Sekte.*"

Elise slowly processed the information. "I think that's the group."

"They used to live near here," Lena whispered, "but they are gone."

"Do you know where they lived?"

"No," Lena said, and Elise's heart sank. Another dead end.

Lena stepped toward her and whispered, "But my father knows."

Adrenaline pumped through her veins. "Could I speak with your father?"

"I will ask him about the house," Lena said. "Can you meet tomorrow?"

Elise clapped. "You bet!"

Lena glanced at Carson for interpretation.

"She means *Ja gerne.*"

"At one o'clock," Lena added as she backed away.

Elise nodded. "I'll be here."

Chapter 17

LENA AND HER LITTLE flock flew away as quickly as they'd landed, but Carson didn't move.

He'd done everything he could to stop Elise from finding the house, but if Lena gave her directions, he would not be able to keep her away.

Elise swiped her hand over the jagged stones, and then hiked her legs over the wall. In seconds, she was on her bike, flying back down the hill.

"Wait up!" Carson yelled as he bolted for his bike to follow her. The sun was starting to set over the trees, but he didn't stop to appreciate the changing light. Instead, he pressed forward, trying to catch up to the girl whose life was about to implode.

Lena's father knew where the Chosen had lived, and now Carson would have to figure out a way to keep Elise from meeting up with Lena tomorrow. He had tried to make himself indispensable with his German, but if he didn't start contributing more to the hunt, she'd probably ditch him.

He couldn't blame her. He was lucky she hadn't gotten a restraining order against him. His whole shtick was creepy—pushy American male with no life chasing a single American woman around Germany. Other travelers might appreciate the company, but Elise just wanted to be left alone.

Next time his mom needed someone to do her dirty work, she was going to have to call on one of the rookies in her office, no matter how inept they were at relationships. At least they were willing to do anything to get ahead.

Elise slowed her speed and pedaled in a circle to wait for him.

"Carson?"

"Hmm?"

The strength had drained from her eyes. "My mother was part of a cult."

Of course it was a cult. What did she think it was—a family camp? Girl's choir?

"What kind of woman gets involved with a cult?"

He hesitated. "Someone who's young and naive."

"But why didn't she run away?"

He paused again. "It sounds like maybe she did."

She started pedaling hard again, as if the very act of spinning her tires would help to sort out the information whirling through her mind.

The orange sky had turned charcoal by the time the two pedaled back into town. Streetlamps carved a winding path down the hill and across the river, which shimmered from the reflection of the castle lights.

Elise held up her end of the bargain and treated Carson to Thai food for dinner. He ordered beef with green curry. She got the chicken with red sauce. They carried their platters to a quiet patio overlooking the river and settled at a table in the corner.

"Are you okay?" Carson asked.

"Not really."

He stirred his meal. "You don't know the whole story."

"I'm going to find out."

He took a bite of the beef and watched her. If he had just found out that his mom had been part of a cult, he would be confused too. And he would want answers. Thankfully, his strong-willed mom would never succumb to anyone's lies—especially those of a cult leader.

"Where are you going in Switzerland?" she asked.

He wiped his face with a napkin. It would have been easier if he had stuck with the truth about his occupation, but at the time, he hadn't wanted her to know he was from Berlin. Hadn't really wanted her to know anything about him.

He looked back at her, and she was waiting for his answer. "I don't know."

"Really?"

"I'd like to go back and ski at Wengen."

"I've never been to Switzerland." She sipped her bottled water. "I've never been anyplace else in Europe."

"You should stay and explore."

She spooned the sauce over her chicken. "If you could only visit one place, where would you go?"

Finally he could tell the truth. "The lake country in Austria."

"Because of the water?"

"Because you can scuba dive, climb, ski, hike."

She smiled. "Bike?"

"You bet."

"And when are you going to get a real job?"

Now she sounded like his mom, circa five years ago. "When I grow up."

"No time soon, huh?"

"Very funny."

Elise took a couple bites of her food and then pushed the plate away. "I'm going to my room."

"Please let me walk you back."

She hesitated. "It's not raining tonight."

"Rain should be the least of your worries."

She relented, and after he finished his meal he escorted her to the Amsel Inn and opened the gate so she could park her bike in the hotel's courtyard. It was only eight o'clock, but between her lack of sleep and her head cold, she'd be down for the night.

She stepped up the stairs, but before she opened the door, she turned around and threw him a quick wave. "Thank you, Carson."

He nodded as he pushed his bike away from the stoop. He didn't suggest getting together in the morning. He had the feeling that if he offered, she would turn him down. After all, she'd found Lena, and Lena could speak English. She didn't need him anymore.

He rode straight out of town to a summer home perched above the river and entered the security code on the pad beside the front gate. The youth hostel would have been fine, but his mom had insisted he sleep here.

The two wings of the Tudor manor ambled through the trees and the tips of each wing commanded a view of the river below. Oak trees loped over the cedar shake roof with a lazy air that might have convinced even Klaas Rudolf, the intense minister of state and lord of the manor, to relax when he was away from Berlin.

Brigitta, the housekeeper, greeted Carson at the door, and he brushed off his jacket before he handed it to her. The Rudolfs weren't here this week—according to Brigitta, they rarely visited even when the weather was warm.

Carson walked across the hardwood floors and glanced out the back window at ship lights cruising along the river. The city lights twinkled to his right. It might be dark, but the clubs in Heidelberg were just waking up. A few years ago, he would have taken a shower and headed out to the bars, but that scene didn't interest him much anymore.

When he was eighteen, he'd thought that hanging out at these clubs was the ultimate in freedom. But then a friend introduced him to Christ and he found out what freedom was really all about. He still liked entertaining a crowd of friends, but he no longer liked the darkness of the bar scene.

Brigitta offered him something to drink, and he asked for a Coke, extra ice. Then he hopped onto the four-poster bed and dialed home on his cell.

"How is she?" his mom asked when she picked up.

"I'm great. Thanks."

"Carson . . ."

He sighed. "She's going to do everything she can to get the information, Mom."

"Stall her."

"I'm trying, but she's not making it easy."

"You have to do this, Carson."

Brigitta knocked on his door. When he opened it, she handed him the cold drink.

"How did you know about the Chosen?" he asked after Brigitta shut the door.

His mom paused as he drained half the glass of soda.

"I met someone from the Chosen when I was young." Her voice cracked. "When Catrina and I were both young."

"The people here called Elise's mom 'Rahab.'"

"You've got to convince her to get out of there!"

"She won't listen to me."

"Someone will start looking for her soon, if they haven't already."

He was trying to make sense of the situation, but ever since his mom had sent him off to befriend Elise, the entire situation had paranoia painted all over it. Addison Wade the ambassador was known for her strength and authority, but every once in a while, as his mom, she slipped off to a place that he didn't understand.

"Who will be looking for her?" he asked.

"A friend of the family."

He groaned. "What family?"

Her voice sounded desperate. "You can't let them find her."

He set the glass on the dresser, trying to figure out a way to ask her to pass the phone to his dad so he could make sure everything was okay. Maybe she hadn't been sleeping well or was on some sort of medication that made her delusional.

"Apparently, the Chosen left Heidelberg years ago," he said.

"Don't mess with them, Carson."

"She met someone today who's supposed to give her directions to their house."

He heard his mom take a sharp breath. "Stop her."

"I'll try, but it isn't easy to distract her." He clanked the ice in his glass.

"Don't bail on me, Carson." She hung up the phone without a good-bye.

He shut the phone and opened the curtains at the far end of his bedroom, gazing over at the lights of the town. Last year, she'd had him stalk a homeless man who she was certain was a predator. He'd followed the guy through the back alleys of Berlin and even slept two benches down from the guy at the Friedrichstrasse train station. As far as he could tell, the man was much more interested in picking through trash bins for fast food than preying on women.

After a full weekend of trailing the man around the city, he told his mom that she'd have to find someone else to stalk the homeless. She hadn't asked him to tail anyone else until she showed up in Humboldthain on Wednesday with his backpack, a train ticket, and the vague description of a woman headed to Heidelberg.

The only one who wanted him to stay in Heidelberg was his mom, and she still hadn't given him a decent reason. She obviously thought that Elise should be afraid of the Chosen, but he didn't know why. And even if he did, it wouldn't matter if he tried to warn Elise. God would have to perform a miracle if he wanted her to stop searching.

He dug a folder out of the backpack and huddled over his desk for an hour translating a research paper about the avian influenza virus. It was good reading to put him to sleep and divert him from the fact that he was deceiving someone who had been completely honest with him.

When he woke up at 6:45, it was still dark outside. If the flu didn't keep Elise in bed, there was only one thing he could think of to detain her this morning.

On the kitchen counter was a spread of salami and cheese alongside some sliced tomatoes and melons. After he devoured the meat and cheese, Brigitta called a car for him. Ten minutes later, he was at the Amsel.

He felt rotten about what he had to do, but if his mother was right about members of the Chosen still being in Heidelberg, then someone needed to take care of Elise.

The back gate was unlocked, and he stole into the parking area behind the hotel. He quietly pushed Elise's bike back through the gate and onto the street before he hopped on and rode to the bike rental shop. It was a lame attempt to stop her from meeting with Lena, but it was the best he could do.

The owner of the store was just opening when Carson walked through the door. He told the man that his girlfriend was in no shape to ride and when he placed a hundred euros on the counter, the man agreed. Someone had stolen Elise's bike, and the man concurred that he couldn't rent her anything else until she'd recovered the lost one.

Chapter 18

THE LACY CURTAIN fluttered over Sara's head, and she brushed it away. In front of her was a feast for breakfast—pancakes, ham, and fresh fruit. She devoured the food on her plate and reached for another slice of ham. But instead of eating it, she set it back on the platter. There were almost forty brothers and sisters at home today, and all of them were hungry.

She leaned back in her chair and rubbed the ache in her shoulder as she took in the simple beauty of the kitchen. It was decorated in navy blue and white with a large vase filled with sunflowers on the glass table. Compared to the stark surroundings at Marienthron, everything in the Berlin house was modern, every room colorful and warm. Sol had invested a lot of their money into this ministry after the Berlin Wall came down, a necessary expense to evangelize guests who were accustomed to worldly things.

The breeze rushed through the window again, and she closed her eyes.

Phoebe had taken her out of her confinement last night, but instead of lecturing her, she'd escorted her straight to the car. Michael was already in the driver's seat, and she had trembled in fear and pain in the back seat as she watched the miles of farmland buzz by the car. Neither Sol nor Michael had told her where they were going.

It was dark when they got to the city, and she almost forgot her fears as they drove through the busy streets, lit with red and white. There were so many people. So many stores. Maybe Sol had brought her to Berlin to scavenge for food.

She couldn't think about the other reason he might have brought her here.

She had slept upstairs with three of the Chosen Girls. Even though they had grown up together, they wouldn't talk to her. It was almost as if they were angry that she had stayed behind.

Her gaze drifted back out the window and down onto the quiet back street. At the end of the row of townhouses, cars and buses raced up and down the busy Unter den Linden. High- and low-ranking government workers frequented this street during lunch, and lonely tourists often wandered down the alley in search of love, both day and night.

It was the heartbeat of their family, the real mission to reach out to those who didn't know how much God loved them. The women were a light to those steeped in darkness, reaching hundreds each year with the message of God's love. Each of the men were given a Bible when they left the home, a reminder that God loved them even more than the women in the house.

The door opened at the side of the kitchen, and Michael started to walk inside. Naomi peeked around the corner and grabbed his arm. She whispered something in his ear, and he laughed.

The food roiled in Sara's stomach. She hadn't heard Michael laugh in years. He was supposed to share God's love with the women in the family, yet—God forgive her—she still wanted him to herself.

Her teeth clenched as she looked back out the window. Even if she had never given him her body, she had given him her heart.

Sara dug her nails into her arms to punish herself for her thoughts. She was Sol's wife, and she was supposed to be faithful to him.

She turned back toward the door, and Michael's eyes flashed with guilt when he saw her.

"I'm going out," he said simply.

She nodded. He didn't have anything to feel guilty about. He was doing the work of the Lord.

"Should I go with you?" she asked.

He shook his head. "Not this time."

She turned away, glad that she didn't have to ride alongside him in silence, glad that she didn't have to beg for food, glad that she didn't have to witness to the men who visited their home like the missionaries who lived here.

Naomi rinsed out a glass from the sink and filled it with water. She had sat on Sara's bed in Marienthron last year and cried when Sol told her she was going to Berlin. She had been scared, but Sara had consoled her, saying God must want her there.

"Are you staying?" Naomi asked.

Sara brushed the wrinkles out of her skirt. "I don't know."

"We need you."

She nodded, hating herself for not wanting to serve like the other women.

"It's not so bad." Naomi took a long sip of water. "Yesterday I witnessed to a man who wanted to devote his life to Christ."

Sara glanced up. "Is he going to join our family?"

"Sol doesn't want anyone new right now." Naomi set the glass on the counter. "But the man said he would come back."

The doorbell rang, and Naomi turned to answer it. Sara heard a man's voice and then watched him breeze past the kitchen as he followed Naomi to her room.

And thou shalt love the LORD thy God with all thine heart, and with all thy soul, and with all thy might.

But where did it say "body"?

She pressed her fingernails into her skin again, trying to purge her doubt. The thoughts wouldn't go away.

Sometimes she wondered if it was wrong for these women to share themselves with so many. Sometimes it even felt wrong to share her body with Sol. Several times she heard other sisters question their faith, their freedom to express love. Sol explained it so simply—God wants us to demonstrate perfect love to one another. His love.

Unto the pure all things are pure.

As part of the Chosen, they were instruments to express God's love as they remained pure in his sight.

Sin came into their hearts when they conformed to the world. And when they doubted God's love, they went back to the worldly system of immorality and injustice and abusing his gifts for personal gain.

She'd abstained from the world, but her soul still felt stained.

She closed her eyes and let the wind breathe on her face. Her faith wasn't based on feelings. It was based on knowing the truth about God. And she knew it. She'd devoted her life to it.

The metal legs on her chair screeched against the tile floor when she stood. She put the leftover food into the refrigerator and washed her dishes along with Naomi's glass.

As she hung up the dishtowel, she heard a shuffle in the hallway and turned. Was someone watching her? She stepped toward the doorway, but she didn't see anyone.

Then she heard a meow.

Her heart quickened as she rose to her feet. She hadn't held a cat since Sol had taken hers away.

"Here, kitty," she whispered as she tiptoed down the carpet so she wouldn't disturb Naomi or the other women. She eased past the gold-framed mirrors and the picture of Jesus on the cross.

The cat meowed again, and she bent down to look under a table. Nothing was there.

The last door on the hallway was open, and she could hear Sol and Jozef arguing again. If they didn't lower their voices, they might turn Naomi's guest away from the kingdom.

"We need to bring in three thousand by the end of the month just to make rent," Sol raged. She wondered how much more they needed for food.

"Eve was a favorite," Jozef replied.

Sol's hand slammed on the desk. "You shouldn't have lost her."

"I didn't know she was going to kill herself."

"You should have seen the signs."

Jozef's voice escalated. "And done what?"

Sara held her breath as she waited for the answer. Too many people from the family chose the wide road to hell instead of the narrow one into heaven's gates. All they had to do was stay strong until God called them home, yet one after another left before it was time. If only they had waited, they could have basked in the light and love of God for eternity.

"Sent her to me."

Jozef laughed. "Like that would help."

"She would still be alive."

The door across the hall moved, and Sara looked down to see a white kitten nudging the door with his front paw. She knelt down and reached out her hand.

"Sara?" Sol called from inside the office.

She looked at the kitten's blue eyes staring back at her. She wanted to pull him close to her chest and feel the soft fur in her arms.

"Wait here," she whispered as she stepped back.

She pushed open Sol's door, and he stood up as his gaze wandered down her dress. She clasped her hands to her chest and waited for him to speak. All she wanted to be was outside in the hall, away from him.

"Yes?" she whispered as she looked toward Jozef and then back at Sol.

Sol held out his hand as he walked toward her, and she had no choice but to take it. His skin was dry, his voice firm. "Do you like it here?"

She opened her mouth, but her words came out garbled. Her eyes focused on the carpet, and she tried to stop her shoulders from shaking. Naomi might be able to do it, but she couldn't love several men a day. She didn't care if their souls were at stake, didn't care if she was the only glimpse they would ever get of heaven. She couldn't do it.

Sol squeezed her shaking hand and let it go. If only she could crawl behind the door like the kitten and hide away.

Jozef took a step, and she cowered back. "I need her, Sol."

Silence hung over the room as Sol leaned down, picked up a white box, and handed it to her. She slowly opened the lid, and inside was an emerald dress with silver buttons. She smoothed her fingers over the silky material and then lifted it out of the box and let the skirt drape on the floor.

It was beautiful, but too big for her.

"I want you to wear it," Sol said.

She didn't answer, her eyes focused on the box. He didn't even have money to buy food. How could he afford a dress?

"You have nothing to worry about Sara." His fingertips grazed her cheek. "I will take care of you."

She tried to smile as she backed out of the room and then covered her ears so she wouldn't hear the vulgar things coming out of Jozef's mouth. Things about her.

After she shut the door behind her, she tossed the box on the floor and pushed open the door across the hall.

"Where are you, kitty?"

The soft meow came from under the bed, and she knelt down on the floor. The kitten stuck his head out, and Sara scratched his ears. Maybe if she had told Sol she didn't want to come to Berlin, he would have listened to her. She'd never been good at witnessing.

The kitten inched out, and she smoothed her fingers over his back.

"Shalom," she whispered. "What shall we call you?"

She rubbed the skin under his neck and smiled.

"I think you will be called Rezon," she pronounced. *Prince.*

She stroked his fur again, but this time he coiled back when she brushed over his back leg. She leaned toward him and saw it was broken.

"Don't worry," she whispered, petting his head again. She would help him heal.

The kitten nuzzled against her hand, brushing her with calm contentment. Carefully, she pulled him close, and the kitten snuggled into her chest.

She stood up and walked back down the hallway.

It could be hours before Sol and Jozef finished talking. And hours before Michael returned. She and Rezon would wait outside until it was time to go home.

She reached out for the doorknob and turned. The door didn't budge so she pushed it with her hip. Still it wouldn't move.

She examined the knob and the wall for a lock. She didn't see one, so she pushed again.

"You just arrived."

She turned to see Jozef's gray eyes bearing down on her. "I need some air."

"I have to keep the girls safe." He lifted a small panel and typed in a code. The door clicked. "There are too many dangerous people on the streets of Berlin."

"Thank you," she muttered as she shoved it open. If Sol decided to send her here, she may never be allowed outside again.

"That was Eve's cat."

She hugged the kitten closer to her chest as Jozef leaned toward her. The heat from his breath singed her skin. "You should keep him."

She shook her head. "Sol won't let me."

"It will be a gift from me." He paused. "A reminder that you're always welcome here."

As she stepped through the doorway, he weaved his fingers through her hair. "You'd like it here."

When he closed the door, she collapsed on the stoop and gulped in the city breeze. God forgive her, but she didn't want to stay with Jozef. And she didn't want to be a missionary. She wanted to go back to Marienthron. She'd even go back into her cell and Sol could lock the door for days. Weeks. As long as he didn't make her share God's love here in Berlin.

She glanced down the alley, and for an instant, she wondered what it would be like to walk away with this kitten and get lost in the crowds.

Jozef wouldn't be able to find her, but where would she go? She had no friends or family outside her family in Grimma. She'd never been allowed to go to school, and she didn't know how to get a job. Sol had taken care of her for her whole life. He was the only one who had loved her.

"Get thee behind me."

Her stomach cramped, and she squeezed Rezon.

She would not let Satan tempt her. Her place was with the Chosen.

Even when she was scared, she wouldn't falter. Even if Sol decided to leave her with Jozef, she wouldn't run. She would do what God required.

Her fingers crept up to the burn on her arm, and she rubbed the seal. She'd already been chosen.

Chapter 19

THE WHIP SNAPPED across the baby's back, and Elise screamed. The woman over the crib laughed, her gray hat shielding her eyes and hair as she raised the whip again.

Elise grabbed the leather cord and tried to wrestle it away, but the woman was stronger and bigger. And she was mean.

The woman ripped the whip out of her fingers and snapped it over the baby.

Elise dove toward the infant, and the leather stung her head and back. The woman cackled at her attempt to rescue the infant, and with a swift hook, the woman snatched a pillow and smothered her face.

Elise shoved her away, fighting for air, reaching out her arms to save the baby.

She had to be strong. Had to survive.

But the woman was stronger. She pushed Elise's head further into the pillow until she couldn't breathe.

Elise flung off the pillow that covered her head and gulped in deep, soothing gasps of air. There was no whip and no baby. It was just a dream—one of the many that had haunted her since she was a kid. Sometimes she was inside a dark room, and other times she was hidden in the trees. But no matter where she was, she always reached for the baby. Yet she could never touch her, never rescue her from whatever made her cry.

Elise rubbed her temples—it felt like someone had swung a wrecking ball and crashed it into her skull. Sometime around 4:00 AM, the flu medicine wore off, but she'd been too tired to even crawl into the bathroom to get the medication. Her shoulders and legs ached from the long bike ride, and her throat was on fire, but it was the pain in her head that paralyzed her.

She pulled the scratchy blanket up to her neck and dreamed about being at home, folded into her warm flannel sheets and goose down comforter. Her dad would pop in one of her favorite movies, and Rachel would bring up a tray with chicken soup and some chamomile tea.

Today she was alone, and she had to get out of bed. Lena was supposed to meet her in three hours.

She pushed her feet over the side of the bed and winced when they hit the cold floor. If she didn't take the medicine soon, she'd never have the strength to make it back up the hill.

She pulled herself out of the bed and moved toward the bathroom to gulp down two more pills. Then she collapsed back into the bed.

At this rate, it would take her eight hours to get back up the mountain.

She stared up at a stain on the ceiling.

Lena had said that her mother was part of a cult, but what type of cult was the Chosen? She'd studied cults in school and learned about cult leaders like David Koresh and Jim Jones. The people who followed these men embraced their leader's beliefs—at least, they did when they first joined the cult. She wondered if they still believed when their leaders tried to kill them.

She could understand how someone might join a supposedly Christian group with good intentions to help other people or save the world. She could even understand how someone might follow a leader who seemed to walk with God.

What she didn't understand was why someone would stay in a group once they realized it was based on the beliefs of man instead of God. How could someone allow another person to trump the words of the Bible and manipulate their mind and actions? Someone like her mother . . .

Her mother had been dedicated to her faith—reading her Bible for hours in the evenings, murmuring prayers as she worked around the house. But in spite of her devotion to God, she had never seemed satisfied in her relationship with him or anyone else. The only time she ever remembered her mother being happy was when she was throwing a party.

Had she ever made her mother smile? Had Dad made her happy? Did God ever satisfy the longings of her soul?

Elise hiked her feet over the side of the mattress and back onto the floor. She had forgotten to call her dad last night!

If he called the hotel in Berlin, they would tell him that she had checked out—two days ago. He was probably boarding an airplane this morning to JFK—next stop, Germany.

For a moment, she forgot about the cult and the pain throbbing through her body. She needed to find a phone.

She washed her face, brushed her teeth, threw on her jeans and a clean sweatshirt, and then pulled her hair back in a sloppy ponytail. Five minutes later, she stepped out into the narrow hallway and plodded down the stairs.

Carson had never mentioned joining her this morning, and there was no reason for him to come. Once Lena gave her directions, she could go to the house by herself. With no interruptions.

She poured lukewarm coffee into a foam cup and guzzled it to jump-start her medication.

After she called her dad, she'd eat a quick lunch and then trek back up the mountain to the abbey. If Carson wanted to find her, he would know where to look.

And a very small part of her hoped he would.

She threw the cup into the trash and stumbled out the back door. The light stung her eyes, and she squinted as she glanced around the courtyard in search of her bike. There was a truck parked behind the small hotel and a couple of newer bikes locked to a stand, but she didn't see the rusty green one that Carson had rented. She stepped around the car and looked behind the small woodpile. No bike.

She had left it out here last night. Hadn't she?

The gate beside the hotel was propped open, and she peeked outside to see if someone had put it on the street. The only bikes she saw were already carrying passengers.

Had one of the other guests taken her bike by mistake? In the darkness, it was probably hard to distinguish between them. Surely no one would have stolen it with so many new bikes available for the taking.

She turned around and jogged back up the stairs and into the cramped lobby. When she rang the bell at the front counter, a woman with a badge that said *Anne* came around the corner, a bucket in one hand and a sponge in the other. She held up the bucket and shrugged like she was embarrassed that one of the guests had caught her cleaning.

Elise didn't care about the bucket. She needed transportation into the Odenwald.

"Someone took my bike."

Anne dropped the sponge into the bucket. "Where was it?"

"Behind the hotel."

"Someone must have taken it by mistake."

She rubbed the back of her neck. "I don't have time to wait."

"Max will rent you another one in Aldstadt. Tell him you'll bring the other one back tomorrow."

"Where's the nearest telephone?" Elise asked, and Anne gave her directions to a square near the hotel.

She lugged her aching body down the road. Even with a new bicycle, she would never get to the old abbey by one o'clock. If God wanted her to continue pursuing this, she needed a miracle. Right now.

At the corner store, she bought a thirty-minute calling card and then located a phone outside the bus station. She dialed home, but no one answered.

Her words jumbled as she tried to explain to the answering machine why she hadn't checked in last night. She hung up, frustrated at the guilt that laced her words. It was silly to be so paranoid. Maybe her dad hadn't even noticed that she didn't call last night.

Right.

She called his cell number, but disconnected when it went to voice mail. She called one last time, just in case he'd been fumbling with his phone while it was ringing and hadn't been able to pick up.

Still no answer.

She leaned back against the plastic side of the booth and listened to his familiar greeting. She was sure he would have his cell by his side for her entire trip.

She left a quick, more coherent message, and then relinquished the telephone booth to another student and turned toward Old Town.

Maybe her dad had agreed to go to a play with Rachel tonight. Usually he avoided anything to do with the arts, but her stepmother loved the theater, so sometimes she roped him into going to a musical or something Shakespearean. Every once in a while, he actually went willingly, though he preferred to be working the farm or hunting wild turkey with a Remington clutched in his hands.

Even if he were at a play tonight, she still would have thought he would run to the lobby to answer her call.

It was selfish of her to think he would be at her beck and call. He was probably enjoying a few quiet days with his family. After all, Devin was his and Rachel's only child. She was Catrina's.

She hopped up onto the bumpy stone sidewalk and sidestepped through crowds of tourists and students. The busy marketplace smelled like spicy meat and sugar.

No matter how much she told herself that her thoughts were ridiculous, the feelings still haunted her whenever she was away from home, especially the feeling that her dad might be waiting for her to leave so he could bond with his real family instead of being interrupted by an abandoned kid who'd been forced under his wing years ago.

Yet, in spite of what had happened to her mother, her dad had never once tried to push her out of the house. Instead, it seemed like he was trying to keep her at home for the rest of her life. Just because he wasn't sitting around waiting for her to call didn't mean that he'd suddenly stopped loving her. A few days away from home and she was getting loopy.

The scent of fresh bread floated out of a café, and she stopped in and ordered a croissant. Her head and legs had stopped hurting, and the haze over her brain was starting to lift.

"Thank you," she whispered. Maybe she could make it back up the mountain.

The bike shop was in a stucco building at the end of Old Town. A yellow sign hanging above the door announced in English that they did indeed rent bikes.

A bell dinged when she walked inside, and a man who she guessed was Max set down a bike wheel and wiped his hands on his Grateful Dead T-shirt.

He didn't even bother with German. "Can I help you?"

She nodded. "My friend and I rented bikes from this shop, and I'm afraid that someone else at the hotel borrowed mine this morning."

His eyes narrowed. "Why did you let them borrow it?"

"They took it without my permission."

He bent down with his wrench and began working on a bike. "It's a nice day to walk."

"Actually I'd like to rent another bike."

"But you have a bike."

"Had one."

He stood up and moved behind the counter. "I'm sorry, but I need you to return the other bike first."

"But I don't know where it is."

"Maybe you should check with *die Polizei*."

She looked around at the clusters of rundown bikes. "Do you sell bicycles?"

"Occasionally."

"I'd like to buy a used one today."

He leafed through a stack of papers. "You will have to buy two bikes."

"What?"

He didn't meet her eye. "Three hundred for each."

"That's crazy."

He shrugged. "I can sell you a bike lock as well."

She stomped her foot before she marched out of the shop, just in case he didn't know she was mad. Over her shoulder, she glanced back through the window, but he had already knelt back down to work on the bike. He'd lost a sale, and he didn't even care.

There was no way she was going to pay a thousand U.S. dollars for a rusty bike that she'd have to leave behind. Her plane ticket to Europe hadn't even cost her a thousand bucks.

She collapsed onto the chilled sidewalk and ticked through her options to get up the trail. A moped? She'd need a license. A taxi? They'd never drive up a bike path. Maybe a small plane and a parachute?

If only it was a couple hours earlier, she would walk up to the old abbey, but it was already eleven o'clock, and even if she had the stamina to hike up the hill, she'd never get there in time to meet Lena.

She stood up and paced past the row of shops. She was so close to finding out what had happened to her mother. But a thousand dollars?

She'd come so far, and now this one man was about to pull the plug on her momentum. If she didn't find a way to get up that hill, Lena would leave, and she would have to start asking questions again. This time without Carson.

She had to find a way to get up to Lena today. If she didn't, she might never find out what happened.

Resigned, she turned back to the bike shop, credit card in hand. Desperation was never a good bargaining chip, but it was all she had. She'd let him rob her with her eyes wide open.

"Elise!"

She turned and saw Carson biking toward her, his hair mashed against his head.

She grinned like a kid. She hadn't expected to see him again, but somehow he'd found her in Old Town.

He parked his bike by the streetlamp. "I thought you'd still be asleep."

She glanced over her shoulder and into the window of the bike shop. A couple was chatting with Max as they picked out their bikes. She tapped her heel on the sidewalk and tried to smile again at him. It was so hard to ask.

"I need your help," she sputtered.

"Really?"

"Someone took my bike."

He pointed toward the shop. "Let's get you another one."

"Max wants the old bike first."

His gaze flickered past her face and into the window of the shop. Max looked up for an instant and waved at him. Carson responded with a nod, ever so slightly, like he didn't want anyone to know he knew the man.

She studied his face. Of course, Max knew Carson. Carson had just rented their bikes yesterday, and he seemed to make friends wherever he went. There was nothing to feel guilty about unless . . . she stared at him as he took a step away from her.

"Can I borrow your bike?"

"I don't think so." He winked and turned toward the store. "Let me talk to Max."

She marched toward the streetlamp and his bike, flung her leg over the seat, and shot him a glare that dared him to try to stop her. "Did you steal my bike, Carson?"

The cheesy grin drained from his face. "Why would I . . ."

A woman wearing a red scarf around her neck and carrying a slick leather briefcase came out of the shop behind him and tapped him on the shoulder.

"Carson?"

The woman wrapped her skinny arms around his neck and squeezed.

Elise didn't bother to wait for an introduction. She didn't want to listen to him stammer out the reason why he'd taken her bike or why he was following her around when he already had a girlfriend in Heidelberg. She had someplace she needed to be in two hours, and now she had a bike to ride.

She pushed away from the curb and clung to the handlebars as she started pedaling away from Heidelberg. And far, far away from Carson Talles.

Chapter 20

CARSON WRESTLED HIMSELF away from Kate's clutch and jogged toward Elise, but she swerved around the corner with his bike and was gone. Anyone else might have been playing games, rounding the block and laughing at him for thinking that she'd actually take his bike.

But Elise wasn't playing. She didn't even bother to glance back as she rode out of town.

How was he supposed to take care of her when she wouldn't cooperate? She was beyond reasoning with, completely incapable of rationalizing the situation. It was like she had lifted her arms to the sky and yelled, "*Bring it on!*"

He scraped his foot across the curb. It was almost as if she thought the very act of risking her life would absolve her from the weight of her mother's death.

But this was more than just taking a risk. Obsession could kill too.

He stuffed his hands into the pockets of his jacket. Now he was standing in Heidelberg. Bikeless. And she was off again, by herself, riding into the forest on a mission to find a group of people that terrified his mom.

And he was powerless to stop her.

Kate clasped his arm again, and he flinched.

"Now I know why you didn't want to do breakfast," she pouted as she followed him toward the door of the bike shop. "But what do you think about lunch?"

"I can't," he replied. There was no time for small talk. He had to get Max to rent him another bike.

"I hate to tell you"—Kate nodded toward the corner—"but it looks like you've been stood up."

"I've got to go after her."

"Lucky girl."

He shook his head. "It's not like that . . ."

She managed a smile. "So then it's just *me*."

He groaned as he opened the door and shuffled back into the store.

It was his mom's fault that he was in this predicament. He didn't want to hurt Kate's feelings, and if he was honest, he didn't want to keep trying to stop Elise from finding out about her mother either. After all, if his mom had committed suicide, he would want to know the reason too.

Why would he want to stop her from discovering the truth?

"What happened to the girl?" Max asked from behind the counter.

Carson tried to smile. It was time to scarf down some humble pie. "She stole my bike."

Max grabbed his bulging stomach and laughed like he hadn't laughed in days.

"Yeah, it's hilarious," Carson muttered.

"So now you need another bike."

"Good observation."

"I'll hook you up for another twenty."

"I don't suppose you'd take it from the hundred I already gave you."

Max drummed his fingers on the side of the cash register. "I worked hard for that money."

"Right." He glanced at the roomful of bikes. "This time I'd like a bike that's not about to fall apart."

"I can't make any promises."

It took ten minutes for Max to find him another bike, in spite of the fact that they were surrounded by at least thirty possibilities. He'd obviously perfected the art of stalling, as well. Maybe Elise had tipped him extra for revenge.

The new bike squeaked as he pushed it outside. Kate was gone, and he didn't look for her to say good-bye. Instead, he pedaled toward a sandwich shop, parked his bike, and went inside.

The aroma of butter and chocolate permeated the warm room, but he didn't buy dessert. Instead he ordered two ham and cheese sandwiches, a couple of grape drinks, and a bag of pretzels. He stuffed the food into his backpack and stepped back outside. Next stop was a drugstore, where he bought two flashlights, batteries, and the German news magazine *Der Spiegel*, so he'd have something to read while he waited.

When he walked back outside, he glanced up the hill at the castle. Beyond the walls he could see the winding path that Elise was probably following, her anger fueling a rapid climb up the hill.

He couldn't blame her for being mad. He'd acted like her friend, her confidant. And then when she'd just started to trust him, he'd swiped her transportation. He'd be irate if someone had done the same thing to him. He had deceived her from the beginning, coming to Heidelberg with the sole intention of keeping her from discovering the Chosen. He'd pretended that he would help her when he was really determined to stop her search.

Even if his mom thought this was all for Elise's good, the deception was exhausting. He should have just said no when his mom asked him to get involved. Now it was time for him to start calling the shots—no matter how angry his mom would be.

Elise could dig as deep as she wanted. It was her family. Her past. Why in the world would his mom want to stop her? And why would he?

His mom was hiding something too, and maybe it was time for everyone to put all their cards on the table so they could sort it out. In the meantime, he wouldn't tell his mom just yet that he was bailing. If he did, she would only dispatch someone else from her office to follow Elise.

What Elise needed was someone to protect her from herself. If he couldn't stop her from tracking down the Chosen, at least he might be able to keep her from getting hurt.

He glanced one more time up at the castle to the right and then turned the other way. It would take Elise a few hours to get directions from Lena and then get back across the river—and she needed that time to cool down about the stolen bike. What Carson needed was to find out exactly what they were dealing with before Elise set foot inside the old commune.

Cars buzzed by him as he crossed over the Neckar on the busy bridge, toward the edge of the university. When he reached the other side, he turned right on Uferstrasse. The sun emerged from the gray clouds, and the scent of toasted oak whisked through the breeze as he watched a barge slide past him on the river.

Even though the woman at the farmhouse had initially denied knowing the Chosen, she had given him detailed directions to their former compound. He pedaled along the riverbank, as she had instructed, and after two miles he turned left onto an unmarked street behind a vacant gas station. A thick canopy of foliage now blocked the sun, and the street narrowed into a curvy, country road as he slowly pedaled the bike uphill. After another mile or so, he parked by a stream and sat down on a log to eat his lunch. There was no reason to hurry. It would still be hours before Elise came this way.

He pulled out his cell phone and checked his voice mail. In her most authoritative voice, his mom reminded him that he was not to let Elise go near the house.

It was too late. Elise deserved to know what had happened, and he wasn't going to stop her.

But no matter what, he would not let her go inside the house alone.

Chapter 21

THE AFTERNOON SUN folded soft rays of light through the trees. Elise zipped up her jacket and hiked around the seemingly endless fence that wound through the forest. The chain links slumped and sagged in spots like stretched elastic, but she had yet to find a place where it was torn.

Lena had given her precise instructions to the property, and she had flown down the mountain and traveled straight to the other side of the river. Her train would leave early tomorrow, so if she was going to find the house and investigate, she had to do it before sunset.

She rattled the chain links of the fence with her toe, but it didn't give. According to Lena, the farmhouse stood on the other side.

She marched forward into the brush. Either she'd find a break in the fence or she'd push it down.

A narrow stream splashed over the rocks beside her, and wind rustled the thick leaves above her head. Something shuffled in the brush, and she shook off the eerie wave that enveloped her. The noise was probably a bird or a mouse, wondering who was invading their territory. She was scaring herself.

All she wanted was one look inside the house to see if it offered any information about the Chosen or where they had gone. If she couldn't find anything, she'd stop searching. She had learned enough to know that her mother's childhood had been tragic and that God had rescued her. Yet, in spite of this new knowledge, there were still so many questions. Why was her mother part of a cult? What did her life look like before she joined the Chosen? And who was her birth father?

Maybe if she told her dad what she'd found, he would finally fill in the blanks.

Something moved in the bushes again, and she swallowed hard. For an instant, she almost wished that Carson was around to distract her from the clatter in the trees.

She clutched her fists and drummed her knuckles together.

Why in the world had Carson stolen her bike? It didn't make any sense, just like it didn't make any sense that a backpacker would delay his journey for three days to help a woman he didn't know.

Maybe meeting Carson wasn't just a coincidence. Maybe it had been ordained by someone who thought her guardian angel needed an extra hand.

She wouldn't put it past her dad to have hired a pro to tail her across Germany—or even a college kid from Virginia who was looking to make a few extra bucks. He was probably calling her dad each night, giving him a play-by-play of her every step. No wonder her dad wasn't home when she called today. He thought someone was watching out for her.

Well she didn't need an escort. She was going to search this house, and she was going to do it by herself.

Hazy clouds dipped over the mountain and settled on the trees. She squinted, and straight ahead she saw a break where the fence had collapsed. She bolted toward the metal pathway, and in seconds, she was on the property.

She crept through a battalion of weathered tree trunks on the other side of the fence. Pockets of fall leaves obscured her view of the sky, and dried leaves blew across her path, crunching under her running shoes as she raced to get out of the cold darkness. After a few minutes, the path began to widen, and she gasped when the trees gave way to a clearing, overgrown with waist-high weeds and grass. She'd been expecting a farmhouse, but in the center of the field was a dilapidated mansion.

Three stories extended out toward the forest, and blue shutters, chipped and faded, dangled over the brown speckled walls. Two of the columns along the wide front porch had cracked, and the roof sagged with them. Plaster cornices that curled up the eaves and a stump of a bronze statue in the fountain hinted of a past elegance. Long before the war, carriages had probably lined the drive, delivering men in top hats and tailcoats and women bound in corsets under their beaded gowns.

At the side of the house was a fountain. And a man!

She jumped back but didn't run. Underneath the man's ball cap was a sandy mop of hair.

How dare Carson follow her up the hill . . . and not even tell her he was here!

"You stole my bike," she muttered.

"I did."

She stepped toward him. "Why?"

"You're pushing yourself too hard." He jumped off the edge of the fountain. "I was afraid you'd end up in the hospital if you didn't get some rest."

"I don't have time for the hospital."

"Right," he smiled. "I'd bet money that we'll be visiting the ER before this trip is over."

"I'm not your problem, Carson."

He stuck his hand into his backpack and took out a sandwich and drink. "Someone needs to look after you."

She glared at him. It was like he'd lifted the words from her father's playbook. "Did my dad hire you?"

He looked stunned. "What?"

"I want to know if my dad paid you to watch out for me."

"Of course not."

She edged her face toward his, but he didn't waver. Instead he smiled at her like he was trying to calm her fears, trying to prove he was a trustworthy kind of guy. Right. It would be easier to convince her if he hadn't stolen her bike.

"I don't need a babysitter."

"Do you really want to debate that?"

She put her hands on her hips. "I'm going into this house."

"Fine. So am I." He extended the food toward her. "After you eat."

She grabbed the drink, guzzled almost half the bottle, and muttered a thank you as she took a bite of the sandwich. Then she glanced up at the mansion and back at Carson. So many things could happen in an old house—she could fall through a floor or get trapped in a room or get bitten by a snake. She shuddered. If something did happen, Carson was the only one who knew she was here.

She looked in his eyes. He may not be the smartest guy she'd ever met, but he had helped her. A little. If he were going to harm her, he would have done it a day or two ago.

She mentally waded through years of her dad's advice. He would tell her to avoid both old houses and men she didn't know. Of course, he probably knew Carson.

She marched past him and walked straight toward the house, stopping only to test one of the few unsplintered floorboards on the porch before she pushed on the front door.

It didn't budge.

Turning back, she saw Carson up on a log, staring in the front window.

She jostled the knob again and shoved it with her shoulder before she stepped back. "It's locked."

He jumped off the wood. "Really?"

"A locked door isn't going to stop me."

"Of course not."

She stepped off the porch and over an old tire. The gray light would be gone in an hour or so. "Why don't you check out the left side of the house, and I'll go right."

Carson didn't move.

"I promise I won't run away."

She rounded the house and pressed her nose against the cold glass of another window, but she couldn't see through the mustard yellow drapes.

What would happen if a rock mistakenly made its way through the glass? Or a tree limb? It wasn't like anyone lived here anymore, and it would hardly damage the facade.

She nixed the breaking-and-entering possibility. God had helped her connect with Lena. If he wanted her to continue, he would get her inside the house.

There was a stone outbuilding in the back yard and some sort of carriage house leaning on its side like a tipped cow. A few stairs led up to a back door, and she reached up to the knob and turned it. It too was locked.

If this property were in the United States, vandals would have pilfered it years ago . . . unless the Chosen had left someone behind to stand guard.

There was a noise behind her, and she whipped around, rubbing the chill from her arms. She scanned the surrounding trees, but the only thing that moved was fluttering branches. Of course no one was behind her. Even with Carson nearby, her head was playing games.

She propped herself up on her toes to look through coated windows. An old refrigerator and a sink filled with dishes. Could someone still be using the home?

"Bingo!" Carson yelled from the other side of the house, and she raced around the building and found him bending over a door in the ground. He reached down and tugged on the scratchy handle until the metal flipped back and the opening erupted with dank air.

"Does the cellar work?" he asked.

"Yeah . . ."

He zipped open his daypack and handed her a flashlight. "I thought we might need these too."

"Thanks." She took it and clicked it on. It should have occurred to her to bring a flashlight.

Cobwebs draped over the entryway. She ducked under the woven curtain and followed Carson down into the darkness. The room smelled like coal, and when she shined her light to the right, she saw the cast-iron door of a furnace. To the left was a blackened staircase.

Her light trailed up the steep stairs to a closed door. If there had been a railing at one time, it was gone.

"Ladies first," Carson quipped.

Her light stopped at a wide crack on a bottom step, and she shook her head. "Not this time."

"Are you sure you can trust me?"

She eyed the concrete floor under the stairs. "Definitely."

"What happens if I fall through?"

She rolled her eyes. "I'll go find help."

He turned around and shone his light toward her chin. "Now I have to decide if I can trust you."

With her flashlight playing on the dark crevices behind him, she watched a critter shuffle toward the side of the room. There was a reason she liked her cats. They hunted mice, and they didn't ask her stupid questions.

She pointed her light back up at the door. "You're stalling."

"You bet I am."

He tested the bottom step with his toe and then the next one. The wood groaned under his weight, but held together.

He slowly pressed ahead, counting steps six, seven, and eight.

With a jolting crack, the next step broke under him. He fell forward and his arms slammed into the wood. His flashlight crashed to the floor.

Elise jumped forward. "Are you okay?"

He groaned as he pushed himself up.

"Avoid step number nine." He planted his feet back onto a more reliable piece of lumber. "And I need your flashlight."

She shined her light onto the floor and saw the cracked plastic case and scattered batteries. Instead of handing her light over, she pointed a beam of light toward the door. "It looks like we'll be sharing."

"Wonderful."

Scrambling on his hands and knees, he slowly crawled to the top of the stairs and grabbed the knob.

Chapter 22

A TOXIC STENCH spilled down the stairs when Carson opened the door. Elise plugged her nose and pressed her toes against the first rickety step. Slowly she began to climb toward the light, skipping over step number nine. And eleven. And fourteen.

Carson grabbed her hand and pulled her up to the top step before they forged through the door and into the living room.

Towels, plates, and a guitar were spread across a green paisley sofa, and four folding chairs lay on the torn carpet. Chipped mugs, spoons, and plastic plates were strewn over a smeared glass coffee table, and mold crept across white paint like the spindly legs of a spider.

She held her breath as she raced toward the hallway, hoping that the spores in the air wouldn't suffocate her.

At the bottom of a wide staircase, she paused and glanced up at the second floor. Carson shook the banister, and the liberated dust coated her face and lungs. She coughed as she pulled the collar of her shirt over her mouth.

"What are you doing?" she mumbled as he shook it again.

"Testing it." He swooped his arm in front of him. "But don't let me get in your way."

She eyed the dark brown wood on the steps and rails. They didn't look deteriorated like the cellar stairs, but even if they were rotten, she wasn't going to let some old wood stop her now.

She slowly moved up to the second floor.

When she made it to the top, she paused to catch her breath then turned down the hallway. Pink floral wallpaper peeled off the walls in giant strips, and the soggy carpet, squashing under her boots like wet sand, smelled like mildew.

Centered in the hallway was a picture of Jesus—his arms outstretched, his head soaked with blood and sweat.

She blinked and looked up again. She remembered this picture, remembered wondering why no one would help the man when he was in so much pain. She'd wanted to pour a pitcher of cold water over his head, wipe away his blood and the pain in his eyes.

No one could help him . . . just like no one could help her.

The memory faded, but she stood frozen in front of the painting.

Carson passed her. "Are you coming?"

She turned to follow him toward the first room in the hallway, a small bedroom with a scraped hardwood floor. Yellowed veins iced the top of the cracked window. A box spring leaned against the wall like a tent, and a pile of filthy clothes rotted on the floor. There was a Bible on a chair, still open, and a plastic plate and cup.

"I can't imagine why no one lives here anymore," Carson said as they backed out of the room. "The place has so much character."

She clenched her nose again. "And the housekeeping is top notch."

"Five stars."

She nodded toward an open suitcase on an unmade bed. Socks and sweaters were scattered on the floor. "When they left here, they left in a hurry."

He pointed to another one of the piles. "Care to dig through a rat's nest?"

"Boys first."

He backed away. "I don't do rats."

"Me neither."

The next four bedrooms were filled with identical piles of clothes and rumpled beds. It was as if someone had shouted "Fire!" and the group had run with whatever they could grab.

She opened up a wooden door at the end of the hall and pointed her flashlight up a circular staircase. This time Carson didn't stop to test the stairs before they climbed, almost like he was as anxious as she was to find out what was on the top floor.

The third floor was dark. Most of the doors were closed. The hardwood creaked as they crossed it.

She put her hand on the knob of a peeling door and turned it.

A crystal chandelier hung from the sloped ceiling on an old ballroom, and the walls were papered with a faded gold. But instead of orchestra chairs or dining tables across the tile floor, the room was filled with cribs and cots. Elise closed her eyes for a moment and felt the breeze rush through a crack in one of the dormer windows.

The children were screaming. Pushing. Crying. Rushing around her legs.

She collapsed back against the wall and clutched her arms to her chest. This was the room where the mean woman was, and she was whipping a toddler with a belt. The girl cried for help, but no one could help her. Elise reached her hands out to rescue the child, but she was gone.

She opened her eyes and stepped toward one of the cots. She remembered this room, these beds. She glanced at the wall. She'd slept on the third one down. It had been so cold. And there had been a trunk—with toys. If they obeyed the woman, they were allowed to play. If not . . .

She shuddered as she turned toward the center of the room. Someone had covered the trunk with a blanket, but it was still there.

She pulled the blanket off the trunk, knelt down on the floor, and opened it. The box was filled with blocks and wooden cars and a tugboat. She rummaged through the toys until she found a carrot-topped girl with big blue eyes and rosy cheeks.

Leah.

They'd left behind her favorite doll.

Metal scraped across the tile floor, and she turned toward Carson. He was moving one of the cribs.

"What are you doing?" she asked as she rescued Leah from the box.

"Looking underneath."

"For what?"

"I have no idea."

That was the problem. He had no idea what to look for, and neither did she. Without databases and files and a stack of books, she was lost.

She held out the doll to Carson. "I've been in this room before."

He leaned back against the wall as he surveyed the cribs. "It looks like a prison."

"I remember the warden."

He turned toward her. "What else do you remember?"

The words stuck in her throat. "Missing my mother."

She took another step, but then she spun around and stared at the far wall. She used to hide Leah from the other kids. In the papers. Mounds of papers.

She shut her eyes, her mind racing as she tried to resurrect the memory. She'd hidden Leah next to the giant window on the wall . . . behind a secret door.

Chapter 23

THERE WAS NO window in the plush red room, but the candle by the bedside flickered like the fireplace in Grimma. Sara dressed quietly in the shadows until Sol flicked on the light switch and turned toward her. Her arms were draped with the brown, ragged dress she'd received as a hand-me-down three years ago.

"I want you to wear the green dress," he said.

"I–I—" she stuttered. "I can't."

His fingers curled over the tip of his cane. "It's not pretty enough for you?"

She shook her head. "It's too pretty."

He studied her face and then he knew. She wasn't being disrespectful. Sara didn't think she was worthy to wear a new dress.

Humility was a quality he encouraged.

He wanted all of Sara—not just her body. He wanted her passion. Her desire. Her devotion. Only he knew that she teetered between faith and distrust. She'd never admit it, but he could see it in her eyes—the cloud of doubt, the questions, the heresy. Someday she wouldn't care about her cats. She would know that he was her king. Her father. Her beginning and end.

He swiped his fingers through the candle's flame. He'd devoted himself to Sara since she was a child, overseeing her education with the delicate balance of adoration and discipline. She was the only toddler allowed into his sanctuary to play games and indulge in chocolates that were banned from the nursery. The other girls had been jealous.

When she was a girl, Sara had fluttered around the old convent like a butterfly. He'd had to work with Phoebe on developing more structure in Sara's schedule. More discipline. They'd had to purify her spirit before she lost focus and became enchanted by the outside.

Phoebe had lashed Sara when she had questioned their authority. She had mandated her fasts, and overseen her days of solitary confinement.

As long as she pleased him, Sol had been her savior.

Even though he delegated most of the discipline to Phoebe, he still had to flex his power when Sara and the others challenged his authority. God commanded their respect. Demanded it. And he demanded it of his children and his wives.

Phoebe and Lily respected him, but he rarely called them to his room anymore, except to stoke the fire and bring his food. Sara, however, was chosen out of all the women in the family to be his rose of Sharon. From the day she was born, she had been pampered and purified, like Esther being prepared for her king. Yet even though she was loved more than any of the other women, she continued to reject him.

Someday the fire of love would blaze in Sara, and when it did . . .

He pinched his fingers over the candle's flame and snuffed it out.

Perhaps Phoebe was too old to continue disciplining Sarah. Perhaps it was time for Michael to step up in his new role as lieutenant and take over this task.

A white kitten stepped out of the corner and brushed against Sara's ankle. When Jozef had told him about the gift, he decided that Sara could keep the cat. If she started slipping away again, a simple trip back to the Mulde River would convince her to remain true.

Sara stepped toward the door, and Sol looked up from the cat and examined the drawn cheekbones that sculpted her sallow skin. Then he reached over, lifted up her worn sleeve, and rubbed his thumb over the etched wounds that lined her arm, until he reached the scar on her shoulder. She shivered under his touch.

"You're pale, Sara."

She didn't look at him. "I haven't been well."

Startled, he let go of her arm. "What's wrong?"

Her eyes wandered over to the dresser at the other side of the room. The last time she'd complained of illness was when she was ten. Phoebe had crushed the Devil's clutch on her body, and she hadn't been sick since.

"I'm tired."

Tired? He forced back a laugh. She might feel fatigued, but it was hardly from hard work. On the days that he sent Sara into town, she rarely returned with food. The only reason he kept sending her was to remind her of what would happen if he sent her into the world for good.

When Sara was at home, she assisted in the kitchen, but she was always available when he needed her—night or day. Lily and Phoebe worked fourteen-hour shifts, but he mandated that Sara get her rest. It was her job to calm him on the nights he couldn't sleep. When *he* was tired.

He leaned toward her. "Is the enemy taunting you?"

She wrung her hands under the fabric of her dress. Her stomach growled, but he ignored it as he stared at her, trying to decipher her motives. In her silence, she was asking to be punished. Resigned to it. Why would she want to be whipped? Remorse maybe. Regret. Or guilt.

He cupped her chin and forced her eyes to meet his. He didn't see that glimmer of hope that he'd seen in her mother. He was looking into eyes devoid of desire. Sara knew her future was with him.

"What have you done, Sara?"

Tears sprang into her eyes unexpectedly, and he sidestepped away from her. She rarely showed emotion to him. Certainly not tears.

Had she met a boy in Grimma? He wouldn't let some kid divert her from her calling. When she lost her desire for the world, she was supposed to embrace her future with pleasure, not despair. He wanted her to beg for his help, guidance, wisdom.

Someone knocked on the door, but Sol ignored it. In Grimma, his family would know not to bother him when he was with one of his wives.

"Sara?" he repeated.

"I don't know what's wrong with me."

He swept his fingers through her soft hair and willed his anger to steady as he lowered his voice. *"He was wounded for our transgressions, he was bruised for our iniquities."*

"Yes, sir."

Now wasn't the time to discipline her—punishment was what she wanted. Now was the time to mend their relationship, remind her that he was her confidant. He was the only one who could heal her wounds.

His fingers brushed over the leather on his sheath. Pity the boy who had been distracting her.

Someone knocked again, and he stepped toward the door and pulled it open.

"What?" he growled when he saw Michael.

Michael pointed down the hallway, and Sol stuck his head out the door to see an emaciated teenage girl huddled on the floor. Spindly collarbones jutted above her chest, and her halter top looked like a black stripe across her pale skin.

"Where did you get her?"

"On Oranienburger," Michael paused. "I think she's a runaway."

"Does she know English?"

"No, sir."

"Good work," he said. It would only be a matter of weeks before Michael would be ready to take over the entire business. "We'll leave for Grimma in an hour."

Michael nodded.

"Get her something to eat and something else to wear." He eyed the girl one more time, and then looked back at Michael. "And tell Jozef we found his new girl."

Chapter 24

DAZED, ELISE INCHED toward the back wall of the old ballroom like she was in a trance. She remembered the darkness. The silence in the room when the lights went out. The children didn't whisper to each other. They weren't allowed to make noise. The only sounds were the snores coming from the woman who slept with her gray hat in her hands.

Once the woman started snoring, Elise would wait patiently in her bed, her body hidden under the covers, her eyes open. As the woman's snoring grew deeper, louder, she'd climb out of her bed, tiptoe over to the wall, and retrieve Leah from the only safe place in the room.

She'd slide Leah out of the room behind the wall and rock her doll in the moonlight. Then she'd kiss Leah's worn cheek and tuck her away again behind the boxes so she'd be . . . safe.

Elise stopped beside the crib and entwined her fingers in the slats.

Why would she need to keep her doll safe? Was another child trying to harm her?

No, that didn't seem right. Safe from the woman? Maybe . . . but there was someone else wanting to wound her doll.

Sorrow rushed through her, whirling around her heart like the winds from a tornado. She gulped back her breath as she fought the tears. She wouldn't cry . . . not now when she was so close to the truth. And not in front of Carson.

The other children had been as terrified as she was. She just didn't remember what they'd been afraid of.

But until she'd returned to this nursery, she hadn't remembered living here, either.

She squinted at the brown paneling in front of her until the thin stripes blurred in the wood. There was something here.

When she shivered, Carson slipped up behind her. She tried to brush off his hand, but he didn't move. "It's okay to cry."

She wiped her eyes on her hand. "Something happened in here."

"You don't have to tell me."

She released her grip on the crib. "I don't remember . . ."

"Let's go back to town." He slid his hands into his jeans pockets. "It's my turn to treat you to dinner."

She dug a tissue out of her pocket and wiped her nose. "Not yet."

She wasn't interested in food. No matter how much the memories hurt, this wasn't the time to turn back. The search was about more than finding out what had happened to her mother. It was also about finding out what had happened to her.

She slowly lowered Leah into the crib and tucked her under the threads of an old afghan. With her back pressed against the slats, she pushed the bed away from the wall.

The seam of the door was barely visible among the panel's stripes, but it was exactly where she remembered. She bent over and tapped, but it didn't move.

She closed her eyes. Maybe it had been a dream. A child's fantasy for a hiding space in a place she was dying to escape. Or maybe not . . .

Her fingers rolled into balls, she shoved her fists into the wood.

"What are you—" Carson stopped talking when the door popped open.

"Okay then," he mumbled as he flicked on the light and shined it into the crawl space. Nothing moved. She held out her hand, and he relinquished the light to her before she stuck her head inside.

Lined up against the wall were fifteen or twenty filing boxes, and scattered across the bare floor were mounds and mounds of paper. She hesitated before she picked up a pamphlet and shook it. Then she backed out of the space and sat down to open the brittle pages.

On the first page was a hand drawn picture of a man and woman drinking mugs of beer in a bar, and Jesus was watching them from behind the counter. The woman looked at Jesus with obvious adoration, but the man was slumped over beside her.

Elise turned the page and saw the man in a hospital bed, with Jesus by his side. Instead of looking at Jesus, he was staring at the wall. The caption under the picture was in German, but she didn't need to read the language to understand that the man had rejected Christ.

On the next page, the man was surrounded by flames. Satan clutched his throat, and the man's arms were flailing as if he were drowning in the fire.

Elise squirmed as she turned the page again, sickened by the crude drawings.

The woman bowed down before Christ, his arms outstretched as streams of light radiated from his face. At the bottom of the page was the text of Matthew 22:14 in bold German and English print. *For many are called, but few are chosen.*

She turned the page and saw Jesus with his hand on the woman's back, her face covered with a veil. He was welcoming her into the gates of heaven as his bride. The woman opened the gate and inside was a crowd, hands raised high, celebrating her arrival.

Elise closed the tract and reached for another one.

This pamphlet featured a scrawny kid on a street corner, his outstretched hand asking strangers for help. One adult kicked him. Another spat in his face. Tears ran down the child's face. No one would stop and help him. No one would give him food . . . until a couple stopped and sat down on the curb beside him.

The woman offered him her hand, and he followed them out of the busy city and into the countryside. She opened the door of a big farmhouse and welcomed him inside to a huge feast. The boy sat at a banquet table and devoured meat and vegetables and fruit.

She handed the tract to Carson. "What does it say?"

"It explains their mission." He scanned the short text. "The Chosen are called to demonstrate God's love to abandoned children around the world by feeding their stomachs and their souls."

Elise took the tract back and flipped to the last page. The same boy was smiling as he stood in a circle with other children.

Carson thumped his finger on the page in front of her. "It says he's finally discovered a family who loves him . . . and a place to belong."

Elise tossed the tract on the floor and dumped out another box. There was a manila file at the bottom, and she opened it to find what looked like a stack of reports. She handed the file back to Carson, and as he skimmed through the German materials, she reached for another pamphlet. The cover was blue . . . the color of her legs after the woman whipped her.

She dropped the paper and closed her eyes as the memory burned through her mind. What had she done to deserve being whipped? And where were all the other kids?

Leaping to her feet, she retrieved Leah from the bed and clutched her to her chest.

Maybe she didn't want to remember.

Carson touched her elbow, but she turned toward the exit and ran. Past the doors. Down the stairs. Through the kitchen and the parlor.

Her fingers shaking, she twisted the deadbolt on the sitting room door and rushed outside.

Sinking down into the tall grass, she gripped Leah to her chest and heaved in fresh air. Carson sat down beside her, and she wished he would go away. Didn't he understand? She needed to be alone.

"Are you okay?" he asked.

"They did bad things in that house." She rubbed her doll's braids. "But someone protected me."

"Your mother?"

She nodded. Thank God, her mother had gotten her out of there.

145

Chapter 25

IT WAS ONLY A FLASH of brown, darting between the ash tree trunks, so slight that Carson would have chalked it up to the tail of a fox or raccoon if he hadn't seen the face. Staring back at him.

Even the gawking wouldn't have spooked him if the guy had nodded or even waved. Instead he ducked back into the dense forest like he was on the lam. Carson searched the trees for another glimpse of the man, but he didn't emerge again.

He was probably a curious neighbor, wondering who was hiking through the property. Or a hunter searching for rabbit or grouse in the woods. Or even an upstanding German citizen ready to dial 1-1-2 and report two Americans on the wrong side of the fence.

No matter how well Carson spoke German, knowing the language couldn't explain away the fact that they were trespassing. It was time to head back to town.

He looked back at the girl beside him. Elise's knees were balled under her in the grass and her arms were clenched around Leah as if she could somehow siphon the doll's strength and courage.

He wrapped his arm around her, and she leaned into his chest. Someone had hurt Elise in this place. Probably her mother too. Without trying, he'd flipped his assignment from professional to personal, and he had no idea how to make her pain go away.

The shadows from the mansion spread over the grass in front of them.

Part of him wanted to demand that they stop their search, not because Addison Wade said so, but because he wanted to protect Elise from the people who had hurt her. Yet sometimes the truth hurt, deeply, and if Elise decided she still wanted to find the Chosen, he wasn't going to mess around anymore. He'd help her find the truth . . . and heal.

When her muscles began to relax, he released his grip and glanced back toward the forest. No movement. Nothing. Maybe the guy he'd seen was just a curious drifter. He was probably already tromping down the other side of the hill.

"Do you still want to find out what happened?" Carson asked.

"Yes." She clutched Leah to her chest. "But there's no place else for us to look."

He uncrumpled one of the papers in his pocket and held it out to her. She glanced down at the German words and looked back up at him.

"It's a list of properties across the former East Germany," he explained. "Values, availability, contact numbers, and proximities to towns."

He pointed down at one that was circled in ink. "This one here is called Marienthron."

When she gasped, he pulled the paper toward him. "Maybe it is time to stop."

"No," she insisted. "I know Marienthron."

He instinctively scanned the trees again, but didn't see anything. "How do you know it?"

"Katharina von Bora lived there." She dropped Leah to her lap. "It's south of Berlin, in Grimma."

Carson could almost hear his mother's voice urging him to stall her . . . divert her. *Tell her there's another convent on the western side of Germany called Marienthron.*

He wasn't going to lie anymore.

"We need to take a little trip east."

"*I* need to take a trip, Carson." She inched away from him. "Not *we.*"

When he glanced back toward the forest, a chill swept over him. He saw the face again, partly obscured in the trees. Maybe it was just one of his mother's cronies checking up on him. But until he called home, he'd consider the man dangerous.

He pushed himself up to his feet. "Let's go get some food."

She looked shocked at his suggestion.

"I'm famished." His eyes searched the forest, but the face had disappeared. He looked up at the fading light in the sky. "And it's going to be dark in a few minutes."

Elise stood up slowly, cradling Leah in her left arm, and followed him toward the break in the fence.

It was a role switch, him trying to motivate her. He wasn't quite sure how to make her move any faster without alarming her. If he told her about the man in the woods, he wasn't sure what she would do if she saw him—probably charge the guy, ask him if he'd known her mother. Sometimes a little fear was healthy.

He stole another glance over his shoulder before he scrambled across the fence. The man was nowhere to be seen.

They retrieved their bikes, and he stuffed the doll in his backpack before they began pedaling back toward town. The sunlight was almost gone, and he held the flashlight in one hand as he guided them toward the Neckar.

Ten minutes into their ride, he glanced back and saw a blue Audi crawling along the road behind them. He stopped the bike, and the car stopped. Not good. Maybe his mom had called in the guard, since she obviously thought he wasn't doing a good enough job keeping tabs on Elise by himself.

How could she possibly think one of her assistants would be better? He'd done everything he could to keep Elise out of trouble.

When he glanced behind him again, the car was gone.

They turned right at the river, and the light from the streetlamps replaced his flashlight. Ahead was the edge of town with a row of shops and a gas station. He motioned to Elise and steered his bike into the small parking lot of a grocery store.

"I need to make a quick call," he said as he parked his bike in the rack.

She glanced down at her watch. "Me too."

As she walked toward the pay phone, he dialed the embassy on his cell. When he identified himself, the receptionist transferred him straight to the top of the food chain.

"Are you done?" Addison asked.

"Hardly," he whispered. "Did you send someone to check up on us?"

"Of course not."

"Mom?"

"I don't want anyone else involved."

"Well, someone was tailing us." He glanced back over at Elise at the phone booth, but he didn't see the car. "If it's one of your rookies . . ."

"It's not."

"Then I'd like to know who it is."

"Did you find the house?" she asked.

"Unfortunately."

"Someone's probably watching it."

"Well, now they're watching us."

"How is she?" Addison asked.

"Traumatized. She remembered the ballroom upstairs and a crawl space filled with literature."

"Get out of there, Carson."

"How do you know so much about this group?"

"It's a long story."

"Try me."

When his mom hesitated, he leaned back against the bike rack and waited.

"I want you to come back to Berlin," she insisted.

"You keep avoiding my questions."

"I want to discuss it in person."

He sighed. "We think we know where the group went."

"Does Elise know that someone is following you?"

He looked back over at her.

"She probably wouldn't care."

"Her father doesn't deserve to lose someone else."

If he didn't stick with Elise, she would go to Grimma on her own.

If the group was still there, they probably wouldn't want some college student sniffing around.

If they still existed, maybe he and Elise could bring the group to justice. She could stop wondering, and his mother wouldn't have to be afraid. "Maybe it's time to stop them."

"That's not a job for either of you."

"How about for the U.S. ambassador?"

"Not everything in life is an easy fix, Carson."

He watched Elise hang up the phone and walk toward the store. "Nor is everything so complicated."

"Come home, honey."

He paused. His mother had never begged him for anything. People usually did what she said, including her most loyal subjects—him and his dad.

"You sent me here to take care of Elise."

"To distract her," she interrupted. "I wanted you to take her on a cruise of the Rhine or go visit a castle."

"I love you, Mom, but I'm not going to quit now."

She actually lingered over her good-bye before they hung up. When he looked across the parking lot, he saw the Audi again. The driver was at the wheel, but his face was hidden by a hat pulled low like he had dozed off while his wife was shopping for groceries.

Carson walked toward the store, and when he stepped inside, he saw Elise unscrewing the lid of a bottled water.

"That was quick," he said as he picked up a liter of Coke.

"No one was home."

"Did you talk to your dad yesterday?"

She shook her head. "I left a message this morning."

"I'm sure he has a few other things to do beside wait by the phone."

She managed a grin. "I guess you don't know my dad."

He took one last look at the Audi. There was no way he was going to leave Elise alone.

He guzzled down half the liter as they stood in line. "Let's go to Grimma tonight."

She studied his face. "Are you serious?"

"Your work is done here, right?"

"I'm supposed to leave for Wittenberg in the morning."

"So we'll take a detour, and then I'll escort you to Wittenberg tomorrow night."

She shook her head, considering the new plan. "When does the next train leave?"

"Forget the train." He paid for his empty bottle. "Let's get a car."

She choked on her water. "I can't drive in Germany."

He grinned. "I can."

Chapter 26

ADDISON WADE HATED two things—darkness and heat. She kept a packed suitcase at the embassy, and when Richard wasn't home, she would work under the fluorescent lights in her office until three or four in the morning before she walked over to the Hotel Adlon and slept for a couple of hours, lights on, air conditioning high.

Unfortunately, Richard was home tonight, and he had to leave before dawn to catch a plane to London. He wanted the room warm and dark so he could get a good night's sleep.

She rolled over and kicked at the sheets. Not even silky 600-thread-count Egyptian cotton could cool her down.

Comfy sheets weren't the answer. Nor was the Tylenol PM she'd choked down before slipping into bed. The last resort was the gin and tonic stashed away in the wet bar downstairs. Maybe that would stop the shivers that ran through her. Hot, then cold.

In the darkness of her bedroom, Addison could almost hear Catrina's desperate pleas, begging Addison to rescue her daughter. For weeks after she'd escaped from the Chosen, Catrina called every day, asking Addison over and over again if she had heard any more information.

Addison had tried to find Catrina's baby. She had hired a private investigator to hunt down the group, but he never caught their trail. And she'd even traveled back to Germany with Catrina and scoured the countryside around Heidelberg to see if anyone could tell them where the group had gone.

There were rumors that she and Catrina followed across the eastern side of Germany, but they never found Sol or his family.

She wanted to find the baby almost as much as Catrina did—even though Catrina didn't believe her. It was almost as if she blamed Addison for losing her child.

Addison shuddered as she tugged the comforter away from Richard. Her husband groaned, but he didn't fight her for the bulky cover. He could have it back in a few seconds anyway, when her body temperature swung hot again.

With a swift push, she rolled over and stared out the window at the dim lights in the exclusive Charlottenburg neighborhood. She had searched for Sol until Catrina died, and she never found him. Yet somehow Elise was narrowing in on their location. Heaven forbid if she actually found them. Catrina was a black eye on the entire group—they were probably still stinging from the punch she threw.

Sweat gushed down Addison's face, burning her eyes.

What would happen if Elise found Sol? It wouldn't take him long to connect the dots, tracing Elise back to Berlin.

She slid out from between the sheets and into the suede slippers tucked under the bed. Wandering into the hallway, she flipped on the lights and shuddered at the lavish floral wallpaper that lined the walls.

The previous ambassador's wife had been fascinated by the nearby Schloss Charlottenburg—the elaborate country retreat of Frederick I. Her passion for all things seventeenth century had taken over the ambassador's residence. Even though Addison and her family had lived here now for three years, she'd never bothered to redecorate. The house was only a stepping-stone for her family. When she retired—thirty years from now—she might have time to pick out things like wallpaper and curtains.

But if the media ever uncovered where she had been in 1983, she wouldn't last another year as an ambassador or in any other office. The story was like lava brewing and bubbling up the throat of a crater. Once it exploded, it would send her rock-solid career spewing out in pieces. No amount of PR would be able to stop the destruction. They would tear her apart, all in the name of education. Or accusation. Or even compassion.

Her colleagues might respect her, but she had no power with the media. If the public found out, they might feel sorry for her, but she didn't want pity. She wanted respect.

Next month, she was retiring her overseas post and leaving for D.C. to be confirmed by the Senate for her new role as ambassador to the United Nations. But if someone leaked this story to the press, the post in Germany would be the last rung on her career ladder. The Senate would never confirm a former member of an abusive religious cult—especially the Chosen.

She shivered again as she moved down the wide stairway and into the formal living room that smelled like ripe lemons from her maid's religious scouring of the wood.

She filled a glass with ice, gin, and tonic and then turned on both lights in the room and collapsed onto the couch. One hand wove through the golden fringe that dangled from the arms of the couch, and her other hand twirled the tumbler. With a mock salute, she lifted the glass and downed the drink.

The alcohol burned as it ran down her throat. A bitter salve. It would blur her memories, but it never made them go away.

Back then, it had all seemed so simple. Pure. She'd been an idealist, convinced that somehow she and Paul Huntington could save all the children of the world.

One stupid decision when she was twenty-one could destroy her entire career.

She picked up the telephone on the side table and called Carson's cell. It was time for him to cut ties with Elise and come home. He didn't know about her year with the Chosen, and even if Elise found Sol, it didn't mean they would trace it back to her. If Elise was so intent on finding trouble, she could find it alone.

She hung up the phone when Carson didn't answer, and then she glanced over to see Richard standing on the stairs.

"What are you doing?" he demanded.

"I couldn't sleep."

He shuffled toward her, wrapped in the threadbare brown robe that he'd bought the year after they were married. Twenty-two years ago.

He leaned toward her and eased the tumbler out of her grip. He stepped toward the sink, rinsed out her glass, and set it back on the counter. The silent treatment was his chosen method to make her think about her actions. The next step would be the inquisition.

The guilt card never worked on her, but Richard kept trying.

She counted down the silent ten seconds that he let her think, and then he sat down beside her. "You want to tell me about it?"

She looked down at her empty hands. "I just wanted a drink."

She also wanted to bury the past and get back to important things like wrapping up her "Three T" agenda before leaving Berlin—meeting with the chancellor for the last time about technology, trade, and terrorism. A good politician made decisions and moved forward with no regrets. Yes, she had to reevaluate her decisions. And yes, she had to study the past to make decisions about the future. But excavating old memories was a waste of time, and it was exhausting, unproductive work.

She'd tried to tell Elise how fruitless it was to go digging around in the past—and dangerous. Elise had whipped up the waters, and Addison had pushed her son overboard—just in time for the predators to feast.

She eyed the tumbler on the counter.

"The gin won't help," Richard said.

It figured that she would marry a teetotaler and a prosecuting attorney.

"It will for the moment."

"What did you do, Addie?"

She melded her fingers around her elbows, pulling her arms to her chest. For an instant she was standing outside Sol's door, waiting to be punished for her refusal to comply. He'd pummeled her with questions, guilt, but she wouldn't answer, wouldn't give him the satisfaction of a response. It only made him hurl insults at her before he turned her over to Phoebe to beat her back and arms.

"Catrina's daughter came to visit me on Wednesday."

He twitched, sending a ripple across the couch. "You didn't tell me?"

"I didn't think she would find anything."

He groaned.

"But she discovered the house in Heidelberg. Some papers."

"How do you know?"

"Carson called."

He clenched his hands together. "What is Carson doing in Heidelberg?"

His tone stiffened her resolve. She'd done the right thing, at the time. She hadn't foreseen that Elise would stay on course. "I sent him to keep her out of trouble."

"To protect *you*."

"And her."

"Right."

Her hands trembled. "If they find out she's searching for them—"

"It may lead to you." He swept his hand through his thinning hair. "You put Carson at risk to protect your career."

She tightened her arms across her chest. It wasn't the only reason why she was worried. "They'll hurt her."

"You're running again, Addie."

One more sip of the gin would help the memories go away. "I've put the Chosen behind me."

"The only way to put it behind you is to confront it. Head on."

She pushed her toes up in her slippers. "You have no idea."

"But you won't do it, because you still feel responsible for Catrina's death."

She met his stare. "I never let guilt mandate my actions."

Besides, she felt even guiltier for not finding Sara and getting her far away from Sol.

"Only God can save the world, Addie, not you."

"Who mentioned salvation?"

He ignored the barb. "You tried to help Catrina find Sara."

She stared down at the ornate rug. "But I failed."

Chapter 27

RAIN PELTED THE BMW's front windshield as Elise struggled to read the map in the dim light. Carson had insisted on taking back roads through farmland and sleepy villages instead of the highway. If they'd hopped on the autobahn, it would have been almost a straight shot up to Leipzig and over to Grimma. But, no, he had to take a midnight tour of the countryside, and now it was three o'clock in the morning.

His cell phone rang, and he glanced at the number on the screen and then ignored it.

"Is it the girl?" she asked.

He glanced over at her. "What girl?"

"From Heidelberg."

He snorted. "No."

She waited for more of an explanation, but he was focused on his driving. He didn't take his hands off the steering wheel or his eyes off the road.

They passed a road sign, and Elise looked down at the map. "This isn't right."

"Turn around?"

"Uh-huh."

He pulled into a parking lot and made a U-turn. They had already backtracked four times during the night, and he had blamed it on her lack of skill at deciphering the map. Right. Most of the roads he'd decided to cruise down weren't even on the crinkled paper that the rental car company had handed them along with the keys. Apparently, naming all the roads in Germany was optional.

Her eyes started to shut, and she forced them back open. She'd already suggested that they stop and rest along the side of the road, since there was no place else they could sleep at this hour. The gas stations weren't even open to buy a cup of coffee.

He had nodded at her persuasive arguments to take a break, but then kept driving.

Carson sped through a yellow light, and she hung on to the door handle as he swerved right.

If she hadn't wanted to find Marienthron, she never would have considered his offer to drive. She may have been groaning about his choice of direction, but she still wanted to get there. Fast.

Carson pointed toward a white sign that glared back at them in the headlights. *Grimma*.

Fog had settled on the half-timbered homes in the old town, blending the stark lines of wood and stucco. A stone steeple climbed up into the misty blanket, and light from the streetlamps muted the dark windows with a soft gray.

After the busy streets of Heidelberg, it was eerie to be in a town that was so still. Solemn. Especially in the middle of the night.

She tried to fold the map, but it wouldn't cooperate so she crumpled it into a ball and tossed it into the back seat. "Does anyone live here?"

"After six AM."

"It feels sort of ghoulish."

"Transylvania is south of here."

She clutched her arms to her chest and coughed.

"You need some sleep," he said.

It hurt to swallow. "Will it help my throat?"

"Probably not, but it will stop the hallucinations."

"Taking a faster route would have helped even more."

He pulled into a gas station—closed—and parked the car.

"What do we do now?" she asked.

He turned off the ignition and leaned back his seat. "We wait."

"All night?"

"Three hours until daylight."

She hugged Leah to her chest as the night air seeped through the windows and chilled the car. Pain swelled her head as her nose began to run again. She reached into her pocket and retrieved a tissue before she gulped down two more pills. Then she zipped her jacket and rested her head.

In spite of the frigid temps, sleep came quickly. The last thing she remembered was Carson tucking his fleece jacket around her shoulders.

Chapter 28

FOOTSTEPS POUNDED THE forest around her, and Elise shivered as the wind pierced her skin. Branches scraped her face, her arms, but she didn't cry.

People were yelling, stomping on the leaves. She wanted to run, but a woman held her close to her chest and whispered in her ear.

She felt the ground around her for the baby, but she was gone. Gone! She was supposed to take care of the girl, make sure nothing bad happened to her. But someone had stolen her away.

A light swooped over her, and someone shouted beside her. The woman pressed her head into the cold dirt, and they waited. She was too terrified to move. Breathe.

When the light faded, she squirmed in the woman's arms, but the woman held her tight.

Didn't she know they had to save the baby?

If they didn't, no one would.

A shout woke Elise from her sleep, and she reached for the ground before she clenched her fists. There were no branches. No baby.

She heard another shout and angled her head toward the window in time to see a straight line of preschoolers marching past the car, anchored at each end by a teacher.

Sunshine had replaced the hedge of fog, though it had forgotten to heat the ground. Under the veil of Carson's jacket, she rubbed her arms until they hurt.

She tried to push the image of the baby from her mind and focus on the day. It was already nine o'clock. And they were in Grimma.

Now they had to find Marienthron.

She shifted in her seat as she glanced over at her rugged companion, still asleep beside her. The tips of his brown hair curled over his eyes, and his flannel-covered arms were wrapped around his chest. He looked like an overgrown puppy—mischievous, playful, and tired.

As hard as she tried, she couldn't be angry with him anymore for stealing her bike. After all, he had translated the documents at the old mansion and brought her to Grimma.

She gulped down two more pills and reached for the car keys beside him. He could sleep as long as he wanted, but even with his lined jacket, she felt like she was about to freeze.

With a flick of her wrist, she turned the ignition, and the car sparked to life. Carson bolted up, whacking her shoulder with his arm.

"What are you doing?" he demanded as she collapsed back against the seat.

She glared at him. "Trying to avoid your punch."

He rubbed his palms together like he was trying to start a fire. "Before that."

"Turning on some heat. This car is like a freezer." She massaged her sore arm. Hidden underneath Carson's flannel was a muscle or two. "Do you always wake up swinging?"

"Only when threatened."

"A little heat might improve your attitude."

"Next time, wake me up first."

She grunted. "There won't *be* a next time."

Tonight she was sleeping in a warm, dry hotel. Alone.

"Coffee first." He rolled his neck and shifted the car into first gear. "Then we fight."

"I'm too tired to fight."

The car crawled forward. "I don't believe it."

He circled the brick-paved square and in front of them was a shop with a maroon awning that topped a row of tinted windows. Café Sperl. She could almost taste the hot latte warming her throat.

She pointed back at the coffee shop as he passed it. "What are you doing?"

"There's no parking."

"So I'll run inside."

"By yourself?"

When he braked at a stop sign, she opened the door. "I can handle it, Carson."

"Get me a ham croissant," he shouted as she slammed the door.

She waved her hand as she walked away.

He rolled down the window. "And a large coffee!"

She didn't turn around. Of course she would get him coffee. Wasn't that the entire reason they were stopping? She liked him much better when he was sleeping.

A bell chimed when she opened the door. Two bar stools pressed up against the window, and a display case with pastries and croissants lined the wall. She stumbled her way through the order, and a few minutes later, the woman at the counter handed her a croissant-filled bag and two lattes.

As she stepped out the door and off the curb, Carson rounded the block. She slid back into the car and held out a latte for him.

He sipped it and sputtered. "I drive all night, and I can't even get a plain cup of coffee."

"I think you're the one who wants to fight." She handed him the croissant stuffed with ham and cheese. "Maybe this will help."

He ripped open the paper and took a bite. "It improves the situation."

She took a long sip of the sweet latte, and the hot, creamy drink blanketed her core. She didn't know what Carson's problem was.

She dug into the bag and took out another croissant. "And I'm hoping this will help as well."

He looked at her warily. What did he think she was going to do? Hand over a snake wrapped in bread?

"Come on," she persisted. "It's good."

He bit into the hazelnut croissant. "It's too sweet."

A car pulled out in front of them, and Carson took the parking spot.

"And I still need my coffee," he said as he got out of the car.

When he dumped his latte on the ground, Elise rolled her eyes like she was one of the preschoolers she'd just watched cross the street. What was it about Carson that made her feel like she was a kid again? Sometimes four and sometimes fourteen. He had an uncanny ability to bring out the worst in her.

She bit into her croissant and let herself relish the sweet hazelnut mixture with a hint of cinnamon and honey. She took another bite. Delicious. She should have told Carson to get her a couple more. She could eat these for lunch and dinner too.

Carson hopped back into the car, jammed his black coffee into the cup holder, and drove toward the stop sign. He didn't hesitate. Hard right.

"Where are you going?" she asked.

"The barista gave me directions."

"I'll bet she did," she smirked. "Probably straight to her front door."

Carson grinned at her, and she caught herself. She had to focus on the task at hand. Carson would be gone in a day, if not hours, in search of a new adventure.

The country roads wound them through another stretch of forest and farmland. At least in the sunlight she could appreciate the scenery. Fifteen minutes later, they were staring at a gray stone wall that rambled down the hill and receded into the trees.

"Apparently, the Chosen is big on barriers," Carson said as he parked the car and got out.

Elise brushed her hands on her jeans, and then joined Carson alongside the rough stone wall. "This wall has been here a long time."

She propped her foot up on a ledge and pulled herself up before she reached again. The top was at least six more feet above her head.

Carson tested a rock. "You want to scale it?"

"Maybe."

"It would be a cinch."

She stretched out her arm, clawing the cold stone until she grasped another hold and lifted her left foot. It would probably shock Carson, but she'd actually climbed once—a rocky cliff along the Blue Ridge Parkway.

She'd gone on a weeklong intensive seminar, studying the struggle of Appalachian women in North Carolina. They'd spent three days listening to lectures and then the professor had released them to the field. It was funny, really—a bunch of history students dangling over a forest of prickly-topped pines. The class had survived the ordeal, but when the professor gave them the option to climb again the next day or research in the local archives, they'd all opted for the library.

Fortunately, this wall was only about twelve feet high, compared to the fifty or sixty feet she'd climbed in North Carolina.

She pressed her palm against another stone. It didn't budge. "I think I can do this."

Carson's hand was on her calf. "I'll spot you."

For an instant, she could almost feel her mother's arms, propping her up to see something. She closed her eyes. It was a koala bear. At the National Zoo.

When she'd tried to climb the links on the cage, she had fallen back in frustration; but then her mother had picked her up and held her tight so they could look at the animal together. At one time, her mother had been strong—strong enough to care for her and lift her high.

She reached again like she was climbing the cage, even though this time she could do it on her own.

When her hand reached the top ledge, she stopped to listen. The group probably had a team of Dobermans guarding the wall.

When she didn't hear barking, she carefully peeked over the flat ridge and drank in the view. There were four buildings left at Marienthron, along with a pond and a small barn. Centered in the old convent was a Cistercian chapel with river stones flecked copper, gray, and muddy brown; the exposed brass bell in its tower was tarnished green. Across the gravel- and grass-covered expanse was a clunky stone dormitory, a library, and probably the kitchen.

For an instant, she forgot about the Chosen.

Katharina von Bora had lived in this convent. She'd strolled along the narrow pathways between the buildings and probably reveled in the surrounding grove of trees that now blazed autumn red and orange. Today, Elise and Carson were trying to get inside, but all Katharina had wanted to do was get out.

At one time, forty nuns had lived in this cloister along with the fifty farmhands, shepherds, woodcutters, carpenters, and reapers that helped them run the place. During the 1500s, it would have resembled a small city with a chapel, fountain, refectory, barns, flour mill, vineyard, and maybe even a brewery.

But no one moved inside the stone walls today.

She glanced down at Carson, and then back at the empty courtyard. What if the guy had deceived her yet again? He had pretended to be on her team, but he knew she was studying Katharina von Bora. Maybe this whole thing was yet another goose chase. The paper he had found in the attic. The long night in the car. She had been so ready to find out where the Chosen went that she hadn't stopped to wonder whether Carson was telling the truth.

Or maybe Carson had told the truth about the paper, but the Chosen had decided not to relocate here. Or maybe they had been here and gone years ago.

She stretched her legs and torso a couple inches higher to see if anything was lurking in the lofty trees beside the compound.

Then she heard voices.

She ducked, her heart pounding, as the voices drew nearer and then faded away. She waited a few seconds before peering back over the ledge. Two women, walking arm in arm, were making their way through the skeleton of a building, its roof and windows open to the sky. Elise released her grip on the top ledge and lowered herself slowly to the ground.

"What did you see?" Carson asked.

"Two women."

"Wearing habits?" he quipped.

She brushed dust off her jeans. "The abbey shut down in 1536."

"Tourists then."

She leaned back against the jagged rock. "I doubt it."

Here she was on the verge of entering the Chosen's hideaway, yet even if she and Carson were able to get inside, what was she supposed to do? Ask these people if they remembered her mother? Ask them what happened to make her commit suicide when she was only twenty years old?

The minister's words returned to her. *There is nothing here worth remembering.*

Too many years had gone by. They probably didn't even remember Catrina . . . or Rahab.

You would honor your mother by remembering her love and her life.

Out of respect for her father, maybe it was time to put an end to this search and send Carson on his way.

Yet if she really wanted to understand why women voluntarily gave up their freedoms, she would have to start with her mother. Did she join the Chosen willingly or was she coerced? What made her stay in the group? And how had she gotten the courage to break free?

She closed her eyes and she could see the baby in the crib. Cold. Scared. Alone.

What if someone else wanted out?

"Elise?"

She blinked. "What?"

"Are you sure you want to do this?"

The seconds passed as she wavered on her decision.

"Because if you do, we should go back to town and ask around."

She pointed to the car. "Let's go."

As soon as she took the first step, she knew: If she didn't get into the compound, she would regret it for the rest of her life.

Chapter 29

SARA PRESSED HER fingers against the window of Café Sperl and stared at the pastries. Her stomach rumbled again, and her shoulders and lower back ached. She'd had dinner last night, but there was no food at Marienthron this morning. Sol told her he wouldn't let her eat again until she confessed her sin.

Her fingers moved to her belly. How could she tell him she was pregnant? He wouldn't want another baby in the home. Not now. They were high maintenance . . . and expensive. At one time, they'd welcomed newborns into the family, but they no longer had enough food to feed the adults, much less growing children. If she told him they would be adding another member to the family, he would discipline her, even though it was his baby.

When she had started cramping and spotting last week, she had tried to tell herself it was just the hunger. But when she found a pregnancy test in the bathroom at the Berlin house, she took it, just in case.

Now she knew the truth. She was more than hungry.

She turned her eyes away from the glass and looked toward the park across the street. Several couples walked their dogs around the square, moms pushed babies in heavily blanketed strollers, and a group of children rode their bikes toward the sandy playground that was centered in the open space across from the café. Bundled in brown coats and colorful scarves, the kids climbed around bridges, soared on the swings, and plunged down the giant slide, seemingly oblivious to the cold.

One of the toddlers fell and her mother swooped in to comfort her and wipe the tears from her eyes.

Sometimes Sara wondered what it would be like to have a mother hug away her fears.

Phoebe was the reigning mother in their family, the queen, but her role was to strengthen their souls by warding off the attacks of Satan. She'd inflicted plenty of pain on Sara, but she'd never tried to take away her pain.

Sara reached for her stomach again. When this baby was born, she would hand it over to Phoebe to be instructed in the ways of God. If it was a boy, the baby would grow up to be one of God's elect. And if it was a girl, Sol would have her serve God in Grimma or Berlin.

Sara shuddered and prayed softly that it would be a boy.

Unto the pure all things are pure.

God had given her this baby, and she would take care of it. Maybe if she could prove to Sol that she could provide food for the family, he wouldn't send her to Berlin. She could stay in Grimma and help Phoebe with the children.

Her stomach rumbled again. She had to find food for herself . . . and her baby.

She peeked into the window again and saw the owner's daughter at the counter, her honey blonde hair pulled back in a knot. She was handing a bag of food to a young couple.

Sara took a deep breath, and the front door chimed as she pushed it open and trudged to the counter. Today, she would get a bag of croissants or bagels for her baby and the other brothers and sisters, and maybe even a couple of sandwiches or some meat and cheese. Today, Sol would see that she could contribute to the family in Grimma as much as the women in Berlin.

The woman smiled at her from behind the counter, and Sara dropped her long spiel in German and simply pleaded with her for some food, *gratis*. The woman nodded, and Sara could see the sympathy etched on her slender features. The woman didn't need to pity her. Even if she was hungry, she was filled with God's strength and love.

The woman reached for a white bag, and Sara's heart raced. She would only steal a few bites for the baby and then take the rest back home.

The woman slipped a croissant into the bag, and then smiled at Sara as she added two more. Sara could almost feel the warmth of the freshly baked bread on her tongue. The food would give her the energy she needed to finish her rounds today and stop the ache in her belly.

Sara reached out for the bag when a shout exploded from the back room. "*Nein!*"

The owner raced out to the counter and plucked the bag out of his daughter's hand. "Please," Sara begged as he whipped the bag over his head. She wouldn't give up now. The woman wanted to give her food, and she needed it.

"*Raus!*" the man yelled. One of the croissants flew out of the bag and slammed into the wall behind him before it hit the ground. She didn't care if it was dirty. She could still eat it.

She pointed at the croissant, but the man screamed again as he raced around the counter.

She pivoted toward the door and ran. Across the street. Around the playground. Through the trampled park. The food had been so close, the bag brushing her fingertips. And the man wouldn't even let her have a bite, not even of a croissant that had landed on the floor.

She collapsed on a bench and hid her head in her knees. All she had to do was get a little food, and she couldn't even do that. Pathetic! She'd never be a good mother or wife or even a child of God.

Someone sat down beside her, and she clutched her arms around her legs. If it was the owner of the café, he could pummel her all he wanted with his words or fists. She deserved it.

"Do you speak English?"

Sara glanced up and saw a girl a few years older than she was with pretty black hair and smooth ivory skin. Her clothes were casual and clean. If the girl were with her friends, she would probably be laughing at her from the coffee shop like all the other girls.

Sara ducked her head and cocooned it back in her legs.

"Are you hungry?" the girl asked.

Her body shuddered as she held back her tears. Of course, she was hungry. Starving! If not, she would never beg someone for food.

"My name is Elise," she continued, and Sara listened. "Let me get you something to eat."

Sara lifted her head and glanced back over her shoulder. It was okay to ask an unbeliever for food, but if Michael saw her fellowshipping with a local, he might report her to Sol, and Sol would never approve of her consorting with a worldly girl.

"The café has some great sandwiches." Elise scooted closer to her. "Ham or turkey. With cheese."

Sara focused on a man riding his bike through the park. "I don't have any money."

"I do," Elise said with a gentle smile. "And it's my treat."

If the woman had money, maybe she would be generous enough to buy several sandwiches. Then she could take the extra home to Sol.

Her stomach rumbled when she released the grip on her legs. Her poor baby was starving too. "Maybe just a sandwich."

"You'll change your mind when you taste their hazelnut croissants."

Sara looked back over her shoulder once more. No sign of Michael. Surely he wouldn't be mad when she told him that this girl was willing to donate food.

Chapter 30

THE DISHEVELED YOUNG girl devoured two sandwiches in less than five minutes and then reached for a hazelnut croissant. After the first sandwich, Elise had stopped asking if she wanted more to eat. She slid the entire tray under Sara's hands, and the girl had glanced up at her gratefully before she picked up more food.

Sara reminded her of the injured kitten in Berlin, with her bony cheeks and matted hair. She couldn't have been more than fifteen or sixteen, yet Elise had watched her march straight to the counter of the café like a soldier going into battle. No one should have to go hungry, especially someone who had the humility to ask for help. What kind of person berates a hungry girl who asks for a little food?

Elise had picked a small table outside for them to sit so Sara wouldn't have to face the café's owner again. Clouds had turned the sky gray, sucking away the warmth along with the sunshine. Elise stuck her hands into her lined pockets, and then pulled them out. She was bundled up like an Eskimo with a turtleneck, jacket, and scarf while Sara didn't even have a coat or a hat. And she wasn't complaining about the cold.

Sara didn't talk much as she ate yet she answered Elise's questions in perfect English, without even a hint of an accent. Elise didn't probe about her family or the fact that she was so proficient in English. Instead she stuck to the basics.

"Where do you go to school?" she asked as Sara bit into another croissant.

Sara lowered her voice. "I'm educated at home."

"That's nothing to be embarrassed about."

"It's a different education than what the world offers. Better." She swallowed the last bite in her hands and then bowed her head and muttered to herself. When she was done, she looked up and smiled. "Ezekiel 34:26—I'm praying that God will shower you with blessings."

A tingle rippled down Elise's back. Most people didn't quote the Old Testament in modern day conversation—unless they hadn't connected with the modern day.

Elise rubbed her fingers together. "You know your Bible."

"Thy word have I hid in mine heart, that I might not sin against thee."

Elise leaned back. Could she have stumbled on a member of the Chosen? She glanced around the park for Carson's burgundy fleece and saw him talking to a young couple. He might be able to get some information from them, but if Sara was part of the Chosen, she'd found an escort to the compound's front door.

"How long have you been studying the Bible?" she asked casually.

Sara looked over her shoulder like someone might be watching her. "My entire life."

"Then perhaps you could help me understand something."

When the girl's eyes lit up, Elise wondered if anyone had ever honored her by asking her opinion. "Certainly."

"If Jesus came to set people free, why do so many people who say they follow Christ seem to be afraid?"

Sara fidgeted with the croissant in her hands. "What do you mean?"

"I've heard the verse that we should give all our worries and cares to God because he cares for us, yet so many Christians don't trust him to provide."

"Most Christians are serving themselves instead of the one true God."

"Which God is that?" she asked.

"The God of . . ." Sara paused and set down the croissant. "I need to go home."

Elise reached for her arm, and the girl recoiled. This wasn't like rescuing the cat. She couldn't pick up the girl and take her someplace safe and warm. But she also wasn't going to lose her yet.

"Let me get you some coffee before you go."

"But I—"

"And another croissant."

"Could I have tea instead?" Sara tried to smile again. "And a couple more croissants?"

"Sure." She stood up warily, praying that the girl wouldn't run. Hopefully, the promise of more food would keep her in her seat.

She opened the door, reveling in the warmth of the bakery. She ordered two herbal teas and two croissants. When she turned around with her order, she smacked into Carson, and the hot liquid splattered onto the front of her jacket and flung across his fleece.

He shook off his sleeve. "So our next stop is a Laundromat?"

"I'm sorry," she said as she scooted past him. "I've got to get back to the table."

"You can't rescue everyone, Elise."

For an instant she felt protective of the girl. "Her name is Sara."

"And she knows about the Chosen?"

She stepped away from him. "I'm guessing that she's in the Chosen."

"You're guessing?"

"If I ask her directly, I'm afraid she'll take off."

"Be careful, Elise."

She grimaced. "Now you sound like my dad."

"Just don't do anything crazy."

She shook her head as she stepped toward the door. Neither Carson nor anyone else was going to stop her from trying to get inside Marienthron.

She balanced the cups and bag of croissants with one hand as she tried to open the door. Carson's arm reached around her and opened it for her.

"Thanks," she muttered as she stepped into the chilly air. Sara hadn't moved from her seat.

Elise set one of the teas in front of her. "I'm intrigued by your faith."

Sara took a long sip. "God's way is narrow . . . and difficult."

"I've been searching for truth my entire life."

"The fear of the LORD is the beginning of wisdom," Sara quoted.

"It doesn't matter what I do," Elise confided, "or how hard I try. I can't seem to find the way to him."

Sara set down the tea and leaned forward. "I can help you."

She willed her voice to be calm, inquisitive. She couldn't blow this chance. "You can?"

"But you have to make sacrifices to serve God."

Elise hesitated. She couldn't sound too anxious to delve into this new world. "I'm willing to make sacrifices."

"When you give your life to God, you can no longer be part of the world."

"I gave up caring about this world a long time ago."

"Then maybe you are ready." Sara smiled. "Would you like to meet again tomorrow?"

Elise glanced back at the coffee shop and saw Carson watching her from the window. "I can't come tomorrow."

Sara's smile dropped from her face. "Why not?"

"I'm traveling to Wittenberg tonight."

Sara stared at the bag of croissants for a moment as she seemed to consider her next move. Then she lifted her head and smiled. "Come with me first."

Elise followed Sara away from the food and the table and the security of Carson's friendship. Before they stepped off the curb, Sara turned, snatched the bag of croissants, and tucked them under her arm.

Elise glanced back and flashed Carson a quick thumbs-up. She was in, but Carson didn't look happy about it. Well, this was what she was here to do, and she wasn't going to blow it. Maybe it was time for him to go to Switzerland.

Sara reached for her hand and squeezed it.

For an instant, she felt guilty about her deception. She hadn't actually lied. She didn't always know if she was on the right path to serving

God, but right now he seemed to be tugging at her heart to follow Sara home.

They stepped off the main street of the tourist district and tromped through an alleyway of tin garbage cans and coal-splattered walls before emerging in a brick-paved square.

The courtyard was quiet. No one was around except a man with a leather jacket and blond ponytail. One of the man's legs was balanced against the bumper of a beat-up Volvo, and he stared at her as Sara handed him the bag of croissants.

"This is Elise." Her voice sounded strained. "She wants to know more about God's plan for her life."

The guy with the ponytail popped open the trunk and put the food inside. "We can't take her home."

"But Michael," Sara pleaded. "She's searching for truth."

He hesitated as he turned toward her. "Are you?"

Elise took a deep breath. She needed courage right now. The courage of her mother in her stronger days. The endurance of her father.

"Yes."

He stuffed his hands into his pocket and closed his eyes, his lips muttering a silent prayer. She'd been so convinced that Sara would lead her to the answers she needed that she hadn't stopped to think that someone else might try to stop her.

When he opened his eyes, he looked at Sara. "We can't support a new member."

Elise cleared her throat. No matter how difficult, this was the next leg of this journey. "I can pay my own way."

Michael turned back toward her before he slid into the car. "What do you mean?"

"My family has money." She managed a laugh that sounded crass, cold. "A lot of it."

When he didn't reply, she scuffed her foot. "I've never cared about money."

"There is so much more to life than what the world offers," Sara said softly.

"I want to serve God," she insisted.

"It's not an easy road," Michael said.

She took a deep breath. "I'm not looking for easy."

Chapter 31

CARSON STOMPED ON the curb, ignoring the pain that shot up his shin. What was Elise thinking? All of the sudden she was some kind of maverick, taking on an entire cult by herself. He didn't care if her escorts were members of the Chosen. She was supposed to stick with him, not go driving off with two people she didn't know.

When the Volvo swerved to the right, he turned and raced back toward the café. He fumbled for the keys in his pocket, and when he reached the rental car, he tugged open the driver's door and slid inside.

As he started the car, he swore at the person who had parked inches from his bumper. He angled up and back four times before he was able to get out of the parking space and speed back toward the main road. At least he knew where they were going.

He whizzed around bicyclists and pedestrians as he sped south on Schulstrasse. Maybe if he got to Marienthron as they arrived, he could confront her at the gate. He didn't care if he exposed her cover. He wasn't going to let her go into that compound by herself. He had no idea what they were capable of, but the Chosen scared his mom—and nobody scared Addison Wade.

How did Elise think she was going to get out of the compound? Or had she even bothered to think? She didn't even have a cell phone with her, and it wasn't like the leaders would let her make a personal call. It was a cult! Contact would be severed the instant those gates closed.

Elise might not care what happened to her, but he wasn't going to let her sacrifice herself for some information.

He pushed down the pedal until he saw the rusty rear bumper of the Volvo up ahead. He punched the accelerator. If the police stopped him now, he'd come clean about the group. Maybe they could escort him to the old abbey.

The Volvo turned right onto Colditzer Strasse. Carson tapped the brakes behind them for a quick stop, but when he lifted his foot to hit the accelerator, he glanced left. A tractor crept away from the stop sign, and Carson stomped his brakes and waited as the vehicle crawled past him at an incredibly slow pace.

He pounded his fist on the steering wheel. Elise thought she was strong, unwavering, but the guilt from her mother's death permeated her decisions. Even at her strongest, she was vulnerable to a power play.

What would happen if he couldn't stop her from going inside?

He turned the corner, and his bumper hovered right below the bright orange triangle on the back of the tractor. Wasn't there some sort of law about driving under 15 kilometers an hour?

He swerved left to pass and then jerked the car back. A line of traffic was spaced out on the other side like an ant parade.

His chest tightened. He had to get to Marienthron before the Volvo and its passengers were locked inside.

He probably should turn around, call Elise's dad in Virginia, and let him drag his daughter away from the commune. But he'd gotten strung into the web, and he was sticking. He didn't care what his mother or anyone else said. He wouldn't let anything happen to Elise.

He opened his window and strained his neck to see around the tractor, but he didn't see a break in the traffic. By the time he got by and made it to Marienthron, Elise would have eaten dinner and gone to bed.

He cringed as he laid on the horn. It was rude. Insolent. But this was an emergency.

The driver pulled to the side, and Carson waved as he passed. Then he shifted up to third and fourth gear as he pushed the accelerator to the floor. Maybe it wasn't too late.

He sped past miles of farmland, and when he came to the forest, he turned onto the wooded lane, gravel and dust spewing up behind him. There was no sign of the rusted bumper ahead.

He dove into each curve like he was competing in the Daytona 500, but no matter how fast he drove, he still didn't see the Volvo.

The edge of the stone wall emerged in front of him, and his car swerved as he sped through the last curve. He wrapped his fists around the wheel to steady the tires.

The gate was in front of him, but no Volvo. He drove past the entrance, parked on the far side, and ran back toward the gate.

The Volvo was parked about fifty yards inside the compound. Empty. Beyond the car was a chapel, and Carson smacked his hand on the cast-iron slats as the doors to the chapel slammed shut.

For an instant, he thought about screaming for help. Causing a scene. Surely, someone would come running out to him. But no matter how hard he yelled, they probably wouldn't open the door. And they certainly wouldn't give him access to Elise.

He retreated back toward the wall. It wouldn't help to alert them to his presence. When he went in for Elise, he needed the least amount of resistance possible.

He hopped in the car and sped back toward Grimma. If he couldn't get to her now, he would arm himself with information until he had something to take to the police station.

Beside the river, he found an eclectic Internet café filled with rusted license plates and faded pictures of Neuschwanstein and Hohenschwangau. The man at the counter offered him a cup of coffee, but he turned it down and bought a half hour of online access instead. Then he sat down at the computer and began to dig through lists of information about cults until he found a profile on the Chosen.

The group had been founded by a man named Paul Huntington. A preacher's kid, Paul had grown up admiring his father's power over the congregation . . . and over the women who frequented their home.

After his father died, Paul had moved from his home in Buffalo, New York, to Seattle, where he worked as a successful car salesman and volunteered as a youth pastor at a local church. He didn't last long at the church—a few months after joining, he splintered his relationship with the church leadership to start a new community, and he took a hundred of the church's younger members with him. Paul preached a message about the freedom and love and community found only in God. Teenagers flocked to his house and they brought their friends.

Using contributions from his new recruits, Paul quit his job and bought a farm near Redmond, Washington, to house a few select followers. Every member received a new biblical name that symbolized the death of their old life before they were anointed into the new fellowship. Only those who committed to leave behind their preconceived notions about Christianity were allowed at the farm. Those who devoted their time and energy and resources to the growth of the group came to be known as the Chosen.

In spite of the public outcry from parents who'd lost their kids, the number of new members surged in the 1970s. Paul appointed an elect leadership and moved his base of operations overseas to a home in Amsterdam. Hundreds of his followers founded communes across the U.S. and Europe.

Paul guided the group around the world through weekly letters filled with wisdom he claimed to receive directly from God. New members of the Chosen were promised a utopian community where they could share God's love and live in humbleness and fellowship. Their mission was to reach out to the poor and the lost—especially to young people in need of a home.

Members of the fellowship had to give up everything to join the Chosen. They were cut off from all communication with the outside world until they were trusted to recruit new members or solicit donations. Followers were taught that all love was pure love in God's eyes—sexual contact being the holiest way to express love for their Father. The leaders began sending "missionaries" into the major European cities, hookers who were supposed to demonstrate God's love with their bodies. The missionaries were called Chosen Girls.

The words on the screen blurred for a moment, and then Carson clicked on the artwork of one of Paul's many letters.

It took only a glance at one of the pictures to tell him that the content was obscene. A girl with a long dress was being beckoned through a tall gate and into the arms of an angel. And then the creature hurt the very girl he'd been designed to guard. In the loving name of God.

He cringed as he closed the page.

Who would publish literature about angels raping a child? And how had the Chosen gotten away with this for so many years?

Carson tried to purge from his mind the images on the letters as he opened another news article about the group.

Paul Huntington had died in 1999, and his oldest son, Titus, had taken the reins of what the writer called a "sex cult." The group still existed in small, secretive clusters around the world. They hadn't changed their philosophy, but they no longer recruited new members like they had in the 1970s and early '80s. Most of their new members were born into the group.

The computer blinked at the end of the half hour, and he pulled his phone from his pocket and called home.

"She found them," he told his mom.

Addison uttered a word he'd never heard burn through her lips.

Chapter 32

ADDISON BATTED THE telephone cord away from her chest. In spite of all she'd done to protect Elise, the girl had jumped into the lion's den. Sol would take one look at her and . . . Addison shook her head to expunge the thought.

She lugged her suitcase out of the back of the closet and threw it on the bed. In seconds, she tossed a couple sweaters into it along with a skirt and some khaki pants.

If only she could ignore this situation. Make it go away. She'd left the Chosen twenty-five years ago, and now Elise insisted on rooting around in the past and digging it back up.

She threw a pair of walking shoes in the suitcase and a bag of toiletries. It was too late to turn back this time. She'd helped rescue Elise before and she'd get her out again. And maybe, just maybe . . .

With a quick push, she slammed shut her suitcase, trying to extinguish even a spark of hope. Sol had promised a long time ago that he would kill Sara, and he wouldn't have reneged on his word.

She rubbed her temples. She had to stop thinking about Catrina's baby and focus on the child who was still alive. The one that had ignored both her and Steve and had run straight into the clutches of the Devil himself.

Steve would be livid when he found out what happened to his daughter. And he would be mad at Addison, even though Elise was the one who had gone searching. Elise was the one who'd decided to hunt down the cult, even though everyone had warned her to stop. Elise was the one who'd pursued the Chosen all the way to Grimma.

If there was anyone to blame for this mess, Steve could blame himself. If he'd just told his daughter the truth, she never would have come scouring for information on her own. A little honesty on his part could have prevented this entire fiasco.

She locked the clasps on the case. A little honesty on her part might have kept both Elise and Carson away from the Grimma compound as well.

She'd skipped her early morning kickboxing class and tried to sleep a few hours after Richard left for London. She hadn't been successful. In a couple of hours, she was supposed to don a black dress and heels and greet the Italian prime minister at a state dinner.

She reached for the telephone again and left a message on her assistant's cell. Jack would have to cancel for her.

She looked up at the antique clock on the wall. Three-thirty.

She rushed to the garage, threw her suitcase into the trunk of her car, and sped south toward the autobahn. Rain splattered across her windshield, and she turned on the wipers.

The sun set rapidly, but she didn't even realize the darkness was approaching. All she could think about was Elise's first night with the Chosen.

If Sol's tactics were still the same, one of the members would become her new best friend, depriving her of food and sleep until her mind began to fry from exhaustion. They would twist the meaning of Bible verses and force them into her mind along with steady doses of guilt and shame and fear.

She shuddered.

She clearly remembered the day Paul had taken her into the compound near Frankfurt. When they'd walked through the gate and into the front door, people had greeted her from their perches on steps, boxes, and the edge of the dining room table. It had been a lonely two months, backpacking through Europe by herself. She suddenly felt welcome. At home.

Paul had taken her hand and introduced her to his brothers and sisters. Family. She'd never had brothers or sisters, or even parents. Her grandparents had raised her after her parents were killed in a car accident the year after she was born. Her grandparents had loved her, but she had always felt like a burden, a kink in their orderly life.

The Chosen gave her something she had always craved—a family who loved each other. It didn't matter that they weren't related by blood. They connected at a much deeper level and were bound together by a common goal as they reached out with God's love.

At the time, she was honored to be part of Paul's group. Enthralled. Paul had selected a biblical name for her. Tirzah. The pleasant one.

She'd called her grandparents back in Virginia and told them that she wasn't coming home. So many people talked about being a Christian, but she'd never understood why someone would give up everything to follow Christ until she met this dynamic man who was actually doing something about his faith. He didn't care what anyone else said about his lack of education or his intense style. Not many people understood Christ or his disciples either.

Paul was different from others in the world. He was truly chosen.

When she joined the group, there were already eleven homes around the world, and Paul was expanding quickly and quietly to reach even more people. He presented God in a way she'd never heard before. Their heavenly Father wasn't about the rules and regulations and confinements that church leaders often tried to impose on their congregations. He was about freedom and love and peace. And as God's messenger to their generation, Paul offered this freedom to the masses. She was ready to help him take this ministry worldwide.

She still remembered the morning Paul had placed his hand on her back and pointed her toward another man, the lieutenant of the Frankfurt house, named Brother Sol. At least, he was "Brother Sol" until Paul left the house—then he wanted to be called "King Solomon" after the wise and wealthy ruler in the Bible. The king who had many wives.

When Sol saw her, he smiled, and as she shook Sol's hand, she remembered very clearly the urge to run away. She didn't move, but she should have run. All the way back to Virginia.

Sol hugged her, welcoming her into their home like the others, and she relaxed her fears. He told her that they would assign someone to help her through the transition of leaving the world. Someone who would help purify her soul. With Paul's assurance that Sol would take care of her, she threw herself into the fire.

Addison steered the car onto the autobahn and floored it to 120 kilometers per hour.

While Paul was a leader and a self-appointed prophet, Sol had been gifted with supernatural insight. It was almost as if he could read people's hearts and souls, and he knew the instant Addison started to have doubts about joining his home.

As the months passed, she beat back the questions in her mind by repeating the Scriptures that the family quoted day and night. She truly thought she had been called out for a higher purpose, that the members of the Chosen were the only ones who communed with the true God.

Every day, they wandered the streets of Frankfurt and told people about the new revolution of love. They sang songs and talked to tourists and brought new converts back to the house in droves. After they were purified, Sol sent most of the converts out as missionaries to new homes around the world, several of them to be one of Paul's new wives.

Addison hadn't asked questions about the many wives. Or the fact that Paul was rarely at the Frankfurt home. Or even about the guns that Sol stockpiled in their barn in preparation for Armageddon.

But her doubts had intensified when Paul sent out a special letter to all his followers and deemed it to be a message from God. One of their missionaries, Bethesda, had been evangelizing in Frankfurt and Berlin for six years and had brought Sol and other leaders into the family.

Paul had christened Bethesda a Chosen Girl and encouraged her freedom in Christ, freedom to express God's love. Using her God-given gift of seduction, Sol encouraged Bethesda to accept donations from the men she slept with, because, in his words, "even a missionary was worthy of her hire."

Bethesda's business in Berlin flourished, as did the money that Bethesda and several other women received for prostituting in God's name. Addison remembered the day that Sol had handed her Paul's letter about being a Chosen Girl and explained that Bethesda needed more women to evangelize in Berlin.

Her rebellion had flared. She'd joined the Chosen to share God's love and serve the needy with Paul. She'd loved Paul and sacrificed her dreams to advance his mission, but she'd seen him only twice since he'd left her in Sol's care. And no matter what he or Sol said, she refused to use her body to lure men to Christ.

Instead of forcing her into prostitution, Sol assigned her to care for the women who returned from West Berlin for days—and sometimes weeks—of R & R. She'd tried to reach out to three of these women and tell them that God would never require that they sell their bodies to tell men about him. But in spite of their brokenness, all three women told Sol about their talks with Addison. He had punished her, and she had shut up.

Until she met Rahab, Bethesda's only daughter.

The cell phone rang, and Addison jumped. She glanced at the ID in the darkness and saw Richard's number.

She squeezed the leather on the wheel as the phone rang three more times and went to voice mail.

The last thing she wanted to do right now was talk to her husband. He would probably tell her to pray, but it would be much better for all of them if she abstained from prayer, because God never listened to her. Richard and Carson could do the praying, and she hoped it would work, because they would need a miracle to get Elise out of the compound.

She turned onto A14 to drive around Leipzig. If God really cared, he would show mercy to those people who truly loved him. He would shower compassion over the children who grew up abused by people who claimed to be hurting them in the name of God.

For I knew that thou art a gracious God, and merciful, slow to anger, and of great kindness.

If God were really great and merciful and kind, he would have saved Sara.

Chapter 33

SOL BALLED UP THE electric bill and threw it toward the fire. They could survive without utilities for a few weeks, but not without a place to live. Marienthron was the perfect kingdom for his family, quiet and secluded. Not even Paul had lived in a place as big as this.

The best way to stay under the radar of the local authorities was to pay their bills on time—paying the rent in Grimma and Berlin topped the list. Until this month, they'd never been late on a single payment.

But tomorrow was their deadline, and without a payment, they'd risk eviction, and an inquisition from the local government.

He picked up his cell phone and stared at the numbers. The last resort was to appeal to Paul's oldest son, Titus, for assistance, and he dreaded making that call.

He'd cut off the umbilical cord to Amsterdam when he found the convent available to rent in Grimma. Paul kept asking for a bigger cut of their funds, and he also demanded that Sol call him "Lord." Sol refused and threatened to send a couple of Paul's letters to the authorities in both the Netherlands and on the other side of the pond. Paul had relented, but he'd excommunicated Sol along with his entire home. Paul's kingdom was still scattered around the world, but Titus didn't have his fingers in Sol's world anymore.

Titus wouldn't dole out money as quickly to their home as Paul had. He was even more tightfisted than his father and stingy with the ministry's funds, even though he was living in an oceanside mansion someplace in South Africa. Most of the remaining members of the Chosen hovered below the poverty line.

Sol clenched the phone as he peeled back the olive-colored curtains and looked down at the courtyard and front gate.

He harbored too many of the group's secrets, and Titus knew it. Neither of them would let the Grimma family go bust.

All Titus had to do was send a little cash this month and a couple of women to work the streets in Berlin.

The phone rang in his hand, and he glanced down at the caller ID. It was Walter, the owner of the dump in Heidelberg.

Walter had let the family live in the place rent-free for seven years, vowing his dedication to the Chosen. While they were in Heidelberg, Sol had even let Walter experience some of the freedom within their family. It had made him an ardent supporter.

"What is it?" he snapped into the receiver.

"There were two people at the house last night," Walter said. "A man and woman."

He curled his fingers around the hem of the drape. "And you waited until now to call me?"

"I didn't want to bother you."

"Where did they go?"

Walter hesitated.

"Where did they go, Walter?" he demanded.

"I don't know."

Sol backed away from the window. He'd tried to erase the trail when they escaped from Heidelberg, but he didn't have time to destroy everything. It would be disastrous if the authorities found out where they went. Or if Walter found the rest of Paul's letters.

He fought for control of his voice. "Tell me what happened."

"I figured they were trekkers, so I followed them into Heidelberg, but then they rented a car and drove out of town."

"To where?"

"I searched for them all morning."

"Where did you lose them?"

"In Gera."

An hour away from Grimma.

Sol hung up the phone and sank into his leather chair. Who would be looking for them? He'd worked hard to establish a tight-knit community in Grimma. He wasn't going to let a couple of nosy tourists stir up the waters . . . or someone returning from the past.

Michael knocked on the door, and when he opened it, Sol motioned for him to sit down. "Did you get food?"

Michael bumped his elbow on the chair when he sat down. "Four bags."

"And Sara?"

"A little food and—"

"And what?" Sol interrupted.

"She was witnessing."

Sol didn't have time to deal with this right now. He needed to call Titus and convince him to wire some money. "We can't afford to take on a new convert."

Michael unzipped his jacket. "I told her that."

Sol picked up the onyx paperweight on his desk and rubbed it in his hands. "Is it a man?"

"A woman."

He leaned forward. "How old is she?"

"Early twenties. An American."

Perhaps the woman snooping through the house in Heidelberg? It didn't matter why she was here. Phoebe could purify her in a matter of days, and he would take her to Berlin. If she was an attractive American, their clientele would pay top dollar.

"Was anyone with her?" he asked.

Michael shook his head. "I wouldn't have brought her home, except she said her family had money."

He set the paperweight down. "Money?"

"She told Sara she was ready to forsake her family if she could find her peace with God."

He licked his front teeth. "Does she have access to this money?"

"Apparently."

It didn't matter if she had been with a husband or boyfriend in Heidelberg. Now she was his. "Bring her in."

When Michael walked back out the door, Sol shoved the papers to the side of his desk. He'd test her dedication as they tested her bank account.

The door opened, and Sol blinked as he watched the woman walk toward him. Her black hair was pulled back in a ponytail, and she wore a denim jacket over her black turtleneck and jeans.

When he met her eye, her gaze didn't waver. Instead, her green eyes sent a jolt through him. They were tinted with yellow, like Bethesda's.

Stunned, he searched for his voice, his air of command. Had Rahab finally come home?

No, that wasn't right. Rahab would be almost thirty-five by now, and she didn't have the yellow flecks like Bethesda. Could it be that Johanna had returned to him? All grown up.

Maybe after all these years, the guilt had worn Rahab down, and she was offering her daughter back to him as the sacrificial lamb.

Yet there was no hint of lamb in this woman's eyes.

"What's your name?" he barked.

She didn't hesitate. "Elise."

He crunched his fingers together. "How did you find us, Elise?"

"I've been searching for a while . . . for answers," she explained. "Sara said that her family might be able to lead me to the truth."

Sol stepped around the desk. Her skin matched Rahab's soft ivory tone, but her posture held Bethesda's strength. A strength that Rahab had never had. "We all have to make sacrifices to be a member of this group."

She nodded. "I'm here to serve."

He took a long breath. "Where are your parents?"

Elise lowered her eyes. "They're dead."

He steadied his emotions as his mind processed her words. She wasn't telling the truth—at least the entire truth. Rahab couldn't be dead. He'd fantasized for years about her return as a broken and repentant woman, grateful for all he had done.

He stared at the lush color in the girl's hair. If Rahab couldn't come, Johanna might do instead.

"What was your mother's name?"

Her eyes shifted, but anything less than the truth was unacceptable. "Catrina."

"How long ago did she die?"

"Thirteen years." Her eyes lowered. "From a stroke."

Rahab deserved a more dramatic exit from this life. "But surely you have other relatives."

"No one that I'm close to." She paused. "When my father died, he left me his estate."

She looked up at him again, and he stared into her face. She was lying, but if she had money, it really didn't matter. After he drained her finances, he'd send her to Berlin.

"Everyone starts their journey with us by giving up their personal possessions."

"I'm ready."

He pointed at her jacket and scarf. "Starting with those."

She slowly unwound her scarf and handed it over with her coat.

Then he pointed at the purse clutched at her side. "And that."

When she hesitated, he knew she wasn't ready to devote herself. Yet. By the end of the week, she'd be ready to do anything for him and their family.

His hand stretched toward her arm. "It's the first step, Elise."

She handed the small satchel to him, and he pried it out of her grip.

"Good girl." He unzipped it and rummaged through her things until he found her passport. With his eyes on her face, he walked over to the fire and tossed it into the blaze.

This girl liked to think she was strong, but she gasped as the flames devoured her identity with the world. It was the first step toward purification.

He took the bank card out of her wallet and held it up. "And now I'll need the PIN."

Her eyes were focused on the fire, watching her passport burn. He wouldn't tell her yet, but they'd get her a new passport. With a new name.

Sol leaned toward her and stroked his thumb down her cheek, stopping at her collar. She shivered.

If he wanted, he could make her beg him for mercy, like the thief on the cross. She needed to experience the pain that he'd lived with for almost twenty years. The anger. The deceit. And she needed to pay . . . pay for her mother's sin.

Chapter 34

ELISE SHOOK HER ARM, but Michael wouldn't let go. He pushed her down a narrow corridor, away from her jacket and purse and burning passport. Did they really think she would give them her PIN?

"I need my medicine." She sneezed as she tried to rub away the emerging headache with her left hand. "It's in my purse."

Michael didn't respond. Instead, he opened a door to his left, shoved her into a small room, and slammed the door. She raced for the knob and twisted it, but it was too late. He'd already locked her in.

She pounded on the wood. "I need my purse!"

When no one answered, she turned around. The gray walls in the room were bare, and a single bulb lit the room from overhead. A lumpy looking bed was pushed against the corner, and a plain oak dresser stood under a small window barred with iron. Daylight was fading, and the night air stole through a crack in the window.

Two battered folding chairs were set up beside the dresser, but she didn't sit down. Sitting would feel like resignation, and she needed to maintain her resolve.

Her head was pounding, but she could battle the pain until someone came to feed her. Then she would ask for ibuprofen and cold medicine. Even if it wasn't as potent as the stuff the pharmacist had given her, she'd stay strong until she met up with Carson on the other side of the wall.

She shivered as she walked toward a second door, this one at the side of the room. She jostled the knob, but it wouldn't budge either.

She backed away and leaned against the cold stone wall.

Even though she had made it into the compound, she wouldn't get answers being locked in a room. Outside the door there must be someone who would remember Catrina as a child.

A key scraped against the lock on the hallway door, and Elise balled up her fists. She might be trapped like an animal in a cage, but she could still fight.

The door to the room opened, and in marched a woman in a black dress with short sleeves that clung to her mottled arms. A red age spot marked her right cheek, and her small mouth was set in a harsh line.

On her head was a gray bucket hat.

Elise closed her eyes and suddenly she was four again. Alone and scared. And she remembered the woman.

All she had wanted was a drink of water. She was so thirsty. She and Leah had crept toward the bathroom, and the woman had captured her before she made it to the door.

Her skin prickled with fear.

Yea, though I walk through the valley of the shadow of death, I will fear no evil: for thou art with me.

She could almost hear her mother's soft voice repeating the familiar verse. Strength rose in her chest, and she opened her eyes and stared into the woman's eyes. She wasn't four anymore. She was twenty-one and able to defend herself against a woman who had to be at least sixty.

"Welcome to our family, Elise," the woman said, like she was delivering a verdict. "I'm Phoebe."

A cough ripped through Elise's lungs and a stitch of pain pierced her side, just below her ribs.

"The first night is the hardest, but it is critical to prepare you for the kingdom."

Phoebe reached behind the door and grabbed a pitcher, drops of water beading on the sides. "Are you thirsty?"

Elise's hands felt clammy, her tongue hot. "Very much."

Phoebe motioned to one of the folding chairs, and Elise dropped down onto the metal seat. Phoebe crossed the room and took a shot glass out of the top dresser drawer and filled it. "This is water for your body, but what we are offering you is living water for your soul."

Elise reached out, and when Phoebe handed her the miniature glass, she guzzled it, pretending it was eight ounces instead of one. If they left her alone, she'd drink the entire pitcher.

Phoebe reached for her hand and she shrank back, but the woman latched onto her fingers like she was bait. "Have you invited Christ into your life?"

She didn't want to divulge anything personal to this woman yet she wasn't ashamed. "When I was six."

Phoebe shifted her chin to look in her eyes. "Are you ready to follow him with your whole heart?"

"I am."

Phoebe pointed to her wrist. "I need that."

She touched the plastic strap. "My watch?"

"*And the multitude of them that believed were of one heart and of one soul: neither said any of them that ought of the things which he possessed was his own; but they had all things common,*" Phoebe said.

Elise slipped off the navy band, and handed it reluctantly to Phoebe, who put it into her pocket. Then she handed Elise a worn, black Bible tagged with thirty or so yellow sticky notes. "Tonight you'll learn all the verses I've marked."

Elise stared down at the collection of tags. "I can't memorize all of these."

Phoebe ignored her protest. "Starting in Matthew."

When Elise continued to stare at the closed Bible in her hands, Phoebe snatched the pitcher from the top of the dresser and stomped toward the second door. She fumbled momentarily for a key, then unlocked the door and stepped inside. Elise heard the sound of water being dumped into a sink, and she groaned as it drained away. All she wanted was one more sip.

She sneezed and a shiver rattled up her spine.

"Are you sick?" Phoebe asked as she set the empty pitcher back on the dresser.

"My head is killing me."

Elise swung her shoulders away when Phoebe reached for her hand again. She didn't want the woman touching her.

"Jesus can heal you, Elise."

"I have no doubt that he could." She sneezed again. "But he might recommend taking medicine instead."

"Medicine won't demonstrate the power of God."

Elise glanced toward the open door on the other side of the room. Inside, she could see the claw foot of a bathtub. Maybe there was also a medicine cabinet in there.

She nodded toward the doorway. "Do you have any ibuprofen?"

"The Devil is attacking you," Phoebe whispered, as if the walls were listening. "Only those who are strong can follow our Lord."

Elise pressed her fingers against her temples. "I thought it was the weak who Christ made strong."

"Memorize the verses, Elise."

Chapter 35

SARA RUBBED HER hand over Michael's arm. He moaned in his sleep but didn't open his eyes. Moonlight flooded the room, washing over his blond hair and the sinew in his neck and arms.

Sometimes she missed the softness in his boyhood cheeks and the spark of mischief in his eyes. He'd grown into a strong, intense man, but as he slept tonight, he looked like the boy she'd danced with as a child. She could never tell him, but she still loved him—at least she loved the memory of him. She could sit here and watch him all night, remembering the times when he'd loved her too.

Rezon purred quietly in her left arm, and peace settled around her like the moonlight. She was with Michael. And her kitten. If she had the choice, she'd never leave this room.

A cramp ripped through her stomach, and she shook Michael harder this time. He rolled over, and she glanced back at the closed door behind her.

If Sol caught her in here, he'd punish them both. And if he suspected that she'd come to do more than just talk, the wounds would be deep. Trying to avoid Sol was like trying to avoid temptation itself; it seemed like he was everywhere, at all hours of the day and night. The man was probably awake in his office right now or roaming the halls. If he opened her door tonight, he would find her gone.

She had debated for hours whether she should step out of her room. Finally, she had decided she had to risk it tonight. If anyone in the family would help her, it would be Michael.

She leaned toward the bed again and whispered. "Wake up."

His eyes flickered open, and longing filled his gaze as he gently pulled her down to him. Her face was almost touching his and for an instant she thought he might kiss her. Instead he bolted up and flung her away like she'd stung him.

"What are you doing?" he growled as he rammed his back against the bed frame.

"I need to talk to you."

He plowed his fingers through his blond hair. "Talk to me in the morning."

"It's urgent."

He looked at the door and back at her, and she realized that he was still as afraid of Sol as she was. "Not in here, Sara."

She stood up and stepped back toward the door. "Ten minutes?"

He sighed. "Okay."

She tightened her robe around her body as she stepped out into the hallway. Phoebe's light was on under her door, but everything else was dark. She tiptoed by Phoebe's room and heard Elise reading a verse from Matthew. At one time, their family had been swelling with new converts, but nowadays the only place where Sol welcomed new converts was in Berlin. She was grateful that Sol had taken in Elise; she could see the questions in the woman's eyes, the longing to know God.

Tonight, the heavens would be celebrating as another soul was captured for the kingdom. If she did nothing else with her life, maybe God would reward her for rescuing Elise from hell's fire.

She rubbed her hand over Rezon's head and smiled. She may not have gotten much food today, but God had used her to evangelize without going to Berlin. Surely Sol would be pleased about that.

With the kitten tucked in her arms, she edged down the stairs at the end of the hallway, avoiding the noisy steps, and crept through the kitchen. She stopped and listened for footsteps, but the room was quiet. If Sol did find her, she would tell him she needed some food.

The door to the pantry creaked as she pushed it open. She slid through the crack, and then eased it closed. Another cramp tore through her, and she fell back against the shelf and waited until it was gone. They were getting stronger by the hour, and her shoulder felt like it was about to explode.

She found the flashlight on the wall, flicked it on, and crept back toward the small door at the end of the shelves.

When Michael was ten, he'd stolen two keys from Sol's office and had given one to her. Sol didn't know, but the cellar had once been her and Michael's secret place to escape. Neither of them had used the keys in a long time, but she had always kept hers secure in her front pocket.

She clutched the key in her hand and slowly turned it in the lock until the door opened. She stepped inside, walked down the rickety flight of stairs, and unlocked the iron gate at the bottom. The hinges groaned when she swung it open, but the noise didn't matter down here. She could scream if she wanted and Sol would never hear her.

Water dripped off the ceiling of the tunnel, and she skirted around a puddle and sat down on one of the benches. She leaned into Rezon's fur, and the kitten purred softly as she slid her fingers across his tiny body. She checked the splint on his leg. It was still intact.

She flicked off her light. "Now we wait."

Sol used the crypt for storage and to practice his many drills. If she could, she would stay here all night, secure in the dark walls.

Some day, when it was time to meet Jesus, her family would meet down here for the ascension into the next kingdom—a glorious transformation filled with light, joy, security, and peace. As long as she could stay strong until the end. As long as she didn't forget what God required of her.

She closed her eyes and thought about the beauty awaiting her in the next life. She would sing and dance down the golden streets. No more sorrow. No more pain. If she were allowed, she would leave this world today.

The door on the far side of the room creaked open. Her heart raced and she held her breath, praying that it was Michael.

"Sara?" he whispered.

She released the air in her lungs and turned on her flashlight. "I'm here."

"What's wrong?" he demanded as he moved toward her.

She hesitated. She wanted to tell him—had to tell him, if she was going to get help. He might be disappointed in her, but even worse than that, she was afraid he wouldn't care.

"How is Elise?" she asked as she gripped Rezon in her arms.

His eyes narrowed. "Why don't you ask Sol?"

"I wanted to know from you."

He groaned in disgust. "This can wait until tomorrow."

"I was worried."

"Phoebe is taking care of her." He stepped back. "Is that all?"

"Michael, I—"

"We can't come down here anymore, Sara." He stepped back. "Sol will punish us both."

"I miss you."

He cleared his throat. "I'm going back to bed."

"Wait," she said softly and took a deep breath. This was agony for her to ask, but she had to think about the baby. "I need help."

"With what?"

She put her hands on her belly. "I—I think I'm pregnant."

She counted the seconds until he responded—eighteen . . . nineteen . . . twenty. His hands clenched at his sides as he glowered down at her. "You think?"

Rezon squirmed in her tight grip, and she set him down. Her elation at converting Elise dissipated.

She had hoped that Michael would have compassion, just enough to take her to a doctor in the morning. At one time, he would have done anything for her.

But things had changed. Maybe she should have kept quiet and beseeched God to terminate this pregnancy, like he'd done the last time. Sol never even knew she'd lost his child.

"I'm certain," she relented. "And something is wrong."

For an instant, she saw sympathy in his eyes. Just a glimpse and then it was gone. "How long have you been pregnant?"

"A month maybe," she muttered. "Or two."

"Sol's child?" he asked.

"Yes," she groaned as she crunched over and tried to breathe. She didn't want Michael to see her like this.

"What's wrong with you?"

"I've been having cramps for a week, but they're getting worse."

"I don't know anything about pregnancy, Sara."

"But you could take me to a doctor who does."

Bitterness permeated his voice. "Does Sol know?"

"No."

"Take it up with your husband, Sara," he said as he stomped toward the door.

Sol would never let her go to the doctor, and he knew it.

"Michael, please . . ."

He opened the door and turned.

"Congratulations," he barked before he left the room.

She sank to the wet floor as another cramp tore through her. She didn't care what happened to her, but if Michael wouldn't help her, who would save the baby?

Chapter 36

DARK CLOUDS GATHERED overhead and an icy wind blew across the bleak landscape. The baby was crawling into a forest and Elise felt a fresh terror clutching at her throat. She sprinted across the clearing toward the line of trees, screaming at the baby to stop, but the baby didn't seem to hear her.

At the edge of a cliff, a giant waterfall roared, its thunderous power echoing through the canyon. Elise raced through the trees, but no matter how fast she ran, she couldn't catch up.

The clouds descended on the cliff, and the baby batted at them with her arms as the swirling wind blew her toward the edge of the cliff. Elise launched herself forward, desperate to grab onto something—the baby's legs, or a foot, or toes. But the baby squirmed away, her arms now hanging over the precipice.

"No!" Elise screeched. If the baby moved another inch, she would fall into the rapids below.

The baby turned around, and Elise was stunned when she saw who it was.

Elise yelled at her to hang on, but Sara leaned back into the cloud and was gone.

The banging of the door jolted her awake, and she dove for the Bible on the floor. Maybe she wasn't here to find out about her mom. Maybe she was really here to help people like Sara get out from under the dark clouds.

Phoebe was beside her. "You're not sleeping, are you?"

"No," she murmured, trying to clear the fog that had settled over her mind.

Phoebe set a mug of hot tea on the dresser and clenched Elise's shoulders. "You will not give in to the enemy tonight."

"I need sleep to fight the enemy."

"Not when you're being purified."

Elise pointed toward the tea. "Could I have a sip?"

"Not yet."

"Then could I use the bathroom?"

"What verses have you learned?"

She stumbled over the words in Matthew 10:38–39: *"And he that taketh not his cross, and followeth after me, is not worthy of me. He that findeth his life shall lose it: and he that loseth his life for my sake shall find it."*

Phoebe's hand slammed against the top of the dresser. "Is that all?"

"Yes," Elise whispered.

Phoebe sat down on the other folding chair and took a long sip of the tea. "Then I will help you learn." She ran her fingers across the Bible. *"Man shall not live by bread alone, but by every word that proceedeth out of the mouth of God."*

Phoebe leaned toward her. "Say it."

Elise could almost taste the sweet, flaky croissant from the café. "I haven't eaten anything since lunch."

"Say it!"

Elise ducked her head and repeated the familiar Bible verse. *"Man shall not live by bread alone, but by every word that proceedeth out of the mouth of God."*

She detected a slight smile on Phoebe's face. She'd learned the verse as a child, but had never practiced it. She needed bread to live. And coffee. And maybe a couple more hazelnut croissants.

When she repeated the verse again, Phoebe leaned toward her. "Elise, in order to enter the kingdom of God, you must die to your own physical self."

Elise rubbed her arms. Is that what Jesus really meant? That she had to starve herself and deprive herself of sleep and medicine and a bathroom? He had also offered freedom . . . hadn't he?

I am come that they might have life, and that they might have it more abundantly.

She blinked, wondering where that verse had come from. She didn't remember memorizing it, but it was stowed in her heart. The enemy was out to destroy her, but Jesus had come to give her life.

Her bladder ached, and she wiggled in her chair. Phoebe was too busy quoting a verse from Isaiah to notice.

"I really need to use the bathroom," she insisted.

The older woman sighed her disappointment. "Go ahead."

Elise gripped her stomach as she rushed inside the tiny room and flipped on the light. The bathtub and toilet were wedged along the same short wall, and a pedestal sink was tucked just inside the door. When she was finished with the toilet, she gulped handfuls of water from the sink. The water soothed her mouth and helped solidify her blurred thinking.

She wouldn't have the strength to help Sara or anyone else if they wouldn't let her rest. Surely Phoebe had to sleep sometime.

She glanced down at her bare wrist, forgetting for a moment that her watch had been snatched from her. It must be two or three in the morning. Phoebe would need a lot more tea to keep them both awake all night.

She closed her eyes and leaned back against the door. She wouldn't be able to stay awake even if they propped up her head. It was a losing battle, and if she believed Phoebe's rhetoric, Satan had the upper hand.

Her head spun as she sat down on the toilet seat and prayed.

She had accepted Christ into her heart at vacation Bible school, but she had never relied on him solely and completely. Yes, she loved him. Yes, she thought she was willing to serve him. And, yes, she tried to apply the principles from the Bible to her life. But she hadn't lived and breathed the depth of her Savior's heart or suffered as he had.

Here she was, complaining about regulated bathroom privileges and food and medication when God may want more from her. He had certainly sacrificed much more for her.

Phoebe knocked on the door.

"Just a minute!" she called as she wiped her hands on a towel.

Right now she needed God more than anything else. Needed him to saturate her mind with his peace and wisdom. And she needed him to give her strength so she could figure out how to get out of here.

If she took an early train, she still had time to get to Wittenberg for her interview. Then she'd worry about getting a new passport so she could go home and be honest with her dad about her journey.

Elise pushed the door open with resolve. It was time to tell Phoebe she was done.

The instant she walked into the room, Phoebe's arm was around her shoulder, her voice calm and low. "I know this is hard for you, Elise, but it will get better. Once you surrender your life, you will be filled with joy and love. And you will belong to a community of brothers and sisters who love and care for you."

Elise blinked. Maybe these brothers and sisters were someplace nearby, safe and secure in their own beds for the night. What would they do if she let out a bloodcurdling scream?

Phoebe seemed to read her mind. "Everyone is asleep now, but you will meet them as soon as we finish cleansing your mind. We don't want to contaminate the others."

Elise stifled a laugh. She'd watched *Finding Nemo* with her brother the night before she'd left for Germany. Phoebe reminded her of those fish calling for the cleaner shrimp—Jake, Jack . . . *Jacques*.

She could almost hear him shout, "He hasn't been decontaminated yet."

She giggled, and Phoebe pressed her fingers into her arm. She was losing it.

"I want to go home, Phoebe."

"Of course you do." The woman pushed her back toward the chair.

Her mind turned fuzzy again as her eyelids drooped. Even the pain in her head had started to feel numb.

Phoebe pointed to the window. "But I can't send you out into the darkness by yourself. We will talk about it in the morning."

Elise looked down at the dresser and saw a spread of bread and cheese and sliced fruit. *Where did that come from?*

"Are you still hungry?" Phoebe asked.

She was beyond hungry. Her hands were shaky, and she felt nauseated, light-headed. "Yes."

Phoebe opened up the Bible and handed it back to her. "I want you to memorize the first chapter of James."

"But—"

Phoebe cut her off. "When you are done, we will celebrate with breakfast."

Elise eyed the plate of food again and began leafing through the pages of the Bible. Maybe she could hang on until morning.

Chapter 37

GRIMMA'S *POLIZEISTATION* WOULD have been quiet at six o'clock on a Monday morning, except that Addison Wade was leaning over the captain's desk, spewing out all sorts of scary legalese. *Liability. Causation. Emotional distress. Obligation. Gross negligence.*

Carson paced the floor at the back of the office, fueled by adrenaline, and watched the irritation expand across the captain's face. The man didn't seem particularly impressed with the information that Carson had found online, his mom's knowledge of all things legal, or even the fact that Addison Wade was the U.S. ambassador. Instead he seemed annoyed that she was stomping all over his territory.

The captain blew another puff of cigar smoke toward them as he explained that Elise was an adult. And a tourist. She was probably taking a spiritual retreat or visiting with friends. But either way, he couldn't get a warrant to search the property. No one had coerced her into going in Marienthron, and it wasn't illegal to travel alone in Germany or to visit a religious group—even if they locked their front door.

When the man stopped talking long enough to write something down on a yellow pad, Carson glanced out the window and saw a few people emerging onto the streets.

He and his mom had spent the night in the car outside Marienthron's front gate—just in case Elise decided to climb the wall in the dark.

When there was no sign of Elise, his mom eventually dozed off. He had passed the time by concocting a dozen rescue schemes. He contemplated everything from crashing the car through the front gate, to tossing a firebomb into the compound, to scaling the wall in the darkness for a clandestine raid. His most sedate idea was to pretend he had a delivery and ring the bell. Then he'd threaten whoever opened the gate and demand to see Elise.

He took a sip of the muddy brew he'd lifted from a half-filled pot in the waiting room.

As they'd driven to the police station, his mom had shot down all his ideas to rescue Elise. But if she didn't come up with a better plan soon, he was going in with the car. It would hardly be a quiet entrance, but it would be enough to alert Elise that she'd better run. If she wouldn't come willingly, he'd sling her over his shoulder and take her someplace where he could talk some sense into her.

Addison took a step toward the captain's desk, and Carson hoped the man was prepared. "Elise is being held against her will."

The captain ignored her statement and handed her some sort of report.

Addison took the paperwork. "You could knock on the door and talk to them without a warrant."

The captain dismissed her with a wave.

Carson hurled his coffee cup into a trash can as he walked out of the room, spattering the gritty liquid on the wall. He should have lied and said the Chosen's leader had clobbered him and taken Elise by force. Maybe aggravated assault would have gotten the captain's attention. Or maybe he needed something more severe, like premeditated murder. He was about ready to provide the murder if the police didn't start taking things more seriously.

"What now?" he asked as he and his mom walked out into the early dawn light.

"I don't know." Addison opened the car door. "If she doesn't come out today, I'm calling *Der Spiegel*."

He checked his watch—it was almost seven. "Why don't you call them right now?"

She got in the car. "Not yet."

He boxed his knuckles together. They had to stop waiting and do something else to get Elise out.

"If you called this morning, they might have the story online by lunch." He got into the driver's seat and started the car. "Maybe then the police would actually go to Marienthron and haul them off to jail."

"The police wouldn't be able to hold them."

"But everything you said—"

"I was bluffing." She sighed. "Attorneys have tried to convict the Chosen leadership all around the world, but they've never been able to pin the abuse on any specific member."

She latched her seat belt as Carson drove through town. "If Sol is still there, they'll run again."

"Who's Sol?"

"The Devil."

Carson gripped the steering wheel with both hands. "It's time for you to tell me how you know about the Chosen."

She stared out the front window.

"Mom?"

"Right," she finally said, and he heard her take a deep breath. "There's a verse in the book of Acts that says, *'Grievous wolves enter in among you, not sparing the flock.'*"

He glanced over at her, stunned. He had never heard her quote the Bible before.

She cleared her throat. "I wasn't spared."

He turned off the highway to follow the country road back up to the compound. "Spared from what?"

When she didn't answer, he repeated his question, and she finally started telling her story.

"After I graduated from college, I decided to spend my summer backpacking around Europe. I was passionate, naive, and lonely." Addison paused. "When I was in Frankfurt, I met a man named Paul and caught his vision for reaching people for Christ. He invited me home, and I didn't look back.

"Three weeks later, I married him."

"What?" Carson pulled the car to the side of the road and turned to face his mom, unsure if he wanted her to continue.

"I know it sounds strange, Carson, but I thought I knew what I was doing." She opened her purse, took out a tube of lipstick, and coated her lips. "What I didn't realize was that Paul had a wife in each of his homes—I was number eleven."

Carson's mind raced through all the materials he had read about Paul and the Chosen. How could his mother have been part of that?

"Our union wasn't even close to being legal." She set the purse back on the floor. "And I discovered later that our marriage wasn't the only thing illegal about the group. The Chosen thought that Paul's so-called messages from God superseded any law—or even Scripture. The Bible had to align with his enlightened prophecies, instead of the other way around."

Carson crossed his arms and stared off into the trees and brush along the side of the road as she continued.

"The strange thing was that, at the time, I really believed that God had called me to this group, called me to reach out to people who needed food and shelter and—above all else—needed him. It took me almost a year to realize that I'd been deceived. I think even Paul himself truly believed that God was speaking through him."

Carson tried to process this revelation. His mother's story. He didn't know what had happened to Elise's mom, but his own mother had volunteered to join the Chosen. He shivered under his jacket. Thank God she was still alive to talk about it.

A million questions raced through his mind. *What was it like? Why had she stayed? Did they hurt her? And why hadn't she told him before now?*

"Does Dad know?" he asked. It was a lame question, but he had to start somewhere . . . safe.

"I told him after he proposed."

His stomach churned. "I wish you would have told me too."

Addison Wade was a fighter, the one to call when things needed to be done. He couldn't imagine his self-confident, persistent mom letting someone else take control of her life and future—not her husband or her colleagues or the president of the United States. And certainly not some con "prophet" who claimed to speak for God.

"I joined the Chosen because I truly believed in its mission to serve God." She twisted her wedding band. "The problem is that I ended up serving men instead, and men can quickly become enamored with wealth and power and pleasure. In the Chosen, they justified their actions with Scripture."

"But surely you knew it was wrong."

"At first, I accepted Paul's theology without question." She cleared her throat. "Unfortunately, after a couple months, I started asking questions."

He wrapped his fingers around the steering wheel. He didn't know if he could listen to any more of her story.

"I tried to convince several of the girls to leave, but the only one interested in talking was Rahab."

"Elise's mom," he muttered.

"I told her that she was being used, and she started asking questions too." She paused. "When Sol found out, he decided to transfer me to a home in Asia so I gave Rahab my grandparents' telephone number in Virginia and told her when she was ready to leave the Chosen, I would help her get out."

"How did you get out?"

"I 'borrowed' one of Sol's guns and snuck out at night."

"Did you use the gun?"

Her tone turned defensive. "You don't know what you're capable of until you've been on the inside."

She was right. He had no idea what he would do if he was trapped in a cult. "How did you help Elise's mom?"

"She called me when she was sixteen and said she wanted to leave. A minister in Heidelberg said she could stay at the church until she flew to Virginia."

"How'd she get a passport?"

"We all had passports." Addison swallowed. "When a new baby was born, Sol would take the child and mother to the nearest U.S.

embassy and apply for a passport. The entire family was prepared, at any moment, to leave the country in case the local authorities started asking questions."

He tapped the wheel. "Will they send Elise away?"

"Not yet. They'll break her down slowly at Marienthron by depriving her of food and sleep and water while they tell her how much they love her." She hesitated. "Then they will begin to break her down mentally by twisting Scripture and making her doubt herself and her faith."

"But Elise knows that they are a cult."

"She did yesterday, but the leaders know how to destroy even the strongest person. If Sol figures out that she's Rahab's daughter, he'll make her pay."

"But you managed to stay strong, Mom."

"If I had been strong, I wouldn't have stayed so long."

"You were deceived!"

"But in spite of what they were telling me, I knew in my heart it wasn't right."

He looked out the window again. Not only was his mom quoting Scripture, but now she was admitting that she had been wrong.

He pulled back onto the roadway and drove toward the abbey, just in case Elise had been able to escape on her own. "You need to call *Der Spiegel*."

He glanced over at his mom, and she looked pale. "I will if we have to."

He wanted to shake her, force her to call the magazine's executive editor and get the story out before it was too late, yet she had to face her greatest fear first. The rescue of Elise Friedman might be the death of her career.

"You think they'll go after *your* story instead of the Chosen?"

Her nod was so slight that he almost missed it. "It would be too good to pass up."

"But a national story would force the police to check on Elise."

"It's not that simple, Carson." She forced a smile. "They might not even mention Elise."

"The story would be all about Elise."

"No." She shook her head. "The story would be about Ambassador Addison Wade aiding hookers in a sex cult."

"But you didn't know it was a cult at the time." He paused as he turned toward her. "Did you?"

"Not until the end." Her gaze dropped to her lap. "And I couldn't make the women leave."

"But you helped Catrina escape!"

"That part wouldn't make the headlines."

"What if you had Jack call the magazine?" he suggested. "If they don't talk about Elise, they don't get the exclusive."

"I made a huge mistake, Carson." She softened the edge in her voice. "The media can pulverize me, but I'm not taking my team down too."

Chapter 38

SARA WAS SPIRALING *in the rapids, her head bobbing up and down as the current plunged her through its rocky course. Elise raced toward her, dodging the rocks. She had to get her out of the water before they hit the falls.*

The current thrust Sara around a bend and washed her onto an exposed boulder. Elise kicked forward. If Sara could cling to the rock, maybe Elise could grab her and swim to shore. She tried to shout to Sara, but the crash of the river swallowed her words.

The clouds descended again, and the icy wind shoved Sara back into the maelstrom of the current.

"Hold on!" Elise shouted again. She was seconds away from rescuing the small girl.

The river rippled in front of her, and Elise stopped and watched in horror as two flaming eyes popped through the surface. A black creature glared at Elise for an instant and then turned toward Sara. Elise lurched forward, but the monster's powerful wake washed her backward as it plucked Sara off the rock and plunged underwater.

Elise screamed and dove beneath the churning surface, probing for Sara in the darkness.

But she was gone.

Someone shook Elise again. And again. She batted the monster away with her fists and rolled over on the cold tile floor. She had to rescue Sara from the monster.

Someone pinched her shoulder, and she groaned.

She had never realized how much she took sleep for granted. Or how disconcerting it was to have it stolen away from her—her inalienable right to rest.

She couldn't open her eyes yet. She needed to sleep for just one more minute. Or two.

"Get up, Elise."

She squinted into the light and saw Phoebe staring back at her. Why wouldn't that woman leave her alone? She could memorize a hundred verses after a few hours of sleep, but if she didn't get some rest, she wouldn't be able to make it another hour . . . forget another day.

Phoebe had kept her up all night, repeating Scripture over and over until the Old English words had blurred in her mind. In spite of her exhaustion, she'd done what was required. She'd memorized the first chapter of James. All twenty-seven verses.

Phoebe had rewarded her diligence with a couple of crackers and a slice of cheddar cheese. She wouldn't let her touch the fruit—that was reserved for Elise's completion of John 15.

"Every branch in me that beareth not fruit he taketh away: and every branch that beareth fruit, he purgeth it, that it may bring forth more fruit," she whispered.

She felt as if she was the one being purged, one limb at a time.

She didn't make it through the first three verses of John 15, even though she muttered them over and over with Phoebe. She couldn't continue.

Phoebe tugged on her arms, but they were anchored to the ground. Her back ached, and the pain in her head raged anew. She could hardly breathe through the congestion in her nose.

If she didn't get out of here soon, they'd have to take her to the hospital.

"C'mon," Phoebe barked.

She coughed. "I can't move."

"Greater is he that is in you, than he that is in the world," Phoebe quoted. The woman seemed to have a verse for everything.

Last night, Elise had fantasized about plush mattresses and blankets, but now all she wanted to do was close her eyes again. She groaned and rolled over as the sunlight warmed the room.

Phoebe tapped her shoulder. "Jesus said, '*Watch ye and pray, lest ye enter into temptation. The spirit truly is ready, but the flesh is weak.*'"

She peeked at the woman. "He also said, '*Come unto me . . . and I will give you rest.*'"

Phoebe yanked on her arm and said, "I will not allow the deceit of Satan to harm me or the other members of our family."

She stood up. "They aren't my family."

"You no longer belong to the world."

Elise stalked to the door and turned the knob, but it was still locked. "You said I could leave in the morning."

Phoebe sat down on the bed. "I'm not finished purifying you, Elise."

"But *I'm* done," she insisted. "I don't want any part of this."

"No, you're not done."

Elise rattled and pulled on the door, but it wouldn't budge.

"I want to go home!" she screamed.

She heard the key in the lock, and her chest swelled with hope. Maybe someone had heard her scream. Maybe someone would finally rescue her from this insanity.

But the man who walked in the door wasn't her savior. It was the bald man with the purple robe who'd taken her purse and burned her passport. The man Michael had called "King Sol."

She turned to Phoebe, but the woman was pretending to be asleep on the bed.

"I do not allow screaming in this household," Sol said. "Especially from new converts."

"I don't want to convert."

He motioned toward one of the chairs. "Sit down."

Elise didn't move. Her mind and body were exhausted, but she willed her brain to keep working. Keep fighting. She wasn't going to let him win.

She mustered a hint of strength back into her voice. "I want to go home," she repeated.

"People who join the Chosen don't walk back out the gates until they are ready to go into the world."

"I'm ready."

"I don't think you are." He brandished the cane in his hand. "But I will help you in your journey."

She took a step back. "You're holding me against my will."

Anger flashed through his eyes. "You left your will on the other side of the wall."

"No, I didn't," she said, but she was too tired to fight. "I just need to rest."

He reached for her shoulder and shoved her toward the open door. She didn't doubt for a second that he'd hurt her if she refused to obey him. He might even hurt her if she did.

"That's not a problem," he said.

A rush of air cleansed her lungs and cleared some of the grogginess out of her mind as she stumbled down the hall. If King Sol wasn't going to let her leave, maybe Carson would get her out. He could probably talk his way in through the front gate.

Unless—she could hardly bear to think about the other option—unless he had already left town.

He wouldn't abandon her . . . would he? Yet he had no reason to risk his life getting her out of here. He didn't even know her—not really. And why would he care? She'd kept insisting that she wanted to find the Chosen, and she had gotten what she wanted. He had no reason to stick around.

Auf Wiedersehen.

What had she been thinking? She had jumped at the chance to get inside the complex, as if she would just walk out the front door again when she was done. Apparently, she hadn't been thinking at all. No one knew where she was, except a backpacker who was probably already on an express train to Switzerland.

Her dad didn't even know where she had gone. He would think that she had simply disappeared off the streets of Berlin, and he'd blame himself for the loss. His heart couldn't handle it.

If only she'd left some sort of trail.

Her heart lurched. *Addison Wade!*

The ambassador knew that she had gone to Heidelberg. Her dad would contact the embassy to report a missing American. And once he told Addison Wade, the ambassador would help him look for her.

Please, God, let her follow the trail.

How long could she stay sane without food or sleep?

Sol pointed down the hallway. "That way."

She looked to her left to see if there was a place she could run. It didn't matter how tired she was. If she could get out of the building, she could scale that wall in record time with the adrenaline still pumping in her system.

"I don't think you understand, Elise." Sol nudged her rib. "I don't tolerate rebellion."

She wanted to taunt him, ask him how exactly he was going to make her follow him. But then again, she was afraid he might show her.

She'd never claim to be a biblical scholar, but she couldn't remember a single incident in the Bible where Jesus forced someone to follow him. He invited people to follow. Some accepted the invitation. Others rejected it.

There was no invitation in Sol's words.

She preceded him down the hallway until he told her to stop. She waited while he fished out a ring of keys from his pocket and unlocked the door to another room. It had the same stone walls and barred window as the last room, but this one had no furniture, only a brown canvas cot against one wall.

She looked back over her shoulder one last time. She'd seen a news story once that said if you were attacked in a parking lot, the best thing you could do to stay alive was not get into a car. The best thing she could probably do right now was not go into the room.

She turned her heels, but Sol's hand shot out, grabbed her arm, and thrust her inside. "Running isn't an option."

Her teeth chattered from the cold as she stumbled across the floor and collapsed onto the cot. As soon as Sol left, she would try to get some sleep.

Sol reached back into his pocket and flashed the medication from the pharmacy in front of her. "Phoebe said you were looking for these."

She swiped her hand in the air like he might actually give it to her.

His voice was calm as he jerked back his hand. "After you give me your PIN number, you can take your medicine and go to sleep."

She bit her lip and slowly shook her head.

"I don't think you understand." He pressed the tip of his cane into her shoulder. "You're no different from the rest of us who have given up everything for the Chosen. But until you show me that you're willing to sacrifice for this family, you're not going to sleep or eat or get another sip of water."

He stuffed the cold medicine back in his pocket. "And you can forget about taking these."

Her eyes slipped shut and she stretched herself out on the cot. Sol prodded her again with his cane. "You don't want to test me on this, Elise."

She groaned in pain as the sharp tip of the cane hit her collarbone. It was as if she'd pried open the very gates of hell and locked herself inside.

"I'm not going to ask you again." He leaned over her. "What's the number?"

It was worth the five hundred dollars to get some rest. Once she figured out a way to escape, she could call her bank and report it as fraud. And if she didn't get out . . . maybe her dad could follow the trail to an ATM in Grimma.

Sol cut the air with a whoosh as he hoisted his cane.

"Wait," she whispered. He could have the number and all the money in the account if he wanted it. She was still going to get out.

"9-2-3-9," she muttered.

"One more time."

She spat it out again.

"Very good." He stepped back and tossed the cold medication at her. "Now you may sleep."

She curled up as tightly as she could on the rigid cot and closed her eyes, praying that God would save her in spite of her stupidity. And that he would rescue Sara from the monster.

Chapter 39

A TAN VOLVO PULLED out of Marienthron's front gate, and Addison squinted into the back window. The passenger had dark hair like Elise, but Sol had never allowed new converts to go into town until they'd been broken.

Carson started the car and followed the Volvo toward Grimma.

"Do you think it's her?" he asked.

"I don't know."

Just like Paul, Sol's strict rules were often amended whenever he had a so-called revelation from God. The erratic changes kept his family on the edge, struggling to follow, and it kept him in control.

If he had let Elise out of isolation today, it didn't really matter why. The instant she stepped away from that car, they would nab her.

Carson followed the Volvo through town until it stopped in front of the Commerze Bank. The image of Patty Hearst flashed in Addison's mind. Surely, Sol wouldn't force Elise to do something so stupid as to rob a bank—even if he was desperate.

The door opened, and a girl slid out of the car seat. Her brown jumper was worn, and she clutched her side as she stepped toward the bank. She was too small to be Elise.

The girl turned toward her for an instant, and Addison's heart lurched when she saw her face. The girl looked exactly like Rahab when she was young, before she got away from the Chosen.

Was it possible?

Addison leaned forward, her fingers shaking against the dashboard. It had to be Sara. Catrina's baby was still alive.

"Are you okay, Mom?"

She couldn't take her eyes off the girl. Somehow God had spared Sara's life.

Carson's hand was on her shoulder. "You're crying."

She reached her hand up to her face and wiped the tears off her damp cheeks. Her chest ached for the child who had grown up in the Chosen all on her own. She'd had no mother to love her. No father to protect her. She'd looked evil in the eye, and somehow she'd survived.

"This is too much." Carson put the car in reverse. "I'm taking you back to the hotel."

"No." Addison blew her nose as the girl walked up to the ATM and punched in a code. When the cash came out, she stuffed it in her pocket and tried the card again.

Carson pointed. "That's the girl that Elise left with yesterday."

Addison hesitated. "It's her sister."

He looked at his mom and then back at Sara. "She didn't tell me . . ."

"She doesn't know."

Carson leaned back against the leather, and they both watched Sara punch the numbers on the ATM again and again like she couldn't make the machine work. Then she hit the buttons one last time and her shoulders slumped as she dragged herself back to the car.

"I can't believe Elise's parents never told her that she had a sister," Carson said as they watched a blond man grab the card from Sara's hand and stomp back toward the machine.

Her eyes stayed focused on the man walking toward the bank machine. "Catrina thought she was dead."

The man stuck the card in the slot, pressing the buttons on the keypad again and again. Finally, he slapped the ATM screen with his palm and jogged back to the car, slamming the door behind him.

"Why did she think Sara was dead?" Carson asked.

Addison pinched the arch on her nose. She remembered the day so clearly. She'd been knocking on doors all morning, ramping up for the next election, when Steve had called her at the office. He was worried about Catrina. She had just returned from Germany yet again and was overcome with depression. He was worried that the guilt over leaving Sara behind would kill her.

"I called her," she said.

Carson restarted the engine. "Mom?"

"I didn't say she was dead." She paused. "Not directly."

He sighed. "What did you say?"

Her shoulders sagged in the seat. First Richard and now Carson was interrogating her.

"Catrina asked if I thought Sara was already in heaven, and I said she probably was."

When Carson groaned, she jumped on the defensive.

"Sol had threatened to kill Sara if Catrina left, and we had no reason to doubt his word." She unclipped her seat belt. "I knew it would be painful to hear, but Steve and I both hoped that if she stopped searching for Sara, she would be able to focus on her health and her family.

"And we were both afraid that if Catrina found Sol, he would kill her too."

The Volvo sped past them, and Carson flipped on the turn signal. "Back to Marienthron?"

Before Carson could pull away from the curb, Addison opened her door and stepped onto the sidewalk. "I need some air."

Blue sky canopied the busy market street as she pressed herself forward, past the fruit stand and café and corner bakery. She could still see Rahab's green eyes, her innocence stolen long before it was time. Rahab hadn't been offered up for prostitution. Her calling from toddlerhood was to be one of Sol's wives.

As his wife, Rahab had special privileges, but she was also subjected to more abuse than anyone else in the group. It was about much more than sex to Sol. It was about power. Control. Commanding the minds of the entire group wasn't enough to satisfy his insatiable desire to be revered. It was almost as if he knew that stealing what was most precious from these young girls would destroy any hope that welled in their souls. They wouldn't speak out, and they would be devoted to him until they died.

And many of them died early.

Most of the girls in Sol's harem were scarred with bitterness, but Rahab had been different. Addison had no idea how someone as crafty as Bethesda could have given birth to such a sweet child. In spite of what ultimately happened, God's hand was on Rahab until the very end.

On a rare day when they were allowed outside, Addison had tried to explain pedophilia to Rahab and then told her that she was serving Sol not God.

It was too much for a nine-year-old to comprehend.

Addison confided in her that she was planning her escape from the Chosen and asked if Rahab wanted to come with her. When Rahab refused to go, Addison slipped her the phone number of her grandparents. If she ever changed her mind, Addison whispered, they would help her start a new life in the United States.

The week before she left Frankfurt, Addison found a pay phone and called her grandmother collect. Her grandparents wired her the money for plane tickets and after the money arrived, she snuck out to the barn and stole one of the many guns that Sol had stockpiled. When she returned to the house, Sol confronted her with his knife and threatened to kill her if she tried to leave. She believed him.

But his smirk faded when she pointed the gun at him. It disappeared when she pulled the trigger. He screamed obscenities at her as she ran out the door and down the street before the other members of the family could stop her. A farmer picked her up along the road and drove her to the airport.

Every minute of that flight back to the States, she regretted that Rahab wasn't with her. And she regretted it seven years later when Rahab called her from Heidelberg. She was ready to get out and wanted to take both of her daughters with her.

Addison had never gotten the chance to meet Sara. She'd only heard stories about Sara, late at night as Catrina fought off the nightmares that haunted her.

Addison crossed the road and walked down to the riverfront. Grass swayed in the wind along the banks, and the water rippled as eight women rowed by in a racing shell.

God forgive her, she never would have stopped searching if she'd known that Sara was alive. She would have found her and taken her away—no matter what the consequences. Nothing was worth letting her suffer at Sol's hand.

She'd made a promise to Catrina years ago, and she wouldn't renege. Now that she knew the truth about Sara, she'd do everything she could to rescue both of Catrina's daughters.

Chapter 40

A BROWN SPIDER CRAWLED across the stone wall, and Elise squashed it with her shoe. Her teeth chattered as she lay back down on the cot, her hands wrapped around her arms. Once the medicine kicked in, maybe she could fall asleep again and drift off, far away from here.

She should have listened to her dad and stayed away from Heidelberg. She should have honored his request to leave the past alone and gone straight to the university when she landed in Berlin.

If only she could go back a few days. A week. She never would have taken the train to Heidelberg. She probably never would have come to Germany. She would have stayed in Virginia and done all of her research in the Library of Congress.

She rolled over and rubbed the goose bumps on her arms. She wouldn't even be here if she could go back further than last week—if she could go back thirteen years.

The walls swirled around her, and she closed her eyes to try to stop the spinning. If only she could go back in time, she would check on her mother after her birthday party instead of speeding up and down their driveway with her new roller skates. If only she had called for help immediately instead of trying to wake her mother up. If only . . .

But her dad had gone to the store, and when the phone rang, her mother had shooed her outside. An hour later, when she had rushed through the front door and called for her mom, no one answered. The familiar sounds of the dishwasher, washing machine, and blender had been replaced by an eerie silence.

She had run to her parents' bedroom and found her mother on the bed.

If she hadn't left her mother alone, maybe she could have stopped her or called for help before she died. Her mother would be here today, answering her questions about the Chosen in the safety and warmth of their home in Virginia.

Elise rolled onto her side and put her head on her arms.

Sleep. She needed to sleep. She squeezed her eyes closed again and tried to pretend she was lying on her bed at home.

Even with her eyes shut, the walls roiled in the darkness and closed in on her.

Elise wrapped her arms around her knees, rubbing her legs to get warm. Where had Sara gone? And Phoebe? Why had they left her alone?

She'd memorize another thirty verses if she had to. Three hundred verses. If only they'd let her out of this room.

Giving up on sleep for the moment, she inched herself up the wall and tried to reach the high window, but it was still a good twelve or thirteen inches above her fingertips. For an instant, she imagined Carson on the other side, rallying the entire Grimma police force, preparing to break her free. Maybe they had snipers surrounding the compound at this exact moment, ready to rescue her from her folly.

She hopped up again, batting the air. Maybe one of the bars would be loose and she could pull herself through the hole. Pain shot through her shins as she fell on the cot, bounced off, and landed on the ground.

When Phoebe told her she wasn't allowed to leave, she should have checked her attitude at the door and done what she was told. How hard would it have been to keep her mouth shut? She should have bitten her tongue instead of demanding to go home.

She had wanted to hear stories about her mother—to get a glimpse of her childhood, even if it was painful. She wanted to understand why her mom had stayed with a cult.

But she didn't need to hear the stories anymore. She understood why it had taken years for her mom to leave. Phoebe—and probably the others—had injected her with a steady dose of anger, feigned love, and guilt until they had forced her to believe their lies.

It wasn't about the fear of God or the love of God. It was about using the fear of God to scare people into doing what Sol wanted.

They'd suffocated the life out of her mother. Driven her crazy. And even when she'd left the walls behind, she couldn't chase away the demons.

Elise touched the cold rock wall with her palms, absorbing the shock of its chill to steady her shaking arms. She couldn't blame Carson if he'd taken the next train out of town. He had tried to save her from herself—swiping her bike to keep her from getting sick, and trying to talk her out of visiting the compound. She hadn't listened and had ended up trapped inside. He probably thought she'd gotten exactly what she wanted—and deserved.

She beat the wall over and over again. Why couldn't she sleep away the misery? She'd only been here for one day, and her mind was already slipping. What would happen if Carson really had left her here? Even if her dad got to Berlin, found Addison, and went to Heidelberg, they would never discover the Chosen's current location. Carson had taken the paperwork out of the Heidelberg home.

Someone jostled the doorknob at the side of the room, and she cowered back against the wall. What were they going to do to her now? As her mind raced through terrifying possibilities, she closed her eyes and pretended to sleep.

God would have to send his angels to get her out of here.

The door swung open, and she heard heavy footsteps tromping across the floor. Someone clenched her arm, and she opened her eyes to see Sol, the steely control in his eyes replaced with rage. He pulled her up and pinned her against the wall. The ragged stone stabbed her back and head, but she didn't have the strength to fight back. "You lied to me, Elise."

She glared at him. "I didn't lie."

"You said you had money."

Money? Her mind whirled. She had fudged a little when she was talking to Sara—but it never occurred to her that they would steal her debit card and try to withdraw all her money.

"It's in the bank," she said.

He held up her ATM card. "Five hundred dollars?"

"There's a—" she coughed as his rancid breath accosted her face.

"A what?"

"A limit. I can only withdraw five hundred a day."

He slid the card into his pocket. "How much more is there?"

"I don't know. A couple thousand."

His eyes raged with anger. "Do you know the penalty for sin?"

"That's just my checking account," she sputtered before he could deliver the penalty.

"Where's the rest?"

"Invested . . . in stocks and mutual funds and a savings account."

"How much is in the savings account?"

"I'm not sure."

He wrung her wrist. "How much?"

The pain commanded her entire body. If she swung back, the penalty would probably be swift.

He twisted her arm until she blurted, "Fifteen thousand."

He dropped her arm, and she rubbed her skin, trying to assuage the pain. He pointed at the door. "I have something to show you, Johanna."

Johanna?

Elise blinked at the name. Suddenly she was back in the attic, her mother holding her tight. They were trying to run away, from the monster.

Elise stumbled backward, her eyes wide. If he knew her name as a child, then he knew her mother. He had probably known about her since the minute she'd walked through those doors.

He grasped her arm again and propelled her toward the door.

"When your mother ran away—" He stopped and waited until she turned toward him. "She left something behind."

Chapter 41

SOL WATCHED THE HORROR permeate Elise's face, the same fear he had seen on her face the night Rahab took her away. She might think she was strong, but she still feared him.

"Your mother chose to disobey God." Sol opened the door. "And God loved her enough to punish her for her sins."

Elise spun around and faced him, the green in her eyes blazing. "God didn't punish her."

"He relinquished her soul to Satan—" He paused. "Just like he'll relinquish yours if you don't surrender."

Her chin rose an inch. "You aren't God, Sol."

He squeezed the handle of his cane as the anger surged in his belly. He would not be undone by this girl. He'd been waiting almost twenty years for Rahab to return, and he would not let her daughter's impertinence unravel him.

He wrenched her arm behind her, and she groaned as he pushed her down the hallway. The second door on the right was already cracked open, and he shoved her toward it.

No matter how impure her intentions, he'd purify her with fire. Like Rahab and Sara, she was destined to be his, and she would revere him as the messenger of God and her king.

Elise clutched the sides of the doorframe until she heard someone moan, then she rushed inside.

Elise's eyes widened when she saw Sara lying on the bed, her wrists tied to the iron headboard. Elise sat down beside her and pushed the sweaty hair off her forehead. As long as he kept Sara as collateral, Elise would do exactly what he asked.

"Are you okay?" Elise whispered.

Sara didn't move.

He pushed up the sleeve on Sara's scarred arm until Elise could see the black tattoo on her shoulder—a large cross branded with the letter *S*. It was the same seal he'd etched on her mother's arm.

"Surely you've seen this before?" he asked.

She turned toward him and hissed. "How dare you."

"It means that Sara belongs to me."

He grasped Elise's arm and pushed up her sleeve to expose the skin on her shoulder. Someday he would mark her like he had her sister and mother.

Elise slapped his hands away, and he laughed as he nodded toward Sara. "Johanna, I'd like you to meet your sister."

Elise stared at him in shock.

"I guess Rahab was good at keeping secrets."

Elise ignored his gibe and began stroking Sara's hair.

"Sara brought you to us," he explained. "Now she's going to ensure that you come back home."

Elise's cheeks were wet from her tears. "What are you talking about?"

"You're going to wire the money from your savings into a new account."

This time she didn't fight him. He was in control, and she would do exactly what he said.

Something shuffled by the door, and Sol looked over his shoulder. Michael was waiting for him, and his face looked almost as pale as Elise's. Sol motioned toward Sara. "Tie her feet."

Michael didn't move.

Sol muttered a curse. If Michael was going to assist him in the leadership of the house, he would have to strengthen his resolve. Without it, they would never be able to keep the other members of the family under control.

"I said to tie her feet."

Michael stepped forward and strung a bandana loosely around Sara's ankles.

"Tighter," Sol demanded.

"It's going to be okay, Sara," Elise whispered as Michael tied the knot.

Sol brushed his hand across Elise's shoulder and smiled. "As long as you come back, you'll both be okay."

—❦—

Sara watched Sol escort Elise out of the room and lock the door. Even when she tried to stop the tremors, her arms twitched and her shoulders and lower back writhed with pain. The room spun around her, and she clenched her eyes shut again. But the spinning didn't stop. Nothing would make it go away. She was done with this life. God could take her and her baby to the other side.

The demons tormented, mocking her from within. Probing. Lying. Squeezing the air out of her lungs.

She couldn't breathe.

She'd doubted Sol. And God. And she'd failed them miserably. How could God ever forgive her selfishness? Her unfaithfulness? She bit her lip.

Or her pregnancy?

Sweat poured down her face, salt stinging her eyes as Sol's words rang in her mind.

This is your sister.

She didn't have a sister. Her mother had abandoned her when she was a child, her love for the world greater than her love for God or her daughter. She'd forsaken her faith and her family. She'd run off and left her baby girl in King Sol's care.

Sol must have meant that Elise was her sister in Christ. Part of the family. Yet Elise had sat down on the bed beside her, stroked her hair, and cried. For her.

No one had ever cried for her before.

Another cramp ripped through her abdomen, and she groaned. It was too late for Michael's love, and Sol was done with her. Someday soon she would be sent to Berlin like the others.

She tugged her arm to reach for her belly, forgetting for an instant that she was tied to the bed.

Sol had to be lying about Elise. She didn't have any real family, nor was she fit to be a mother. Or a sister. Or a member of the Chosen. Every day, she failed God. Over and over. She would never be worthy of him or her baby or this group.

Why didn't Sol just kill her?

She heard a shuffle at the side of the room, and she looked down in time to see Rezon creeping out from under the chair. With his back leg tied up in a splint, he leapt onto the bed and nudged her arm.

She jerked on the bandanas, twisting her arms as she tried to comfort her kitten. She tried to sing softly to him, but she couldn't pull him to her chest.

How could she possibly take care of a child when she couldn't even care for a cat?

The only way she could save her baby was to stop fighting the pain.

Chapter 42

THE SUNLIGHT BLINDED Elise for a moment when Michael opened the front door. He didn't push her down the walkway. Didn't need to. Even if Sol was lying about Sara being her sister, she would still go to town, transfer the money, and then figure out how to get Sara away from the monster.

And if Sol was telling the truth, why hadn't her mother told her she had a sister? And why had she left her with Sol?

The resignation in Sara's face disturbed her even more than the bloody lines and scars on her arms. When she'd seen the black tattoo on Sara's shoulder, she'd wanted to lunge at Sol and choke the life out of him for branding his followers like they were livestock. But he was pulling the strings right now and all she could do was dance.

If only she could cut the bandanas off Sara's arms, pick her up, and run out of this compound. Sol might think he could still hurt Sara, but Elise didn't think it was possible for him to hurt the girl anymore.

They walked through the courtyard, and Michael nodded toward a group of men and women picking vegetables in a garden. There were a couple of kids working beside them, but the rest of the faces were middle-aged. The men all had beards, and the women wore baggy dresses with hair cascading down to their waists. They stared at her like they'd never seen an American before.

She felt like racing through the yard and shouting, "Don't you want out?"

There was freedom outside these walls. Freedom in Christ. Sol and Michael might make a formidable team, but they wouldn't be able to

stop the surge if these people flooded out the doors and over the wall . . .
unless Sol was ready to shoot any member who tried to defect.

She climbed into the passenger seat of the Volvo and choked on the
stench. The cracked leather seats—or Michael—reeked of sweat. Or
maybe she was the one who stunk. She hadn't had a shower in three
days.

Michael stopped at the front gate and released the padlock. On the
other side, he relocked it, and they started their drive toward town.

Elise rolled down the window and drank in the afternoon air. It
would be so easy to jump out of the car at a stoplight or when they got
to the bank, but she wouldn't run until she could take Sara with her.
Unfortunately, Sol also knew she wasn't going anywhere.

What she didn't understand was why Sara didn't run away when she
was in Grimma. Sol let her roam free to ask for food. Even if she didn't
have any money to get on a train, she could go to the police station or
find someone else to help her. Yet, in spite of what Sol did to her, she
chose to return home.

Elise glanced at the blond man to her left. Carson had exuded calm
and friendliness, but not this man. He was intense . . . just like her.

She leaned her tired head back against the seat. "So why did you join
the Chosen?"

His voice was as cold as his eyes. "I didn't join."

"Were you born into the group?"

She sneezed, but Michael didn't even bother with a *Gesundheit*.

"This group is my family."

"But surely someone misses you on the outside," she prodded. All
she wanted to do was understand why any man would surrender to an
obvious lunatic who claimed to be a prophet of God.

His face was stoic. "Someone left me with the Chosen when I was
two."

"And Sol never let you go."

He straightened his shoulders. "He and Phoebe took care of me
when no one else would."

"So you think you owe them something?"

"Some people don't understand the importance of loyalty and family."

If he would tie an innocent girl to a bed, how far would he go to prove he was loyal?

Michael stopped the car under a yellow and black sign, and Elise followed him up the stairs and into the Commerze Bank. Beside the line of tellers was a manager with a striped suit and thinning hair. After Michael shook his hand, the man pointed toward a side room with a tinted window.

When they walked into the room, Michael pulled out the chair for Elise, but as she sat down, she glanced toward the lobby and squinted. There was Carson, grinning back at her. She sprung out of her seat.

"Bathroom!" she exclaimed.

The manager looked at Michael and then back at her.

She tried to calm the fervor in her voice. "*Badezimmer?*"

Michael shook his head, but the manager was already motioning her toward the door. Michael leapt to his feet and clamped his fingers around her elbow as he walked her through the lobby.

She tried to act nonchalant as she searched the room for Carson. But like a mirage, he was gone. Maybe the exhaustion was catching up to her and she was imagining people who weren't really there.

Her body slumped as she and Michael moved in lockstep toward the hallway at the side of the bank. She was alone, and there was nothing she could do. No matter how much she wanted Carson to be there, an imaginary friend couldn't help get her and Sara out of Marienthron.

Just then, a flash of burgundy caught her eye from the corner of the lobby. She turned her head and blinked slowly at the familiar sight of Carson's jacket.

He nodded at her, and she blinked again. This time he didn't go away.

She forced her hands to stay at her side and stifled the smile that tried to creep up her face as he smiled at her.

Thank God he hadn't left her. He was still here. In Grimma. And he knew where she was.

With Michael's hand on her elbow, Elise walked into the narrow hallway that led back to the bathrooms. When they reached the ladies' room, Michael reached across her and opened the door to a dark room. He relaxed his grip on her arm and nodded. "Make it quick."

Elise slipped inside the door, locked it behind her, and flipped on the light.

"Shhh!"

Elise jumped, and with her fists clenched in the air, she jerked her head around to face Addison Wade.

She caught her breath and stammered, "Wh–what are you doing here?"

"Trying to get you out of this mess." The ambassador whispered. "Are you okay?"

Her hands collapsed at her side. "A little tired."

Addison searched her face as she reached for Elise's hand. "I bet."

"How did you know I was here?"

Addison's gaze sank to the tile floor. "Carson called me."

Elise froze, her hand going limp in Addison's grasp. How did the ambassador know Carson? She pulled her hand away as she tried to process this new revelation, but her brain was already fried from hunger, fear, and sleep deprivation.

"Does he work for you?" she asked quietly.

"It doesn't matter."

The realization hit her slowly. "Carson Talles . . ."

"Carson Talles Wade."

"He's—he's . . . ?"

"Carson is my son."

Her mind raced back to her first encounter with Carson. He had whipped the marriage application out of her hand and had taken it back to the counter. She had thought he was an easygoing backpacker headed for Switzerland, but he had known who she was from the very beginning. His mother had probably sent him to keep her from finding the Chosen, and he had almost succeeded.

She clutched her cold hands together. She wanted to be mad at

Carson and his deception. Angry at his feigned interest in her and her story. But right now she was grateful that he hadn't left her alone. She couldn't imagine what would have happened if she had stumbled onto Sara and the Chosen by herself. Carson had stuck with her, and now he had brought the U.S. ambassador down to help.

Addison pressed something into Elise's hands, and she looked down to see a sandwich and bottle of water.

"Eat," the ambassador urged, and Elise didn't argue. She gobbled down the ham and cheese and then guzzled the water.

"There's a girl at the compound," Elise said when she finished the food. "Sol says that she's my sister."

Addison stepped back. "I know."

Michael knocked on the door, but Elise didn't move.

"You knew I had a sister?"

"I thought—" Addison hesitated. "We thought she was dead."

Her mother had thought Sara was dead.

She stared at the mirror, a hundred questions racing through her mind, but Michael pounded again. When she reached for the door, Addison blocked her arm. "You don't have to go back."

"I do if we want to save Sara."

Addison took the sandwich wrapper and the bottle from her hand. "We're going to get you out of there."

Elise nodded and walked back outside.

—⁓⁓○

Addison counted to sixty before cracking open the door. She listened for a moment but didn't hear anyone in the hallway. Elise and her escort were gone.

Draping her purse over her shoulder, she slipped out of the bathroom and made her way toward the lobby. With a quick glance to her left, she saw Elise's outline in one of the conference rooms, but she didn't stop.

Carson followed her across the lobby, but he was watching the same room. "What's she doing?"

"Staying."

He stopped walking. "No, she's not."

She pointed toward the door. "Let's talk outside."

He glanced back toward the room one last time before he jogged out the door and down the stairs. "If we don't take her with us now—"

"She's not coming."

He groaned as he turned around. "Of all the—"

Addison grabbed his arm and tugged him toward the car. "C'mon, Carson."

He unlocked the door for her and she climbed into the passenger seat. "Tell me what happened."

Addison clipped her seat belt. "I'll explain when you get in."

They had to keep focused right now—as a team. Their mission had grown even bigger than rescuing Elise. It was about saving Sara as well . . . and exposing Sol. The German authorities wouldn't care about the Chosen's brand of religion, but they would be very interested in the corruption and abuse of kids. And if they still had their little operation going on in Berlin, she would take it down.

As Carson walked around the car and slid into the driver's seat, Addison took another deep breath to steady her nerves. "Sol introduced Elise to her sister, Sara . . ."

"And now she won't leave." Carson finished her sentence for her.

"You got it."

Carson started the car and pulled out onto the street. "Then we've got to get Sara out right now."

"Sol won't do anything to her until he gets Elise's money."

Carson slammed on the brakes. "Elise and that guy are at the bank!"

"And we're going to the police station."

Carson looked over at his mom and threw up his hands. "The captain wouldn't listen."

Addison took a deep breath. "He will now."

Chapter 43

STRANDS OF SARA'S HAIR were plastered onto her wet forehead, and Sol watched her legs writhe like flames on the bed. He had sealed his bond for her with the fire, seared into her heart a love that was even stronger than death. Yet she continued to fight his love for her.

She looked at him, and he saw the terror in her eyes.

"Are you ready to get out, Sara?"

When he reached down to touch her hair, the cat clawed his arm. He swore as he bunched up its paws and hoisted it over his head. The cat gnawed at him with its tiny teeth, and he squeezed.

Sara struggled to reach the cat, but she couldn't. Just like he hadn't been able to reach out to Johanna when Rahab had stolen her away.

With his other hand, Sol reached for his knife, and Sara screamed for him to stop.

He held the knife up to the cat's throat. "*Thou shalt have no other gods before me.*"

Sara shut her eyes, muttering with her lips. She wasn't begging him to save the cat. She was praying. The anger rose like bile in his throat.

"Who is your lord?" he demanded as he pressed the knife into the cat's flesh. Its wail pierced his ears.

If Sara really cared that much for this animal, he wouldn't kill it, but he'd mark it just like he'd marked her.

He stepped closer to her as the tears poured down her face. "Who?"

A loud whistle erupted over the howl of the cat, and Sol stopped. He threw the cat back onto the bed, grabbed his cane, and hobbled into the hallway to look out the window. With the exception of an occasional hunter's shot, the forest around Marienthron was usually silent. Once, a couple of curious boys from Grimma had scaled the wall, but when Sol pulled out his knife, the kids scrambled back over the wall and never returned.

The steady whine of the whistle grew louder, and Sol squinted as a cloud of dust billowed up in the distance. Someone was coming down the road.

He realized in an instant that he wasn't hearing a whistle. It was a siren. Sirens. And they were drawing closer.

Ignoring the pain in his leg, he raced to the end of the hall and pounded on Phoebe's door. She flung it open, fear etched in her face. He had never seen her terrified before.

"I need you to ring the bells."

Phoebe stepped into the hall. "Three times?"

"Yes." He stepped away from the door. "And get the fire."

Her left eye twitched. "You want me to burn everything?"

"Everything." This time they wouldn't leave behind a mountain of paperwork like they'd done in Heidelberg.

He grabbed her arm as she turned. "Is Michael back?"

Phoebe shook her head. "I don't know."

"Find him," he shouted as she rushed away. He needed Michael to sweep the house while he locked Sara and Elise away. Then they would open the front gate to the police.

He glanced down at his robe. He'd have to change into his suit as well.

Lily ran out of a nearby room and when she saw Sol's face, she rushed back inside. If the family could stay calm, they could get through this. No problem. They'd drilled for a crisis like this a hundred times. Everyone had a specific task, a specific place to be. In minutes, the compound would resemble a peaceful retreat center. An oasis.

Sol rushed back toward Sara's room. He'd thought that Elise's loyalty to her sister would stop her from causing a scene at the bank. What had she said to the authorities? And why in the world hadn't Michael stopped her?

The sirens grew louder.

It didn't matter what she said. He wasn't playing her game. They had escaped the scrutiny of the world and its petty laws over and over. And they'd do it again.

When he walked back through Sara's door, she recoiled. He didn't have time to revel in her fear. Instead, he slipped his knife out of its sheath and slit the bandanas from her wrists and ankles. She screamed as blood dripped from her skin, and he slapped her for her weakness. It was only a small nick compared to the chasms she'd already carved into her arms herself.

He ripped the bandanas off the bed frame and stuffed them into his pocket. Then he pushed her out the door with the cat in her arms. The bells in the tower gonged their warning.

From the front window, he could see a line of gray and green cars outside the gate.

For an instant he was thirteen years old and back in Texas, the police kicking down his front door and hauling his father off to prison. The strength he'd seen in his father disintegrated that day. His father had not even fought as the pigs handcuffed him and dragged him away.

When his father died in jail five years later, Sol had vowed that he would never let anyone control his life . . . or his death.

He shoved Sara down the hallway. She didn't squirm in his grasp, but the cat's cries intensified as they rushed toward the kitchen. When it was time for him to go, it would be glorious—a blaze like Germany had never seen before.

A side door opened, and Sol banged his bad leg against the leg of a table when he turned to look. He groaned. How had the police gotten inside? He hadn't unlocked the gate.

But instead of the police, it was Michael who walked through the door. His hand was clasped firmly onto Elise's shoulder, and when she turned to look at Sol, he saw hope flicker in her eyes.

"What happened?" Sol demanded over the cat's cries.

"I have no idea."

The intercom from the gate buzzed.

"Did you lock the gate?" Sol demanded.

"Of course."

Sol shoved Sara toward Michael. "Take her too!"

Michael wrapped his fingers around Sara's arm as Sol pointed to the pantry door. "Inside!"

When Michael hesitated, Sol pushed them with his cane. Then he stepped back and smoothed his robe before tapping the intercom button. "Yes?"

The man at the other end mumbled something in German.

"English, *bitte*," Sol replied.

He heard a shuffle, and someone else came to the box. "This is Sergeant Braun. We have several questions for you."

"About what?"

"We are searching for a missing person."

Sol stepped back. Elise had lied to him again. Someone was looking for her, and their search had led them to Marienthron.

He cleared his throat and hit the button again.

"Everyone here is a resident, sir."

"Could you please come to the gate?"

"Certainly." He paused. "I'll be right there."

He turned and rushed back toward the pantry, flinging the light on when he opened the door. Rahab had tried to take them down once. He wouldn't let her daughter do the same. He would punish Elise later, but right now he needed her to walk. Fast.

He took the ring of keys out of his pocket and unlocked the small door at the back of the pantry. As soon as it was opened, Michael thrust Elise and Sara ahead of him and forced them down the stone stairs. The cat whined in Sara's arms.

Sol followed Michael and the two sisters down the staircase. At the bottom of the steps, a metal gate blocked the entrance to a dark tunnel, and Sol unlocked it. This cold underbelly had been one of Marienthron's selling points. His family was well acquainted with its walls.

Michael shoved the two girls into the tunnel, and Sara stumbled onto the damp floor. She grabbed Michael's pant leg and held the cat up. "He's hurt."

Michael backed away.

Her eyes pleaded with him. "He'll die down here."

"You're right," Sol said, grabbing the cat from her arms. He didn't need a howling cat to alert the police.

He slammed the gate shut, stuffed the key in his pocket, and shuffled back up the stairs behind Michael. He threw the cat on the pantry floor and rushed toward his office.

Inside, Phoebe had kindled a roaring fire in the fireplace and was dumping papers into the blaze. Sol grimaced when he saw the fire devouring his meticulous records. Turning to his desk, he unlocked the bottom drawer, pulled out two more files, and tossed them into the flames. The buzzer from the front gate rang again.

If the police had evidence against him, they'd get a warrant. Otherwise, he would open the gate when he was ready.

Chapter 44

THE LIGHT FADED INTO a dark blanket, enveloping Elise and Sara in the thick, cold air. Elise shook the gate, screamed for Sol and Michael to come back, but her pleas only reverberated off the walls of the tunnel. Sol would never leave her alone down here with Sara . . . unless he didn't plan to come back. And why should he return? He'd gotten what he wanted—money and revenge. His work was complete.

She pounded her hands against the metal. King Sol had buried them alive.

"Sara?" She reached out in the darkness, and her boots slipped on the mossy floor as she stepped forward. "Where are you?"

She heard breathing to her right. She turned and moved toward the sound. The Chosen had sucked the life out of her mother, but she could still save Sara . . . if she could convince her to fight.

When she reached out again, she felt Sara's hair, and she crouched down beside her.

"Leave me alone," Sara whispered.

"We're going to get out of here." She wrapped her fingers over her sister's sweaty hands and massaged them, trying to infuse life back into her body. Sara didn't respond.

Elise sank down on the wet floor, cold muck seeping through her jeans, chilling her skin. The dankness infiltrated her nose and lungs as she breathed deeply, trying to steady her racing heart. Even stale oxygen was better than none. As long as she had air, she could figure a way out of this tunnel.

She clenched her jaw to silence her chattering teeth. Had Sol locked them into a crypt?

She didn't really know much about crypts. In the old abbeys, people were usually buried in the walls or the floor . . . weren't they? Only a few of the old Catholic churches actually piled bones below ground. There wouldn't be any bones . . . unless Sol had locked other people down here before them.

She shivered, rubbing her hands over her arms.

This wasn't a crypt. The crypt would be below the chapel, and they were under the kitchen. This was probably a wine cellar. Or a medieval refrigerator.

Her eyes tried to adjust to the darkness, but she couldn't even make out shadows. She blinked again and again as her eyes searched for a hint of light. No windows or cracks in the foundation. Just a deep, dark tomb.

She crunched her arms to her chest.

Yesterday, she'd been a woman on a mission, eating croissants at a café and asking questions about her mother. Today, she was trapped under an old convent by a man who clearly wanted her dead. Her very core had been shaken, and here she was, thousands of miles from home, just trying to stay alive.

The sound of dripping water echoed around the room. Her brain was already groggy from lack of sleep. Her body was numb. She flattened her palms on the wet floor. It would be easy to lie down on the soggy mattress and succumb to the darkness. But she was afraid that if she fell asleep in this cold, she might not wake up again.

She gulped another deep breath. It was a miserable attempt to calm her nerves. The air chilled her skin just like the night . . . just like the night her mother had picked her up from her bed and ran.

"*I'll never let you go.*"

Elise flinched as the memory flooded back.

She clung to her mother's neck in the darkness. For hours, they hid in the brush as people stomped by, calling her name over and over. Her mother put her fingers over her lips.

"*What about Sara?*" *she asked as they finally paddled across the river.*

"Don't worry," her mother whispered. *"I'll go back and get her."*

"Right now?"

She shook her head. "Very soon."

A rush of adrenaline warmed her. Her mother had loved her. And she had loved Sara, even if she had never been able to rescue her youngest daughter.

Water splashed on the floor beside her, and she leapt to her feet. She may have lost her mom, but she wasn't going to lose Sara. This time they were going to escape together.

"We're going to get out of here," she told Sara.

The girl took a deep breath. "Are you really my sister?"

"I think so."

"Our mother ran away from God."

"She ran away from Sol." Elise pressed her fingers against the stone wall and searched for a break. "She knew that in order to truly serve God, she had to get out of the Chosen."

"There is only one way to God," Sara replied, her voice flat.

Elise nodded even though Sara couldn't see her. "The way is through Jesus Christ."

"And his messengers."

Elise paused. "That's not in the Bible."

Sara's breath sounded shallow. "We have to prove our love to him."

Elise murmured a silent prayer for wisdom. She'd never been good at sharing her faith—she preferred demonstrating God's love through her actions rather than through her words. Yet now wasn't the time to shrink back. She had to share the truth.

"There is nothing we can do to earn God's love, Sara," Elise explained as she leaned back against the cold stone.

"That's not true," Sara muttered, but Elise heard the longing in her voice. She desperately needed to see the purity and compassion of God's love. And the freedom that only he could give her.

"He already loves you, Sara. You can't do anything to make him love you more, and you don't have to destroy your body to prove your devotion."

"But . . ."

Water dripped on Elise's forehead, and she brushed it off. "Being a child of the Chosen does not get you into the kingdom of heaven, but being a child of God does."

"Sol said—"

"Our mother learned that Sol was not speaking with God's authority. He was only using the Bible to get what he wanted."

Elise crossed her arms over her chest. If only she could expunge the anguish from Sara's heart and burn it. This was a girl who had grown up believing that Sol was the voice of God, a messenger of his love. Her entire life, she'd been told that following Sol was the way to God. That she had to act a certain way in order to please Sol. And when she pleased Sol, she pleased God.

It didn't matter what he said—she had to obey. Disobedience was penalized swiftly and painfully. Not believing was the ultimate sin.

Sara had no idea what it really meant to have Jesus die for her. Sol had stepped into the place of Christ, and she had had to sacrifice her body in an attempt to win his love. The thing was, Sol could never offer the peace that her heart desired. Or genuine love.

Elise tried again. "Sol is not loving to you."

"But he demonstrates God's love to us."

"The reason he doesn't want the world involved with your group is because he knows that the world would punish him for what he does to you and the other girls."

Elise remembered the verse from Mark and she quoted it. "*Whosoever shall offend one of these little ones that believe in me, it is better for him that a millstone were hanged around his neck, and he were cast into the sea.*"

A sob escaped Sara's lips.

"It's not your fault," Elise whispered.

Sara moaned. "Why did she leave me with him?"

"She didn't want to leave you, Sara." Elise rubbed her hands on her sleeves. "She planned to take us both."

"But why didn't she come back?"

Elise hesitated. "I don't know." She squeezed her eyes shut. If their mother could figure out how to escape, then so would they. She would get Sara out before Sol destroyed her.

She opened her eyes and squinted into the darkness. Surely Sol wouldn't have put them in a place where they could escape . . . unless he didn't have time to find another hiding place. Or maybe he didn't think they would crawl back into the tunnel.

With her hands stretched out in front of her, she shuffled along the wall, cringing as her fingers brushed over the slimy surface.

She stopped and listened for any scurrying of little feet. It was silent, except for the steady patter of water on the ground.

As she inched away from Sara, the bumpy rock turned smooth, and her knee cracked against a flat stone. She scooted around it, telling herself it was a bench instead of a tomb.

She turned her head back toward Sara. "I'm going to find a way out." Sara didn't respond.

"Are you okay?" she asked the darkness. Even if Sara thought she didn't need Elise, Elise needed the comfort of Sara's voice.

Elise took a step toward the opposite side of the tunnel. Sara may have given up, but she wasn't going to surrender. She inched past the blocks of stone or concrete and pretended that she was back at the Holocaust memorial in Berlin, just trying to find the best way out.

When she slid her toe forward again, there was some sort of hole. She bent down on her knees and felt the open space in front of her. Her heart pounded faster. Maybe this was the tunnel that Katharina had used when she ran away from the abbey.

"I've found something." Her words echoed off the walls. "I think it's a staircase."

"It doesn't go anywhere."

Elise tried to steady her voice. "You've been down here before?"

Sara didn't answer.

"Is there another way out?" Elise wanted to shake the girl, convince her to fight for her life. Her freedom.

"There's a door." Sara hesitated. "But it's locked."

Chapter 45

CARSON STOOD OUTSIDE the wall at Marienthron and paced along the gravel, waiting for someone to unlock the front gate. The Chosen had been stalling for almost a half hour—plenty of time for them to hide Elise and dispose of decades worth of evidence.

He stepped back and stuck his head through the open window of the car. Addison was in the front seat, spilling her story to a reporter at *Der Spiegel*.

The police captain had been skeptical of Addison's story when they returned to the station, until she explained that she was going to call a national news magazine. Then he suddenly decided to knock on the gate to see if Elise was there. If Sol refused entrance, he said he would petition for a warrant to search the convent.

One of the four police officers on the scene pushed the intercom button beside the gate yet again and waited. When no one answered, Carson's fingers curled over a rock jutting out from the wall. It would take him less than five minutes to scale it and be inside. The police might frown on his entering without permission, but it wasn't like they hadn't given the Chosen plenty of time to open the gate.

He was about to pull himself up onto the rock when he felt a hand on his shoulder.

"He's coming," Addison said, nodding toward the gate.

Carson released his hold and dropped to the ground.

A grim-faced man hobbled toward the gate with the help of a cane. He wore a tailored suit, but there was nothing else tailored about him. His messy black tie coiled like a snake around his neck, his head was bald, and his unruly beard reminded Carson of a picture he'd once seen of Moses after he'd descended from Mount Sinai.

"Good afternoon." The man greeted the collection of officers with the carved tip of his cane. Strong body odor wafted through the iron rails. "I'm Solomon Lucien."

An English-speaking officer stepped toward the gate. "We are looking for an American tourist."

Sol feigned concern. "Near here?"

"We suspect she may be inside Marienthron."

The man shrugged his shoulders. "Many pilgrims stop here to rest and renew their spirits."

"We want to search for her."

"The only reason we lock the gate is to keep out trespassers." Sol pulled a key out of his pocket, stuck it into the lock, and snapped open the padlock. "Everyone is here at their request."

Carson stepped forward. "Not Elise."

Sol turned toward him. "Who?"

He wanted to knock the smirk off the man's face. "Where's Elise Friedman?"

"I'm sorry." The man flashed his yellowed teeth. "I don't know of anyone by that name."

Sol turned back toward Sergeant Braun. "I have nothing to hide."

Trees loped over the stone buildings on the inside of the compound. The bushes had been trimmed, and dark red and white chrysanthemums lined the walkways. The cops fanned out in the courtyard to search, and Carson tailed two of them through the arched cloister, under a portico, and into a musty residential hall.

Inside the first room, a man sat on a bed reading his Bible. He nodded at Carson and then looked back down at the book. In the next room, another man was writing in a notebook. At the far end of the hall, a kid peeked out of another door and ducked back inside.

The police strode toward the stairwell and glanced into the rooms along the hallway. Carson didn't know what they were expecting to find—maybe Elise, with her feet propped up, reading a novel on one of the beds.

If she was reading, it wouldn't be casually. When he'd seen her at the bank, she had looked terrified—probably for both Sara and herself.

The hallway was as quiet as a convent, the people contemplative. If he didn't know the truth about this group, he would think it was some type of Zen retreat center.

The police tromped up the staircase at the end of the hallway, but Carson pushed open the back door and walked out into the fresh air. In front of him were the remains of a brick walkway. There were two other gray buildings in the compound and next to him was a stone church with three arched windows and a crumbled bell tower. The church was tiny compared to the cathedrals in Berlin, and missing were the lavish domes and columns from the Baroque era.

This design was simple. Plain.

He walked toward the open doors of the church and slipped inside. While he didn't expect the grandeur of the Berliner Dom, he thought he would find rows of pews along with a relief of Jesus and a carved altar in front.

But the interior of this church had been stripped; the pews were gone. Even the altar was in shambles. If there'd ever been any sculptures along the walls, the Stasi—East Germany's secret police—had probably destroyed it in the 1970s. The only color was the faded blue and copper tiles that had once been an aisle.

Something moved in his peripheral vision, and he turned. Beside him was the man who'd escorted Elise to Grimma.

The man stepped forward, his eyes focused on the front. "Why are you here?"

"I'm trying to find my friend, Elise."

The man shook his head. "I can't help you."

Carson tried to control his frustration. "Where did you take her after the bank?"

The man continued to stare at the front of the church, his lips moving as if he was praying.

"We're not going to leave until we find her," Carson insisted. "And you'll be prosecuted for kidnapping."

The man turned slowly toward him. "Kidnapping involves taking someone against their will."

Carson wiped the sweat from his forehead. "She doesn't belong here."

"Maybe God is pursuing her."

Carson pushed his foot over a cracked piece of tile. Arguing would never convince this man that his group wasn't of God. And if he pulled the sympathy card, the man might shut him down.

He opted for the raw truth. "She's trying to help her sister."

The man hesitated. "Sara?"

Carson nodded.

The man glanced toward the windows and then leaned back against the wall. "Sara is sick."

Carson steadied his voice. "What's wrong?"

"She needs a doctor."

Carson scanned the room. "Do you know where she is?"

The man pushed away from the wall and stomped toward the front of the church and up the steps. When he knelt down, he stretched out his hands until his forehead hit the ground.

Minutes passed as Carson prayed that God would soften the man's heart. Like his mother, most of the people here had probably joined the Chosen because they truly thought they were following Christ. Carson hoped that this man still had the desire within him to demonstrate the love of Christ to Sara . . . and to Elise.

Slowly, the man rose, turned around, and marched back down the stairs. He didn't say anything as he passed Carson, but in his silence was the invitation to follow him.

Carson didn't hesitate. He tailed him to the side of the chapel and into a smaller anteroom. At the side were two carrels that were probably once used as study bays. In the center of the floor was a staircase.

The man motioned to the steps, and Carson followed him down the short flight. The walls were stone, and on each side were empty alcoves that once held vases or sculptures.

The man plucked a flashlight off one of the shelves and then reached inside his shirt, pulling out a key that was attached to a leather strap. He slipped the strap over his head, and as he pointed the key toward the lock, someone on the other side yelled for help. He dropped the key.

Carson dove toward him. "Hurry."

The man tossed him the flashlight, and Carson leaned down to help him look for the key. When the man stood back up, his fingers shook.

"You're doing the right thing," Carson whispered.

The man stared at the wooden door, frozen. "*We walk by faith, not by sight.*"

"God would want you to save Sara."

The man's shoulders slumped. "I don't know what to do."

Carson closed his eyes, trying to recall the verse in Matthew. "Jesus said that whatever you do for the least of these, you do for him."

The man turned, unlocked the door, and shoved Carson toward the abyss. Carson looked back at him and then into the darkness. It would be a cinch to lock him inside.

Chapter 46

ELISE'S SCREAMS ECHOED around the tunnel as she pounded her fists against the locked door. She twisted the handle, shoving the wood with her shoulder and knee, but it wouldn't budge. She yelled again, hoping that the policemen had infiltrated the convent and would hear her cries.

If the police didn't hear her, she would keep searching for another door or shaft or vent leading out of here. Sara might have given up, but she wasn't going to stop until she found a way out.

Blood rushed to her head as she shouted into the darkness. Sol's madness had already taken her mother's life. He was not going to take hers and her sister's as well.

She shrieked again, the sound echoing around her. It was the sound of fear. Hope. Life.

"They won't be able to hear you," Sara said from the other side of the room.

Elise took a deep breath and faced the direction of her sister. She could understand hesitation or anger, but she couldn't comprehend her apathy. If she'd ever been compelled to fight, she'd lost it.

"Don't you want to get out of this place?"

Sara paused. "I like the quiet."

Elise wanted to shake her. Without food and warmth, they would die in this tunnel, and Sara was enjoying the solitude.

"You don't have to go back to Sol." Elise stepped toward her. "You can come with me."

Sara hesitated. "I can't leave him."

"Yes, you can. When all this is over, you can walk right out the front door."

"He's my husband," she insisted.

"Would you *choose* to marry a man like him?"

"I don't know," Sara muttered.

"What Sol has done to you is wrong."

Sara began to sob, and Elise edged back toward her sister and sat down. She reached out in the darkness and Sara leaned against her shoulder, her tears soaking through Elise's turtleneck.

Elise smoothed her hand over Sara's hair. "It's not your fault."

"But I let him . . ."

"You were a child."

She shuddered. "I couldn't make him stop."

Elise wanted to hug her and shake her at the same time. She would not let Sara punish herself for Sol's sin. Sara had been born into the Chosen, and the only way she knew to express her love for God was to submit to the man she'd been told was his messenger. She'd sacrificed everything with her devotion. Sacrificed for a man who didn't know how to love.

If her mother hadn't rescued her, Elise would be sitting here today like Sara—abused, tormented. Her nightmares were nothing compared to living every day within the Chosen.

A clanging noise echoed across the room, and Elise arched her back as the door at the back of the tunnel banged open. Was Sol coming back to torture them? Maybe he'd been waiting until the police left to finish his revenge.

Elise thrust her hands in front of her. If he tried to touch her, she would claw, pound, pummel him until he stopped.

A flashlight rounded the room, and she shielded her eyes as a man whispered her name.

She leapt to her feet. "Carson?"

"Thank God!"

She ran to him, and when he wrapped his arms around her, she didn't push him away.

"Are you sure you want me to rescue you?" he asked.

"Very funny."

He stepped back. "Because I don't want to get in your way."

"You were in my way most of this trip, Carson *Talles*."

He shrugged. "My mother's maiden name."

"You lied to me."

"I was trying to keep you out of trouble . . . which I obviously failed to do." Following Carson's gaze around the dark room, Elise noticed engravings on the stone walls.

"I'm still angry with you."

"Oh, no." He shook his head. "You can't turn this on me. I'm the one who's supposed to be angry with you, going inside the compound of a cult with no cell phone and absolutely no plan."

Another man edged around him, and she squinted to see his face. Michael.

She cringed and took a step back, but Michael didn't even look at her as he bolted toward Sara. When he reached her, he kneeled down and whispered in her ear.

Sara didn't move. "What about Rezon?"

"He's upstairs."

Michael tugged on her arm, but Sara still didn't stand.

"Sara?" Michael asked quietly at first and then he shook her. "Sara!"

Carson shined the beam of the flashlight over toward Michael, and he and Elise raced across the room. Sara had passed out in a pool of blood.

Chapter 47

MICHAEL'S WHITE SLEEVES turned red as he rushed Sara up the stairs and collapsed onto the church floor. Elise sat down beside him and held Sara's limp hand as she pushed the wet hair out of her sister's ashen face. Sara might want to give up on life, but Elise wouldn't let her go.

She would fight even if Sara didn't have the energy left. She couldn't lose her sister.

Carson tossed her his jacket and she wrapped it over Sara as he called for help on his cell.

Michael wiped his eyes with the back of his hand and cradled her in his arms. "She can't die."

"She won't," Elise said as she prayed that Sara's body would struggle to survive, even if her mind had lost its will to live.

Michael slipped his hand into Sara's front pocket and pulled out a key. Tears dripped down his cheeks. "She could have gotten out."

Elise turned toward him. "What?"

"She had the key to the gate and the pantry door." He waved it in front of Elise's face and then crushed it in his hand. "I thought she would escape."

Elise fell back against the wall. Sara had had the key, yet she had chosen to stay in the dark dungeon where she would be safe from Sol . . . and Michael.

Sara had probably never known what it was like to be loved. The people who were supposed to love her had hurt her instead. Sol had abused her, and Michael had helped him. It must have seemed as if God had disappeared.

"Does she know that you love her?" she asked him.

His head dropped. "No."

"It's too bad," she muttered as she stared at the man who had helped Sol assault her sister. The man who had tied Sara to a bed. The man who had given his life to someone who claimed to be a messenger of God. Someday he would wake up and realize he had been serving the wrong master. God help him when he did.

The door of the crypt banged below them, and Elise jumped. She did a quick head count—Michael, Sara, Carson. She leaned over the stone staircase and saw Sol hobbling up the steps.

Without thinking, she stepped toward Carson. Sol might be coming for her and Sara, but she wasn't going to let him lock her back into one of his rooms.

"The ambulance will be here soon," Carson whispered. She prayed that Sara would hang on until the medics arrived.

Sol ignored her and Carson as he stared at the blood on Michael's sleeves. "It's time to ascend."

When Michael didn't move, Sol held out his arms. "I'll take her."

Michael's glance ricocheted between Sol and Sara. For a moment, Elise thought he might actually hand Sara over to Sol, but instead he rested his hand on her forehead. "She's going to the hospital."

Sol stepped toward him. "God's calling her home."

Michael thrust his bloody arm toward Sol. "Just like he called her to be pregnant?"

Elise shuddered at his words. A child bearing another child in the name of God. And this man who purported to know God had tied her to a bed and locked her in a crypt when she was carrying a baby.

Michael stood up, clasping Sara in his arms. "She needs a doctor."

Sol spoke with slow, deliberate words. "God has entrusted Sara to my care, and you will not question how I implement the plan for her life."

Elise cleared her throat. "What about God's plan for her life?"

Sol glared at her for an instant and then focused back on Michael. "I want you downstairs."

When Michael turned to walk away, Sol reached for the leather sheath around his waist and drew out a hunting knife. The steel tip gleamed in a shaft of fading sunlight.

Elise stood tall as a steady calm suppressed her fear. She wasn't going to run and leave Sara behind. A quick glance at Carson told her he wasn't going to run either.

Michael turned to face Sol, his voice quaking. "What are you doing?"

Sol brandished the knife toward him. "You betrayed me."

Michael hugged Sara to his chest. "I won't let you hurt her again."

Sol lunged forward, and Michael swept Sara to the side.

"Traitor," Sol seethed.

Carson edged to the right of Sol. He twirled his finger slightly, and she nodded at his signal to distract Sol.

Her voice trembled. "The police are going to arrest you, Sol."

He sneered and pointed the knife at her. "The police are already gone."

Carson's shoe scraped on the stone floor, and when Sol turned to face him again, the blade glinted in the meager light. He thrust the knife at Carson's head. "Not another step."

None of them moved until Addison Wade stepped out of the shadows.

"Put down the knife," Addison said. Her eyes were locked on Sol, her voice calm but razor sharp. "You're not going to hurt any of these kids."

Sol didn't blink, but disbelief slowly registered on his face when he turned to face her.

"Tirzah," he spat. "And I always thought Rahab would be the one to come back."

She ignored his taunt.

"You don't want Sara." Addison edged toward him. "You've already destroyed her."

Elise glanced at Carson and watched his head volley back and forth like he was trying to determine the distance between Sol's knife and his mother.

"Are you volunteering to take Sara's place?" Sol scoffed.

Addison didn't waver. "You're going to prison, Sol."

"I'm not going anywhere."

Carson leapt forward, and with a swift kick, he knocked Sol's cane from his hand. Sol swore as he watched his cane skitter across the floor.

"Don't move." Sol flashed his knife at Carson.

Dragging his bum leg behind him, Sol crawled toward his cane, but before he could reach it, Addison scooped it up from the ground.

Silence engulfed the room as Sol struggled to stand on one foot. Elise glanced around and wondered where the rest of the family had hidden. Why weren't they all wielding guns beside Sol, demanding that Sara be returned to the fold?

Either they had deserted him or they were preparing to defend their leader.

The old man lurched toward Addison, his eyes blazing. "Give me the cane."

"Sit down, Sol."

The knife shook in his hand, but his voice was defiant. "I'm King Solomon."

Sara moaned, and when Addison whirled to look at her, Sol lunged again. Elise screamed, and the ambassador sidestepped Sol's advance and swung the cane at his head. The sharp crack of wood against his skull echoed through the chapel.

Elise gasped and her hand enveloped her mouth as Sol stumbled sideways. He struggled to regain his balance, but his bad leg faltered beneath him. Face forward, he pitched down the stone staircase.

Elise rushed over, but it was too late. King Solomon lay in a crumpled heap at the bottom of the stairs.

Addison took charge. "We need another ambulance," she instructed. Carson was already dialing his cell phone.

"You." She pointed at Michael. "Take Sara out to the front gate and wait for the medics." Michael nodded and clung to Sara as he backed away from the staircase.

Addison spun toward Elise. "And you—"

Elise patted the ambassador's shaking arm. "Breathe, Mrs. Wade."

Addison took a deep breath and then they both looked down at the lifeless form at the bottom of the stairs. King Sol's power didn't exist outside this compound . . . and certainly not outside this world. Even he would have to bow down.

"You asked me once who your birth father was," Addison whispered.

Elise felt sick to her stomach. She had wanted answers, but not like this. She didn't want the truth anymore.

"Please tell me it was a pilot from Montana."

Addison pulled her close. "Steve loves you like a father should."

Chapter 48

AS DARKNESS FILLED the arched windows on both sides of the sanctuary, Addison placed her hands on Elise's shoulders and swung her away from the staircase. She wished she could modify the truth and make Elise's birth father a kind, loving man who was thrilled to find out he had a daughter. She wished she could change a lot of things, but at least Elise had an adoptive father who loved her more than someone like Sol ever could, and a mother who had risked her life to get her away from the abuse.

"Are you going to be okay?" she asked.

Elise nodded.

She pointed toward the open door. "Why don't you go check on Sara?"

Elise glanced down at Sol one last time and then turned and rushed out of the room.

Addison picked up a flashlight from the ground, and shined the light across the tile floor of the church. With her back pressed against the plaster wall, she reveled in the silence.

The man she'd despised for most of her life was gone, and he'd left behind a houseful of wounded men and women. But the destruction would end here, in this old church, in the place he had deemed his kingdom.

She stepped slowly down the staircase, avoiding a small puddle of blood near Solomon's head. She wanted to see him one last time before they took him away. Just to make sure he was really gone.

His body was contorted and his eyes stared blankly at the ceiling. His mouth circled as if he'd screamed his last breath.

She stepped over the body and through the doorway, scouring the dungeon with the light. In front of her lay the entrance to a rocky tunnel, layered with browns and gray, brick and plaster. On the other side of the room hung a wooden cross, and under it was a row of concrete tombs. To her right, she saw a faded mural of Jesus dying on the cross, and etched at her feet were engravings. Burial plots. A padlock dangled from an iron gate on the other side of the room.

She shone her light toward a brick archway and maneuvered past the tombs. Inside a smaller anteroom was another staircase in the floor, and she shined her flashlight down into the crypt's lower level.

With a quick glance behind her, she stepped onto the narrow stone stairs and went down.

There was no door to this level. Just a plain entrance leading into a room with a low ceiling and dark nubs along the wall. There weren't any murals in this crypt, but like the upper level, the floor was carved with engravings.

To one side of the room were four metal filing cabinets, hardly relics left over from the medieval era.

She walked toward them and yanked open one of the top drawers. Inside was a row of manila files, and each file was labeled with a biblical name. Elijah. Elon. Ephron. Esther. Eve. All people who had once lived in Frankfurt or Heidelberg or Marienthron and had been transferred to other missions around the world.

She'd known Sol was meticulous, but she'd never imagined he would keep a file on every person in the group.

A black line crossed out Eve's name, and she tugged a sheaf of papers out of the file. It was a biography of a girl named Sally Toplin before she joined the Chosen in 1989. Originally from Arkansas, Sally had joined the cult during a spring break in Florida. Listed were her bank account numbers, her home telephone, and the names of her family members. At the end of the profile, someone had scribbled in ink that she'd died in Berlin.

Tragic.

Addison slipped the file back and opened the drawer above it. She thumbed through the B files until she found the one she was looking for.

Bethesda.

She whipped open the folder and began skimming the details.

Bethesda's real name was Nadine Alcott, born in Beverly Hills to a wealthy family. She joined the Chosen during her freshman year at Loyola Marymount and traveled with the group when they moved their commune from Southern California to Europe. Her mother was an actress and her father was an executive in the entertainment industry.

Nadine had one child. Catrina. Father unknown. She died in 1985.

Listed at the end of her profile was her personal information—bank account, address, and home telephone in California. She folded the sheet of paper and slipped it into her pocket.

She heard footsteps in the tunnel, and she stuffed the file back into the cabinet so the police wouldn't think she was tampering with evidence. Two boys raced around the corner, and when they saw her, they froze and began to back away.

"What are you doing?" she asked.

They glanced at each other, and the older one stepped forward. He couldn't have been more than nine or ten, but the determination in his eyes made him look like a man.

"Ascending," he said bravely.

She remembered the ascension drills from Frankfurt. Sol would blare a siren in the middle of the night, and they would all rush out to the barn.

She hesitated. "Can I practice with you?"

The boy shook his head. "Only people who are part of our family are allowed to go."

"I joined the Chosen in Frankfurt," she assured them, "but no one ever showed me this drill."

He stared at her like he was trying to determine whether she was telling the truth. "Has he chosen you?"

"Father Paul chose me years ago." She leaned down and whispered, *"For many are called, but few are chosen."*

The boys stepped toward the alcove behind the filing cabinets. "Should we wait for the rest of them?"

Addison shined her light in front of them. There was a hump on the ground, covered by a ratty army blanket. On top of the blanket was a small black box with a switch.

A bomb.

Knowing Sol, it was probably dirty enough to collapse the cellar and poison everyone above them. And he'd probably shown the youngest members of the family how to detonate it.

The oldest boy took a step toward the bomb, and Addison choked back the anxiety in her voice.

"We should definitely wait," she said with authority. "Sol would want us to do this as a family."

"But no one else is around," the younger one insisted.

Addison thought for an instant, watching the older boy's hand. If he got any closer to the bomb, she'd have to tackle him, and who knows what type of self-defense moves he'd learned from Sol. It wouldn't be pretty.

"We need to go find them first," she said to the older boy. "Sol wants us to stay together until the end."

He nodded. "The very end."

"Exactly." She thumped her fist in her palm. "We can't let the world win."

"We will conquer them," he said.

She motioned toward the door. "As a family."

Chapter 49

ELISE FOUGHT THE current as she ducked her head under the dark water. She had to get to Sara before she drowned. She had to rescue her sister.

"Swim, Johanna," a voice commanded, still and strong.

She pushed through the water. The monster thrashed against her as she fought; its scales cut her arms and legs. But she wouldn't let go until he gave up Sara.

The water suddenly stilled, and a white light overpowered the darkness. The monster twisted as if in pain and cowered toward the edge of the river like it was afraid of the light.

Peace surged through her heart. Relief.

The light grew brighter and brighter, and the monster disappeared.

When Elise opened her eyes, she saw gold striped wallpaper and the outline of a dresser at the foot of her bed. A double-layer curtain covered the window, and the only light in the room was seeping under a door to her right.

She was in a hotel suite. In Grimma. Addison and Carson had brought her here to rest. She had taken a hot shower and collapsed into bed while they visited Sara in the hospital.

She closed her eyes again, and the details came rushing back. The crypt. The knife. The horrible sound of wood and bone. The revelation about her birth father. She shuddered. No wonder her mother had tried to hide her past.

In the dim light, she looked at the clock on the nightstand. Six-thirty. Was it morning or night? Not that she really cared—as long as she wasn't in Marienthron.

She rubbed her eyes, wondering how long she'd slept. It felt like days.

She turned on the bedside lamp and saw clothes draped over a chair. Someone had replaced her wet jeans with a dry pair, and they had left a clean T-shirt and cardigan.

She dressed slowly and brushed her teeth in the sink before she ambled over to the door. It opened onto a small sitting area.

She flinched when she saw a man at the corner of the room, slumped in one of the chairs, but when she took another step, she saw a suede cowboy hat crushed in his lap.

"Dad?" she whispered.

Steve Friedman opened his eyes slowly, and his hat fell to the floor when jumped out of his chair. "Hey, sweetie, are you okay?"

"I think so." She hadn't felt so rested since she'd left Virginia. "How did you get here?"

"I was already at JFK when Addison called."

"But you hate to fly . . ."

He took her hand and squeezed it. "What were you thinking, Elise?"

"I'm sorry, Daddy."

She looked into her dad's brown eyes, full of concern and love. How could she have doubted his love for her for a second? He'd flown all the way to Germany to be with her, even though he despised both airports and airplanes.

He made her sit on the couch before he walked to the kitchenette to fill a glass of water. He handed her the water, and she took a long sip.

"I always thought it was my fault that Mom died," she said as he sat down beside her. "Like I could have saved her if I hadn't left the house or if I'd only come back sooner."

He shook his head. "It was never your fault."

"And then when I found out she committed suicide . . ."

His head dropped. "You weren't supposed to know that."

"But I did. And then I really thought it was my fault."

"Never, honey."

"Now I understand what happened to Mom, and what happened to me." She paused. "Though I still don't understand what happened to Sara."

He reached for his hat and fumbled with it. "You know most of the story now."

She pulled a blanket over her legs. "But I want to hear the rest from you."

He took a deep breath. "The night she ran away, your mom took you to a church in Heidelberg. She begged the minister to go back and get Sara, but he convinced her to wait until morning. When they returned with the police, they found the group had vanished during the night and had taken Sara with them."

No wonder the house in Heidelberg was such a wreck . . . and why they left all those papers behind.

"Your mother went back to Germany six times to search for Sara, but Sol had hidden her well."

She twisted her hands under the blanket. "The death certificate said Mom overdosed on drugs and alcohol."

"She overdosed on a medication for depression, but we don't know that she was trying to kill herself."

"What else would it be?"

"The Chosen destroyed Catrina from the inside out." He cleared his throat. She couldn't imagine how hard it must be for him to talk about losing his wife.

"She wrestled with depression and regret and guilt for leaving Sara with Sol, and guilt for what she did while she was part of the Chosen." He curled the edges of the hat. "I've always believed that she was just trying to drown out the pain and went too far. I don't think she intended to kill herself."

"You should have told me this before!"

Steve tried to smile, but his mouth quivered. "She wanted to leave the Chosen far behind and offer you the opportunity to live free—even of the memories."

Elise slid forward, wrapped her arms around her dad's neck, and hugged him. She'd never been more grateful for the man who had picked her to be his daughter.

There was a knock at the door, and Steve walked over to open it.

When Carson stepped into the room, he held out a bouquet of roses and smiled at her. "I heard you had a rough week."

Her face felt warm as he handed her the flowers.

"Thanks, Carson."

Something squirmed under his fleece jacket, and a tiny white head peeked out. Carson pulled out the kitten and set it on the floor, his back leg secured in a fresh splint.

"Apparently the hospital staff isn't so fond of cats."

Elise stared at the kitten that Sara had taken to the cellar. He looked like a cleaned-up version of the one she'd found in Berlin. "What's his name?"

"Rezon." Carson smiled. "He's named after a prince in the Old Testament. An enemy of Solomon."

She knelt down and ran her fingers over the kitten's head as he nudged his nose into her leg. "Is Sara going to be okay?"

Carson sat down on a chair and leaned back. "She's recovering."

"The baby?"

He shook his head, and the emotions swelled inside her. She was angry at Sol for what he did to Sara. Sad for the baby who never got a chance at life. Terrified for Sara who would have to deal with the same guilt as their mother had for not being able to save her baby.

And any relief Sara felt at losing Sol's child would only be another burden for her to carry.

Elise picked up Rezon and scratched the fur on his head.

It would be a long time before Sara was okay.

Chapter 50

THE PRESS CROWDED THE steps of the town hall in Grimma as Ambassador Addison Wade straightened her blazer and stepped onto the platform. Jack had called twenty or thirty times with major media requests, but she hadn't spoken to a reporter since she'd hung up the phone with the guy from *Der Spiegel*. The past four days had been spent at the hospital and on the telephone to just about everyone—except the media.

She cleared her throat as she moved to the microphone and clutched the podium. Hands popped up from the crowd, and she pointed to a man in the first row.

"What is the status of your confirmation for the UN?" he asked.

Addison straightened her shoulders and leaned into the microphone. "I've asked the White House to withdraw my nomination."

A flurry of cameras clicked, and she blinked. Within seconds, that sound bite would air around the world.

She picked a hand from the middle of the crowd, a woman in a navy suit and white blouse.

"What will you do next?"

Another deep breath. Another smile. "I've accepted the job of executive director of Hatzolah International, an organization dedicated to rescuing the hundreds of thousands of women and children forced into prostitution each year."

"Do you regret your decision to talk about your involvement in the Chosen?"

For an instant, she was back inside the compound, following the two boys upstairs to a cramped room on the second floor. Phoebe had vanished, along with most of the adults in the house, and they had left a roomful of scared children alone with the sirens and the police.

No wonder the boys had gone downstairs. It was the only thing left for them to do.

"The police rescued seven children from the Marienthron compound and are working to place them in safe homes. I could never regret securing their freedom."

A breeze rushed through the trees around the square and across the makeshift podium. Addison batted the hair out of her eyes as she pointed to another reporter.

"The police recently raided an illegal brothel in Berlin, allegedly operated by the Chosen."

"Yes," she replied. The police had gone in the same night that Sol's kingdom at Marienthron had crumbled.

"Why would a religious organization operate a brothel?" he asked.

"The Chosen is a cult, not a 'religious organization,' and the leadership viewed sex as the manifestation of God's love. They encouraged the women in the group to use their bodies to 'evangelize.'"

A reporter from the front row raised her hand and stopped to adjust her glasses before asking her question. "Does the Chosen support prostitution in their other homes around the world?"

"The brothel in Berlin was affiliated with the home in Grimma, but I hope the authorities will investigate other Chosen homes about their involvement in prostitution."

The woman's hand was still up. "One follow-up question."

Addison took a long sip of water from a plastic bottle. "Go ahead."

"Did you use your body to evangelize?"

She bristled. "No."

The woman ignored the other hands around her. "But you were married to the leader."

"It wasn't a legal marriage."

The woman typed something into her laptop. "But you thought he spoke to God?"

"I discovered later that he thought he *was* God."

"Were you a so-called Chosen Girl?"

"I believe I've already answered that question." She managed a smile. "Next?"

A reporter in the back shouted, "Do you know what is going to happen to these women?"

"My hope is that they will begin to recover at one of the Hatzolah homes scattered across Europe."

"What happened to the pimp in Berlin?" another reporter called out.

"I'll turn that question over to Sergeant Braun," Addison said as she stepped back from the microphone.

"A Polish national named Jozef Ogitzak was arrested at a border checkpoint this morning," the sergeant explained. "He is currently in jail and under investigation for human trafficking."

And for creating a dirty bomb, Addison thought, but the police wouldn't talk about that for a long time—if ever. They were more interested in how he had acquired the Cs-137 needed to make it.

Addison looked out over the crowd of cameras, microphones, and reporters as the police sergeant answered a rapid fire series of questions. Her story would top the news for days—sex, money, religion, and the U.S. ambassador.

The headlines should have been about her confirmation to the UN post, but she'd known the instant she placed the call to *Der Spiegel* that she would not be going to the UN. Even though she had left the Chosen twenty-five years ago, her name would forever be aligned with forced prostitution and a religious cult.

She had decided to do what she had hoped to do so many years before when she was part of the Chosen, back when she was an idealist. Her position with Hatzolah would give her the opportunity to rescue even more women and children.

She stepped toward the podium for one last question.

"Why did you decide to tell your story, Ambassador?"

She glanced across the square at the hotel where two women waited for her—one of them terrified of moving into the world; the other anxious to be home.

"I had no choice."

With a quick nod, she exited down the stairs and opened the door to the hall. She crossed the lobby, walked out a side door, and followed the street to the hotel.

Sara had left the hospital yesterday, but it would be a long time before she recovered from Sol's abuse. The man who had controlled every aspect of her life was now dead, and Michael, the one man who seemed to care about her, had disappeared after she was taken to the hospital.

When Addison sat down on a chair in the suite, Elise pushed a white bag and a latte across the coffee table.

Sara had what many of the other women didn't—a sister who loved her and a man who was willing to step in as her father and care for her as well. If she started fighting, she might be one of the survivors.

Addison took a sip of the coffee. She wanted to be finished with the questions yet there were still some unanswered ones in this room. "What do you want to know, Sara?"

The girl slowly petted the kitten, and Rezon purred as he nuzzled closer to her. "Why didn't she come back and get me?"

Addison wished she could take the girl in her arms and pet her sorrow away too. It was easy to console a kitten, but unfortunately, it wouldn't be as easy to comfort Sara.

"Your mother scoured Germany searching for you, Sara." She cleared her throat. "Sol had hidden you and the rest of the group at Marienthron."

Doubt still hung over Sara like a dark cloud. "Yes, ma'am."

Addison took her hand. "She loved you so much, Sara. She would have faced down Sol in a second to get you out."

Sara's eyes lowered. She didn't believe it, and why should she? No one had helped her before; at least, no one without an agenda.

Sara's voice cracked. "Where do I go now?"

Steve gave her an awkward smile. "Elise and I want you to come stay with us in Chesapeake . . . but Addison has another option that may be better for now."

Addison pulled out a file from her briefcase. "I found some information in Sol's records about your grandmother."

Elise's mouth dropped open, but Sara didn't move.

"Grandmother?" Elise asked.

"Her name was Nadine Alcott, and she joined the Chosen when she was in college." She smoothed her fingers across the table. "She was the first woman to go to Berlin."

Addison wished she could reach over and shut Elise's gaping mouth before she scared Sara. "Our grandmother was a prostitute?"

Addison cleared her throat and marveled at the fact that she was about to defend Bethesda. "She thought she was a missionary."

Sara didn't move, but the red in Elise's cheeks deepened. She turned toward Steve. "Did you know that?"

He looked down at the floor.

Elise shook her head. "What else should we know?"

"Nadine died in 1985, but your great-grandmother is still alive." Addison paused. "I had my assistant make some calls, and he located her in Malibu."

"Where's that?" Sara whispered.

Addison's heart ached for the girl who had never gone to school. "In the United States."

"What did she say?" Elise asked.

"She would very much like you both to come visit her."

Elise glanced at Steve, and he took her hand in his. "You should go."

"And she's invited Sara to come stay."

Addison leaned back and waited. She wouldn't even have told Sara about Teresa Alcott, except she had spent an hour on the phone with the woman, and discovered that she knew what to expect. Teresa was processing her own emotions, as well. She had been stunned by the revelation that her runaway daughter had a child and two grandchildren; and that the grandchildren were still alive.

After they'd lost their only child to the Chosen, the Alcotts had done extensive research on cults. Teresa knew it might take a long time for Sara to recover, but she also knew that recovery was possible.

Hours after Addison contacted her, Teresa had already lined up a counselor and a tutor to help Sara through the transition.

Sara turned toward her sister. "What should I do?"

Elise didn't hesitate. "Go to Malibu."

Sara looked down at the kitten one last time and then back up at Addison. Her eyes were full of trepidation. Fear.

"Carson's got the car out back, and when you're ready, he can take the three of you to the airport."

Sara's voice shook when she spoke again. "Rezon goes with me."

Addison nodded. "You bet he does."

Chapter 51

THE BREEZE BLEW Sara's bangs across her face, and she brushed back her hair to watch the deep blue water roll away from the rocks and collide with the horizon. She was thousands of miles away from Marienthron and Berlin and the Mulde River.

And she was scared.

For God hath not given us the spirit of fear; but of power, and of love, and of a sound mind.

More than anything, she needed a sound mind.

She sat down on a patio chair, and Rezon nudged her ankle. She reached down and picked him up so he could enjoy the view from Teresa's porch.

Rezon may not care about the view, but he sure liked Teresa. She had taken him to a veterinarian when they arrived, and the man had set his leg properly and given him some medicine. Sara had almost asked Teresa if the doctor would give her some medicine too, to ease her pain.

Her baby was gone, and so were Sol and Michael. Elise had flown with her to California, stayed overnight, and then she had left as well.

Her first day in Malibu, Sara had locked herself in her bedroom.

Teresa had knocked on her door from time to time with offers of food and sparkling water and juice, but mostly she had just let Sara rest. She'd huddled under the covers for hours, shocked at the light that streamed in around the edges of the curtains and amazed by the connecting bathroom that Teresa had said was just for her.

On the second day, she'd spent almost two hours soaking in the bathtub, relishing the hot water and the lavender aroma in the suds. Then she'd opened the closet, picked out a soft pale blue skirt and white blouse, and ventured out onto the balcony with Rezon to watch the ships in the distance.

By the third day, she had opened the door of her bedroom and peeked into the hallway. Teresa's house was almost as big as Marienthron, but there were no dark corners or crypts or raging fires. She crept out to the living room and then ran back to the safety of her room.

For her entire life, she had been living in the darkness with Sol while there was so much light on the other side of the world. He had never let her see the light. She shivered in her short sleeve blouse as her fingers crept up to her shoulder. Sol was dead, and Teresa said a doctor could get rid of the tattoo along with the rest of the scars on her arms.

Her fourth day in Malibu, Teresa had taken her into town, and the people who worked at the restaurants and shops and the boutique could actually understand her when she spoke English. She shopped for new clothes—cotton tops, bright-colored skirts, her first pair of capris. A man cut her hair and showed her how to style it with a brush and blow dryer. Then Teresa had taken her to lunch along the oceanfront, and she'd discovered that she liked the taste of seafood. And butter.

She wanted to share all these new things with Michael, but he wasn't there.

You turned my wailing into dancing; you removed my sackcloth and clothed me with joy.

Sara brushed her hair out of her face again as she glanced down one last time at the swift tide. The water might be able to take her far away, but she no longer wanted to bury herself in its folds.

See! The winter is past;
the rains are over and gone.
Flowers appear on the earth;
the season of singing has come.

SONG OF SONGS 2:11–12

Epilogue

TEN MONTHS LATER

ELISE LISTENED TO Sara pound out the final bars of "Ode to Joy" on the baby grand piano while Rezon slept in her lap. Music was more than a talent for her sister; it was a calling. A God-given gift that welled up within her and cascaded down onto the keys.

The counselor had helped Sara deal with her guilt, but the music helped her express her emotions in a way that words never could. It spilled out of her heart with passion and anger and joy. God had blessed her with something that no one could take away.

"That was beautiful, Sara," Teresa said, and Elise hid her grin with her hand. Their great-grandmother said that every time Sara finished playing a hymn.

Teresa shifted the blanket on her lap. "Could you do 'How Great Thou Art'?"

Sara began to play.

Their great-grandmother had a long list of favorites that she requested daily, and Sara always complied. The two of them had bonded soon after Sara stepped off the airplane. The mother who had lost her daughter, and the daughter who had never had a mom.

Even though Elise had been out to Malibu three times to visit, she still felt like an outsider in Teresa's home. She'd already found her place in Virginia, with memories of her mother and a father who loved her. Sara had found stability with Teresa, this warm, compassionate woman who exuded God's love, and she was thriving under Teresa's care.

This house tucked into the bluffs was a pillar for Sara, and Teresa was the foundation. She had cleared her social calendar when Sara arrived and had devoted herself to her great-granddaughter's recovery.

While Teresa helped Sara heal in California, Elise had pounded out the remainder of her thesis in Virginia. In spite of missing her interview in Wittenberg, she was able to complete her work by interviewing Professor Reimann over the phone and spending a couple days camped out at the Library of Congress.

She glanced across the room, and Carson winked at her. She would be forever grateful that he had followed her across Germany, and grateful that he helped convince Addison to get her and Sara out of Marienthron.

Almost a year ago, she had stopped asking him to leave her alone, and their friendship was slowly evolving into something more. She had wanted to start over and so had he.

When she left for the States, he had returned to his job in Berlin. He had sent her a long apology for deceiving her via e-mail, and since then they had either e-mailed or talked every day. They were slowly building back a foundation of trust, grounded on their common faith and friendship.

A couple of months after she returned to Virginia, Carson invited himself to her family's farm in Virginia. Last week, when he found out she was flying to California, he offered to take her scuba diving near Catalina. She'd agreed—not because she had any real interest in diving, but because she wanted to see him again.

After surviving her short stay at Marienthron, she was suddenly ready to do things she'd never dreamed of before . . . like flying back to Berlin in the spring to assist Addison with the hundreds of woman who had arrived at Hatzolah for help. With Addison's passion and drive, the organization grew quickly as word got out on the street that Hatzolah would harbor abused women and children and help them start a new life.

It was a risky business for Addison and her staff, but Addison was no longer afraid.

Someone buzzed the intercom, and Elise slid out of her seat.

"I'll check it," she said.

Teresa didn't move, her eyes closed as she breathed in the music of the old hymn like it was a fragrant oil.

"Yes?" Elise said when she pressed the button.

A male voice answered. "I'm, uh, looking for Sara . . . Alcott."

Elise looked back toward the piano. Was Sara dating someone? All she talked about was her music and studies and her desire to learn more and more. Nothing about a boy. But whenever a cloud of concern passed over Sara's face, Elise wondered if she wasn't remembering the man who had saved her last year and then walked out of her life without even saying good-bye.

Elise punched the "talk" button. "May I tell her who's calling?"

There was a long pause. "My name's Michael . . ."

Elise released the button and motioned to Carson. Teresa and Sara were too wrapped up in their musical world to notice her and Carson walk out the door.

When they reached the front gate, she saw Michael, standing with one hand buried in his pocket and the other gripping a motorcycle helmet. The last time she had seen him, he had been covered in Sara's blood as he shielded her from Sol's blade.

His blond hair was cut short, and he wore a plain T-shirt and jeans. When he looked down at her, she could see the uncertainty in his eyes.

She clasped her fingers around the wrought iron. "What are you doing here?"

"I'd like to see Sara."

"You left her at the hospital!"

He hung his head. "I'm so sorry."

"She kept asking for you over and over, but you weren't there to take her hand."

"Calm down," Carson whispered, but she couldn't calm down. This man had not only wounded the woman he supposedly loved, he'd abandoned her. Yet, in spite of what he'd done to her, Sara had still wanted him.

"I'll never forgive myself," Michael said quietly. "Not just for leaving her, but for hurting her . . . before."

Elise's shoulders stiffened as Carson put his arms around her and breathed into her ear. "Think about it, Elise."

She stood frozen. Here was the man who had abused and then abandoned her sister. But he was also a man who had grown up in the Chosen. A man who, like Sara, had had no choice but to follow Sol. It was only by God's grace that Elise had not grown up right beside him.

Elise leaned toward the gate. "I don't want Sara to get hurt again."

"I understand." He cleared his throat, his eyes focused on the helmet in his hand. "I just wanted to ask her to forgive me."

He took a step back toward his motorcycle. "Please tell her that in spite of what I did, I still love her."

As Michael put his helmet on and climbed back onto his motorcycle, Carson nudged her. Tears welled up in her eyes and she brushed them away. With a sigh, she opened the gate. "I'm not going to tell her that."

Michael nodded his head in resignation and reached for the ignition on the bike. "I get it."

"No you don't," she said. She grabbed his arm and motioned toward the courtyard. "If you want Sara to forgive you, you're going to have to ask her yourself."

Michael's hands shook as he took off his helmet and followed Elise inside.

Discussion Questions

1. What is the similarity between Elise's journey through the granite blocks at the Holocaust Memorial and her journey behind the walls of Marienthron?

2. How can well-meaning Christians get trapped in toxic churches and cults?

3. Have you ever had someone in your life use the Bible for manipulation instead of truth? How did you react?

4. Even though she knew she might die, why didn't Sara tell Elise that she could get out of the crypt?

5. James 2:25 says that the biblical Rahab was "considered righteous for what she did when she gave lodging to the spies and sent them off in a different direction." Even though she may have thought she was worthless, how did God use Rahab (Catrina) in *The Black Cloister*?

6. During the Protestant Reformation, Martin Luther preached that salvation is by grace and not works. What is the balance between our freedom in Christ and our service to him?

7. Elise was prompted to move forward by her nightmares of the baby and the monster. Has God ever spoken to you in a dream?

8. As a follower of Christ, it is essential to be a part of a community with other believers, but how can you protect yourself and those you love from a leader who is misusing God's name?

Author's Note

SEVERAL YEARS AGO, my family and I lived for a season in the former East Berlin. Our flat was a block from the old wall, and my life was changed as I stumbled my way through conversations with local merchants, roamed the back streets of the city, visited Martin Luther's Wittenberg, and learned about both the triumph of the Reformation and the terrifying days of Communist rule.

Before we came back to the United States, a story began to form in my mind about Katharina von Bora's escape from the abbey and the freedom she found in Christ—but a thread was still missing. I waited (and waited) for inspiration until I met a woman who had been raised overseas in a sexually abusive cult. As I listened to her heart-wrenching stories and started researching abusive cults, I knew it was time to write.

I have attempted to be as factually accurate as possible with the landmarks in Germany, and historically accurate with regard to Katharina von Bora. The only exception is my portrayal of the ruins at Marienthron. Though the remains of the abbey are still outside Grimma, they are no longer habitable.

Like the leadership in the Chosen, cult leaders often misuse their spiritual gifts as they demand obedience, exclusivity, and sacrifice from their followers. Those who join a religious cult are usually attracted to it because of a group's dedication to community, outreach, and Bible study. It isn't until after they have joined that they discover the darker side of deception and manipulation.

Though this novel is not meant to mirror one specific religious group, my hope is that it portrays the confusion of children who are born into a cult and are often abused. There is opportunity for healing. For more information about toxic religion and recovery, please visit my Web site at http://www.melaniedobson.com.